BEYOND
the PLAY

OUT OF REACH BOOK THREE

NEW YORK TIMES BESTSELLING AUTHOR

KAYLEE RYAN

Cover Design: Perfect Pear Creative Covers
Cover Photography: Wander Aguair
Editing: Hot Tree Editing
Proofreading: Deaton Author Services & Editing 4 Indies
Formatting: Integrity Formatting

BEYOND
the PLAY

OUT OF REACH BOOK THREE

KAYLEE RYAN

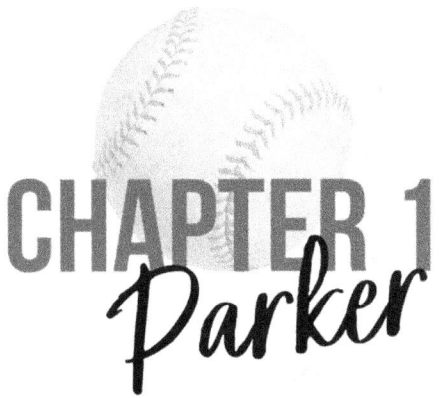

CHAPTER 1
Parker

F ALL IS MY FAVORITE SEASON. Don't tell my family because choosing any other season than baseball season in the Monroe household is a travesty. I do love baseball season. How could I not? My dad played professional ball my entire childhood. It's in my blood and that of my sisters as well. My older sister, Paisley, played college softball like me. Our little sister, Peyton, is a freshman in college this year, and she plays as well. It's almost as if it's a Monroe family tradition.

Anyway, back to fall. I love to watch the leaves and the weather change. I live for the months that I get to break out my leggings, oversized sweaters, and knee-high boots. And don't get me started on the pumpkin-flavored coffee sold at the campus coffee shop. They would make a killing if they sold that stuff year-round. Then again, that would take away one more thing to look forward to during my favorite time of year.

Honestly, I think a big part of why I love this time of year is that my dad was home every fall. It was a couple of months every year that we got to be a family. All five of us were home to eat dinner together and for the holidays. It was the time of year I looked forward to the most.

"Hey, are you ready to head out?" my best friend, Autumn, asks from my bedroom door.

"Yep." Grabbing my phone, I shove it into my small crossbody purse and follow her to the living room of our two-bedroom apartment.

We've been living in the same place, just off campus, since our sophomore year. Paisley still takes credit for that miracle. She claims she wore Dad down, so he was too tired to fight with me by the time I got to college. I think she might be half right. It was surprisingly easy to convince my dad to let us move off-campus as sophomores.

"I'm so ready to let loose," Autumn says as we climb into the back of our Uber. "Midterms just about killed me."

"You say that every single time, and I've hardly seen you crack open a book." Autumn is smart as hell. She hears it once and retains the information. I, however, am not. Having my best friend be a genius is helpful when it comes time to cram. She's the best study partner.

"It's the stress of it all. Everyone on campus is on edge and has their nose buried in a book. There's so much tension." She rolls her neck as if she can feel all the tension she's talking about right this moment.

"Not all of us can be super-geniuses," I tease.

"Hey, you benefit too," she fires back.

I smile because she's totally right. "Who else is coming tonight?"

"The usual. Kate and Bridgett are meeting us there, and you know if Bridgett is there, Garrett and his shadow Troy will be there too."

"Are you ever going to tell me what happened between the two of you?" I ask. She knows I'm referring to Troy.

She exhales, resting her head back against the seat. "Nothing happened. We kissed. He wanted more, I said no, and that was it."

"Did he pressure you?"

"No. He never pushed it past kissing the rest of the night. He was gone the next morning when I woke up, and he acts as if it never happened."

"You should talk to him."

"He's not interested."

"How do you know?" I challenge.

"Can we not do this? Tonight is about going out and relaxing our minds from midterms. The last thing I want to do is try to wrap my head around Troy and what he does or doesn't want." Her eyes are pleading, so I relent. I don't want to upset her, but I see the way he looks at her, and I know for a fact—because she's told me on multiple occasions—she has a thing for him.

"Fine, but we are tabling this discussion for a later time. As in any time but tonight." I give her a pointed look, raising my eyebrows for dramatics to make sure I get my point across. We will be discussing this. She can't hide from how she feels forever.

"Thank you. Now, come on." She reaches for the door handle and steps out of the car. I follow her, and as soon as my feet hit the sidewalk, she's linking her arm with mine. "We need drinks and some sexy hard bodies to grind against."

I nod because that sounds like a damn good time to me after the hellish week of midterms. We pay our cover to get into the club, and with a quick text message to Kate, we head to the back where our friends have secured a booth.

"About damn time!" Troy stands from the table and wraps his arms around Autumn in a hug. He smiles at me over her shoulder. His eyes are glassy, which tells me he's well on his way to being drunk off his ass. More than that, drunk Troy is an emotional Troy. Tonight just got a little more interesting.

"Parker," Troy slurs and teams it with a big cheesy smile. He doesn't let go of Autumn, and the way that she grins up at him tells me she's not the least bit upset about it. Yeah, we are definitely going to have that conversation.

"You need drinks," Kate announces. "Let's go, Monroe." She grabs my hand and pulls me to the bar.

"Vodka cranberry!" Autumn calls after us, not bothering to leave Troy's embrace to follow.

"Are they ever going to be official and put the rest of us out of our misery?" Kate asks as we reach the bar.

I shrug. "I don't know. They're both stubborn as hell." I toss my long dark hair over my shoulder. I haven't even hit the dance floor, and I'm already burning up in here. It's packed, not that I'm surprised. This is a college town, after all.

"We can all see it," Kate says with a sigh. "I hate feeling like we're in the middle. We all know they want each other."

I nod because she's right. It's crystal clear to those on the outside, but I also know that it's not always that easy if you're the one living it. I watched that with my older sister, Paisley, and her now husband, Cameron.

Kate's hand clamps down on my arm where it's resting on the bar while I wait for the bartender to notice me. "What?" I ask her.

"Hottie, nine o'clock. He's not stopped looking at you since we stepped up to the bar," she tells me in an excited whisper-yell over the music of the club.

"Really?" I ask enthusiastically. I've been single for far too long. Not that I think this hottie that Katie speaks of will change that, but I'm definitely ready to let loose and have some fun. If there's a hot guy included in that, that's just a bonus.

Slowly, I turn my head to casually look at where she stated, and my eyes lock with his. I suck in a breath when I realize who he is. Dark, messy hair, a crooked grin, and the tight black T-shirt he's wearing shows me he's fit. Not that I didn't already know. I can't see them from this far away, but his bright blue eyes remind me of a bright sunny day. How do I know? Because the sexy man staring me down like I might be his next meal is none other than Holden Bailey. The star shortstop for the Tomahawks. He's admittedly the best shortstop in the league, which is what he's known for—in addition to his playboy ways. He doesn't even hide the fact or try to deny it when reporters ask him about the rotating arm candy he's photographed with. He might be sexy as hell, but he's not the fun I'm looking for. The last thing I want is to be labeled as another one of his many women.

Growing up with my dad and now having a brother-in-law who is a professional athlete, I know all too well what the media is capable of. Not to mention my dad would flip his shit if he thought I was dating Holden.

"He's pretty," Kate whispers, pulling my attention back to her.

"He's pretty, but he's a playboy." It's a crying shame too. Kate's description is a little off. He's more than pretty. He's sex personified. I've always had a thing for athletic men. That's the hardship of growing up around them, I guess. Regardless, Holden Bailey is every girl's dream guy, except for the notches on his bedpost. Sure, I know the media can blow things out of proportion, but when the man does nothing to dissuade the rumors, well, it has to be true, right?

"You looking for forever, Park?" she teases.

"Nope. But not looking for an STD either." I shrug and raise my hand in the air, finally getting the bartender's attention.

"What can I get you, ladies?" he asks.

I order a vodka cranberry for Autumn and me and pass him some cash. "I guess I should have made sure no one else needed a drink," I say, turning to look at Kate.

"Nah, we all just refreshed with a new round right before you got here."

"How long have you been here? It's obvious that Troy is already three sheets to the wind."

"Just about a half an hour. We did a little pregame at our place before we left."

"Here you go." The bartender places two vodka cranberries in front of me and slides my cash back as well. "Paid for," he says, nodding to the other end of the bar where Holden sits.

"Thank you," I say, feeling myself blush. It's not the first time a handsome stranger has bought me a drink, but this is Holden Bailey. Yeah, I know he's a manwhore extraordinaire, but still. Holden Bailey!

Pulling a few dollars from the cash he gave back, I drop it into the tip jar. Slowly, I lift my drink and turn toward the end of the bar. My eyes automatically lock with his, and I hold up my drink and mouth, "Thank you," before grabbing the second drink and walking back to our table. I ignore the way my body heats from just his gaze. I ignore the intensity of those blue eyes I've seen staring at me on the television screen. And of course, I ignore the fact that even though he plays for our rival team, I've always thought he was sexy as hell. I'll take that one to the grave with me.

"Hey, Parker, wait up," Kate says, rushing to keep up with me. "What was that?"

"Nothing. He bought our drinks. I said thank you." It was more than nothing. Just the look he was giving me has my body lit up like the Fourth of July. That man is way too sexy for his own good, and I need to keep my distance. Those blue eyes, they're dangerous, and so is he.

"That man was devouring you with his eyes. You should go talk to him."

"Not interested." My mind knows this is true. My body, on the other hand, is all for going to thank Holden in person.

"It's not like you have to marry the guy. Have some hot, sweaty sex to wash away the stress of midterms and call it a night. Or two," she adds with a wink.

"What part of not interested in an STD did you not understand?"

"Come on, Parker. He can't be that bad. You dated Dalton from the football team for like six months. I didn't hear you complaining then."

"I'm older and wiser. Besides, the notches on Holden's bedpost make those on Dalton's look like child's play." Dating Dalton was a good time. We were compatible as in we were both focused on our respective sports, and neither one of us needed or wanted much from the other. We would meet up at parties, hang out, and the sex wasn't terrible. When I found out I was the only one treating us exclusively, I ended things. Sure, we weren't serious, and he didn't break my heart, but I'm a one-man kind of girl, serious or not. So, sadly, I said goodbye to Dalton and his six-pack, and I've been, as my friends like to call it, in a dry spell ever since.

"Well, if you don't get some action soon, they're going to need a machete to whack down all the cobwebs."

"Ha-ha," I reply dryly. She's not wrong, but still.

"What are we talking about?" Autumn asks when I finally slide into my seat at the table and pass over her drink.

"Nothing."

"Oh, it's something. Some baseball sex god is sitting at the bar eyeing our girl here. He even bought your drinks," Kate says, grinning as she reaches for her own drink that she left at the table.

"Stop." I laugh. "It's nothing. He bought us a drink. No big deal." It's also not a big deal that one look from him and my panties are ruined, right? I think I'll keep that little slice of information to myself.

"Hate to break it to you, Monroe, but when a man buys you a drink, it's a big deal," Garret speaks up.

"He's right," his girlfriend and one of my close friends, Bridgett, adds. "He's into you."

"He's just flirting. It happens all the time."

"Trust me on this," Garrett adds. "He's not going to waste his money to just randomly buy you a drink unless he wants you."

"G's right," Troy chimes in. "He wants you."

"What in the hell are you waiting for? Go talk to him. Have some fun," Autumn urges.

"You"—I point at my best friend and roommate—"need to drink that so we can hit the dance floor." In a show of solidarity, or just to get them all to shut up about me going to talk to Holden freaking Bailey, I bring my drink to my lips and chug it. Probably not my smartest move of the night, but desperate times call for desperate measures. With one look, he has my body on fire. We have to stop talking about him. I need to get my ass out on the dance floor and clear my mind of everything but the beat of the music.

Slamming my now-empty glass on the table, I push back in my chair and stand. Autumn is quick to follow, as are Bridgett and Kate. Troy and Garrett hold up their beers with a nod that they're watching us. Garrett never lets Bridgett out of his sight when we're out like this, and it's comforting to know he's got eyes on all of us. I'd usually say that about Troy as well, but from the glassiness of his eyes, he's not seeing things all that clearly tonight. Besides, I know my friends, and we might get two songs of dancing in before they join us. Garrett can't seem to stay away from Bridgett much longer than that, and Troy, well, he's pretty much the same way when it comes to Autumn.

I've never experienced that kind of relationship that gives you a deep need to be with someone like that. I hope that one day I'll find a man who can't stand the thought of being away from me and vice versa. That's my last thought as we reach the dance floor, and I throw my hands over my head and rock my hips to the beat.

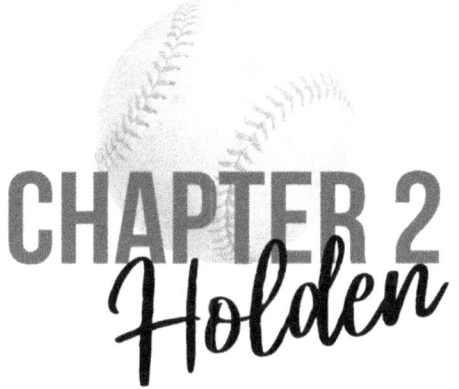

CHAPTER 2
Holden

T ODAY BLOWS. NO, IT MORE than blows. It sucks hairy donkey balls. Why, might you ask? Well, I got the call today while sitting in a small café having lunch with my parents that I'm being traded. That's right, traded. Apparently, the Tomahawks mastered a multiplayer deal with the Blaze, and I'm a part of the deal. I've only completed two years of my three-year contract with the Tomahawks, and now, according to my agent, Harold, I'm being traded to the Tennessee Blaze.

Of course my parents, especially my mother, are thrilled about the news. The Blaze is our home team. Me being traded means that this visit in the off-season is turning into me moving home. Sure, that's a perk, but I'm still blindsided.

I'm salty about it. No, I'm more than salty. I'm pissed. The Tomahawks were my team growing up, and to play for them has been a dream, but apparently, according to my agent, the media hype that follows me everywhere I fucking go was too much for them. It's not uncommon for a team to broker a multiplayer deal. I just never thought I'd be one of them. I'm the top-ranked shortstop in the league, but according to Harold, they don't want the press. Apparently, they're, and I quote, "taking the team in a new direction." I call bullshit. It has nothing to do with the press and everything to do with the Blaze's top shortstop getting injured last year. The team has kept his prognosis quiet, but to me, they are screaming loud and clear. Gerald Baylor is not coming back.

It's bullshit. Sixty percent of the shit written about me is complete and utter shit. The other 40 percent, I'll claim. I'm a single man, and I'm dating. That's life, but since my life is in the spotlight, I look like my dick sees more action than a public restroom. It doesn't, by the way, in case you're wondering. Sure, I've been with my fair share of ladies, but I don't fuck them all. Most nights, I fall into bed exhausted and send them home in a cab, but that's not what the paparazzi like to report. How they latched onto me, I'll never know, but those fuckers got me traded. Okay, fine, I played a role in it as well. I don't dissuade the rumors, but I blame that on Harold. He claimed any press was good press, and well, here we fucking are. Add in the fact that I play the field, not ever committing to one woman, and you have Holden "the playboy" Bailey.

It's a crock of shit.

Kind of.

Mostly.

I do like to play the field, and committing to one woman, well, it's not something I've ever considered. I'm still young. Still trying on the many varieties.

Luckily for me, Harold's contract is up for renewal as well. As soon as I speak to the management of my new team, I'm going to ask for leads for a new agent. Harold can kiss my ass.

Don't get me wrong. The Blaze is a good team. Hell, they're kicking ass and have done so the past several years, having won two World Series in the last ten years and several attempts at almost making it there. That's further than I've gone with the Tomahawks, so this might be a good thing for me. It's every player's dream to make it to the World Series. It's an even bigger dream to actually win it. The Tomahawks are a strong team, but the Blaze, well, they're kicking ass and taking names. So, I guess I'm not as pissed as I once thought now that I think about it. I just hate being blindsided and fuck them, and fuck Gerald for saying it was my "media reputation." Call a spade a spade and just be up front about Baylor being out this season.

That brings me to the present. I'm in town staying with my parents until I find a new place. That's what every twenty-three-year-old wants to be doing—moving back home to live with their parental units. Sure, it's only temporary, but after you've lived on your own, it's weird as fuck to move back in with Mom and Dad. I guess the trade isn't so bad, bringing me home to my family.

Regardless, I needed to get out of the house. Since I have yet to meet my new teammates, I'm flying solo tonight. Most of my friends I grew up with moved away for college and never came back home. And the others I've fallen out of touch with. You know, the ones who only call when they need a loan or have a great business venture they want me to invest in. Yeah, I won't be calling those so-called friends. Being alone tongiht suits me just fine. All I want to do is have a drink or five and then call an Uber to take my ass back to my parents' place.

So, here I am, sitting at the bar of the crowded club, minding my own business when I see *her*. Long dark hair that looks like it would feel like silk between my fingers. Her eyes, they're a bright blue, similar to my own, and although it could be the lighting, they look like they're sparkling. She's with a friend who is cute but doesn't hold a candle to the dark-haired beauty. I've been sitting here for the better part of two hours, and she's the first woman to approach the bar who's caught my eye. I'm selective, unlike what the tabloids like to report.

After calling the bartender over and sliding him some cash to pay for the beauty and her friend's drinks, I keep my eyes on her.

They're deep in discussion, and neither one seems to notice they've captured the attention of every man sitting at the bar and even that of those standing close by.

I watch as she shakes her head and tries to give her money back to the bartender. I bring my beer to my lips to help fight my smile. The bartender nods my way, and she turns her head. Our gazes lock, and it's like a shock to my nervous system. I can't seem to look away. Hell, I can't seem to move from her stare; it's locking me into place. Finally, she turns to her friend, and they walk away.

Draining my beer, I signal for another and turn in my seat to look for her. She's easy to spot with that gorgeous hair, and did I mention she has a tight little body too? She's with a group—two other girls besides the friend with her at the bar and two guys. I pay close attention, not caring that I'm blatantly staring at their table. Both guys appear to be with the other girls. I didn't see a ring, so that means she's available, or at least not legally attached. Not that I'm one to poach on another guy's girl, but damn, if she has a man in her life, he should be here with her. I know I would be.

I don't even pretend to casually watch her. I stare openly, and let me tell you, the view is spectacular. When the girls move to the dance floor, my eyes move with them. I have to adjust my stance to follow them. My eyes are locked on her. Every sway of her hips, her arms held high in the air over her head. The way her long dark hair cascades down her back when she tilts her head back as she belts out the lyrics. I could stand here and watch her all damn night.

I'm well on my way to doing just that when the two guys from their table join them. They go to their girls, which leaves mine and her friend dancing alone. Yeah, I called her mine. She will be too. She just doesn't know it yet. When some jackass slides up beside her, getting way too close for my liking, I set my warm beer on the bar and start toward her.

Cocksucker.

I saw her first.

It's as if I'm on autopilot as I head her way. My feet eat up the distance between us. I don't have a single claim to her. Hell, I don't even know her name. What I do know is that if someone is going to be putting their hands all over her on the dance floor, it's going to be me.

I walk up behind her, and the guy's eyes widen. Ah, he must recognize me. I don't say a word as I keep my eyes on his and place my hands on her hips, pulling her into me. She glances over her shoulder, and to my surprise, she rolls those big blue eyes. However, what she doesn't do is pull away.

The douche who thought he had a chance backs away, and once he's out of sight, he's also out of mind. Not that I can think of anything but the beauty in my arms as she rolls her hips. When she lifts her hands in the air, I grab her wrist, pressing my lips to her sensitive skin before bending so she can place her hands on my hair. She tugs, and my cock twitches against her ass.

I don't know how long we're on the dance floor. One song bleeds into another, and that's just fine with me. This night that started as complete shit has moved to having this gorgeous woman in my arms, grinding against me. I still don't know her name, but I know the taste of her skin as I press my lips to her neck. I know the smell of her hair as I bury my face in it. I know the feel of her ass pressed against my cock, and I know the curve of her hips beneath my palms.

I fucking love it all.

Every. Piece.

Normally, I'm ready for this part of the night to end and get to the sex, but she feels too damn good in my arms to rush this. It's the most fun I've had at foreplay in... well... ever. I'm content to be right here, grinding into her. It's just going to make taking her later tonight that much sweeter. I might sound presumptuous, but the way she's grinding on my dick and pressing her tight little body against mine, I know she wants it just as bad as I do.

Electricity courses through my veins. Very rarely do I get this worked up. It's usually me sitting at the bar. We make eye contact, I buy her a drink, and she comes over to say thank you. She mentions that she knows who I am, and that's when I spell it out for her.

One night.

No strings.

No exchange of numbers.

No happily ever after.

Just sex.

Those are the rules, and I've never had anyone balk at them, and I've never been tempted for a repeat. Although if anyone was going to tempt me, it would be this beauty in my arms.

She turns in my arms, locking her hands behind my neck. Her body is pressed against mine, and my cock is as hard as it's ever been in my life. My hands are on her hips, but I need her closer. I'm not sure if that's even possible. What I do know is that this woman is intoxicating, and I can't get enough of her. Sliding my hands from her waist, I let them fall to the top of her ass and hold her close. My forehead lowers to her as we sway to the music. My chest is rapidly rising and falling, and hers matches my rhythm.

Good to know I'm not the only one affected by the intensity flowing between us. Song after song plays over the speakers, and neither one of us seems ready to let go. When she lifts her head, I lower mine. I lick my lips in anticipation as she bites down on hers. I'm going to kiss her, and she's going to let me. I lean in a little closer. I can feel her hot breath mingle with my own. This is it. I lower a little closer, but before I get a chance to see if her lips are as soft as they look, we're bombarded by her friends. One of them taps on her shoulder, pulling her attention from me to them.

One of them motions that she needs a drink, and my dancing partner nods in agreement. She pulls away from me and loops arms with her friend as they make their way to the bar. I stand there and stare after her. She doesn't even look back at me. Two women slide up next to me. One moves to my front while the other takes my back. However, I can't even appreciate the hot girl sandwich they're making out of me because I'm still staring after the girl with the long dark hair and big blue eyes. Who just... dismissed me?

What. The. Fuck?

Stepping away from the handsy twins, I make my way to the bar. I slide up next to her and place my hand on the small of her back. "What are you drinking?"

She turns to look at me. "I'm good, thanks."

"Come on, love. I just had my cock and my hands all over you. The least you can do is let me buy you a drink before we get out of here."

I see her shoulders stiffen as she turns to face me. "First of all"—she holds up one slender finger—"I'm not your love. Second of all, we were dancing. That's it. Nothing more, nothing less."

"Come on." I laugh. "You don't really believe that. We were practically fucking out there," I say, trying to keep my voice smooth and the irritation I feel at bay. I've never had someone so blatantly push me away. Not even in high school.

"Dancing," she says again.

"He's right, you know," her friend chimes in. "It was hot." She smiles over at me. "Hi, I'm Kate." She grins mischievously at her friend. "This is Parker."

I wink at Kate. "See. We're hot together."

"Sorry to disappoint you, but we're done here." She grabs her drink, slides some cash toward the bartender, and walks away.

I stand frozen for a second or two before jumping into action and grab Kate's arm before she can get too far away. "Kate, is it?" I ask her.

"Yep." She grins.

"What's up with Parker? She got a man?"

"Nope."

"Can you give me her number?" I ask

"Nope. If she wants you to have it, she'll give it to you."

"Here I thought you were on my team."

She shakes her head, tsking. "You see, that's where you're wrong. I'm on her team, always. Just because I think she needs to let loose"—her eyes rake over my body—"and that you would be the perfect candidate for that doesn't mean I'll be giving up her details."

I run a frustrated hand through my hair. "At least tell me where I can find her." I'm aware that I sound like a whiny bitch, and that's not me. This isn't who I am, but she walked away. That's never happened to me before. I need the chance to redeem myself.

"We're here a lot. Tonight we're blowing off steam from midterms."

"Is she eighteen?" I ask, feeling the blood rush from my face.

Kate throws her head back in laughter. "You're safe, Casanova. She's twenty-one."

She looks twenty-one, and she was buying drinks, but you never know these days. Some good fake IDs are floating around out there, and I was a college student. I know how crafty some people can be when they want to be.

"That's all you're going to give me?" I ask as Parker and the rest of their group step up beside us.

"We're heading out," Parker announces. She doesn't give me a single glance of recognition.

"How are you getting home?" I ask her. She ignores me. Reaching out, I gently place my hand on her arm. "Parker." I wait until she turns her irritated gaze my way. "How are you getting home?" I don't know why but I need to know she's going to get home safe. All of them have been drinking.

"Not that it's any of your business, but we took an Uber." She turns back to Kate. "Ready?"

"See you around, Casanova." Kate waves and follows her group of friends out the door.

I'm left standing there with my dick in my hands. Well, not really, but I might as well be. I don't know what the fuck just happened, but Parker, whatever her last name is, just sealed her fate. Maybe I should have told her that I'm a playmaker.

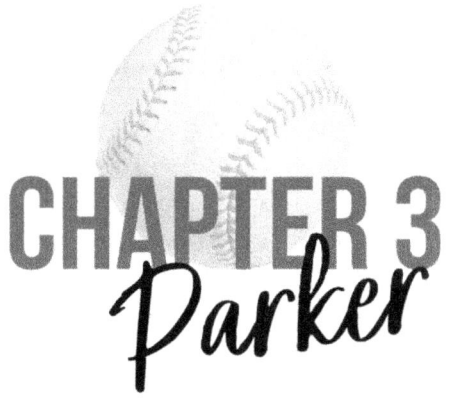

CHAPTER 3
Parker

I MARCH OUT OF THE club like my ass is on fire. And in a way, it is. I'm turned on, which pisses me off. I knew better than to dance with him. I know who he is and what he's known for, but I did it anyway. His body felt too damn good pressed against mine. And the way he moved his body in time with mine... hot as hell. I'm so turned on right now I can't see straight. If he were anyone else, I'd have given him my number. Hell, I might have dragged their sexy ass back to the dance floor, and who knows, maybe, just maybe, taken him home with me.

But this is Holden Bailey.

I know better.

Too bad my body didn't get the memo.

"Slow down," Kate calls after me.

I stop at the curb and take in a deep breath. My hands hang at my sides as I tilt my head back, closing my eyes, letting the fall air cool my heated skin.

"Parker, what the hell?" Autumn says, linking her arm through mine.

"Did he hurt you?" This comes from Troy. His words are a little slower, a sign of his alcohol consumption of the evening.

"No." I lift my head and open my eyes. "He didn't hurt me. I'm just not interested."

Troy studies me. "That why you're squeezing your thighs together, and your nipples look like they could cut glass?" he asks. He suddenly doesn't sound as inebriated as I first suspected. He folds his arms over his massive chest and stares down at me.

"He's right," Garrett chimes in.

"Hey!" Autumn and Bridgette smack them on the arms.

"Not helping," Autumn huffs.

"What she said," Bridgette agrees.

"It's the cold air." We all know I'm lying. "Can we go?" I ask.

"Uber is on its way," Autumn tells me, holding up her phone to show me the app.

"Thank you." The cool night air is starting to get to me. Just as a shiver races down my spine, the Uber driver pulls up. Autumn and I say our goodbyes and climb in while Kate, Bridgette, Troy, and Garrett take the one behind us.

"Holy shit, Parker. Holden Bailey had his hands all over you," Autumn exclaims as we pull away from the curb. At her excitement, the Uber driver glances in the rearview mirror, but I ignore him.

"We were dancing."

"Which is code for fucking with your clothes on."

"Stop," I say, not able to hide my smile. "You're ridiculous."

"What's ridiculous is you pushing him away. This is Holden Bailey we're talking about. Hot as hell baseball player. In fact, I've heard you say more than once how hot he is. That's how I know who he is. You've pointed him out to me several times."

"He is hot. I'm not denying that. He's arguably the most gorgeous man I've ever laid eyes on." It's more than that. Holden has this way about him. His confidence shines through in everything he does, and that makes him even sexier. Pushing aside his tendency to sleep around, he's a man who knows what he wants and goes after it. You can see that in him with every play he makes on the field. It's a sight to see.

"And he wants you."

"He wants in my pants. There's a difference." A big difference. He's not interested in the person I am. He's only interested in what's between my legs.

"And that's a problem because?" Autumn asks.

"Come on, Autumn. You know that's not me. One-night stands are not my thing." I don't bother to mention that if he were anyone else, or if his reputation didn't proceed him, I would have seriously considered a one and done with him.

"Maybe they should be. At least for one night. One night with Holden Bailey."

"Do you hear how ridiculous that sounds?"

She shrugs. "He's hot as sin, and from the moves I witnessed on the dance floor, the two of you have chemistry in spades. Can you imagine... ?"

She doesn't finish her question, but she doesn't have to. I know exactly what she's thinking about, and she's right. There was something there. Something hot and all-consuming, but I refused to let it suck me in. We danced, we had a good time, and that's that. I'll never see him again. I knew that going into this, which is why I walked away.

"Enough about Holden," I say as the Uber pulls up outside of our apartment building. With cash handed over, we slide out and make our way inside.

"Fine, I'll stop, but I still can't believe you passed up a once-in-a-lifetime orgasm."

"He could suck in bed," I toss out. Again, we both know that's not the case. A man can't move like that on the dance floor and not bring it in the bedroom. It's just not possible.

I try to remain serious but lose it, and we both start laughing. "Fine," I reluctantly agree. "He might have been amazing in bed, and sure, I'll never have the opportunity again, but that's okay. He would have forgotten me the minute he pulled out, and that knowledge is worse than never having what you refer to as a once-in-a-lifetime orgasm."

"Fine," she huffs. "I see your point."

"Love you, A," I say, hugging her tight. "I'll see you in the morning." Rushing down the hall to my room, I close and lock the door. Quickly, I strip out of my clothes. I reach for pajamas, and I pause before getting dressed. I'm hot and sticky and in need of a shower. Pulling my silk robe from the back of my bedroom door, I grab my clothes and head across the hall to take a quick shower.

All I can think about is him and the way it felt to have every inch of him press against me. I'm horny as hell, and all we did was dance, but I refuse to do anything about it. Instead, I deny myself the release that I need and rush through my shower. Tonight was fun, but it's over, and there is no use wishing it wasn't.

I wake to the sound of my cell phone vibrating across my nightstand. I groan before blindly reaching over and tapping the stand until I find it. Carefully, I unplug my phone from the charger and squint to look at the screen. When I see my older sister calling, my heart drops, and I'm pushing accept.

"What's wrong?" I ask Paisley. She never calls me in the mornings.

"Are you sleeping? It's noon."

"I got home late." I also had a hard time falling asleep thinking about a pair of light blue eyes attached to a man with big strong hands and a hard body. That's not the only thing that was hard, but we're not thinking about that.

"Well, get up, lazybones."

"I'm up," I groan.

"Good. Are you coming to Mom and Dad's for dinner tonight?"

"That's the plan."

"Great. Are you bringing Peyton?"

"I don't know. I haven't talked to her. Why?" She's acting weird.

"Can I not miss my little sisters?"

"Your husband is home after being on the road for months. Don't you have better things to do than bother me?"

"Oh, trust me. Cam and I got some us time." She laughs.

"I don't need to hear that, Paisley," I complain, which only makes her laugh harder.

"Oh, hush. Now, make sure you pick Peyton up and bring her with you."

"What's going on?"

"Nothing. I just miss my little sisters."

"I'm not buying it, Paisley Taylor. Spill."

She laughs again. It's a carefree sound that makes me smile too. She's so happy, and Cameron adores her and their three-year-old son, Jett. My sister fell in love with a man who loves her like our dad loves our mom, and I couldn't be happier for her. For both of them.

"Well, if you're that worried that something is wrong, you better be there to find out."

"To find out what?" I counter.

"Love you, Parker." She makes a kissing noise, and then the call goes silent.

I'm pulling up my favorites list to call Peyton when my phone rings, and I see the image of my baby sister smiling back at me. "Hey, I was just getting ready to call you."

"Let me guess, Paisley?" she asks.

"Yep. Did she call you too?"

"No, but she sent me a text that said you were picking me up to take both of us to Mom and Dad's and that I needed to call you to make sure you were up and moving."

"It's noon. Dinner isn't until five. We have plenty of time," I assure her.

"I'm guessing she woke you up too?"

"Yep. I didn't get home until late last night, and it's Sunday. I'm sleeping in."

"I think you've already slept in, Parker." She chuckles. "Anyway, I was up late too. Karina and I were making plans for spring break."

"Nice. However, the planning isn't going to be the issue. It's convincing Dad to let you go."

"Well, I have you, Mom, and Paisley on my side, so I'm sure we can convince him. Besides, you and Paisley have softened him up over the years. I'm not worried."

"Such confidence, baby sister," I tease.

"Yeah, yeah. Get your ass moving and come and get me."

"We have five hours."

"I want to go early to get some laundry done. It's so much better than the dorms."

"Fine. I'll be there in an hour. Wait, make that two," I amend, and she chuckles.

"If you're not here by two, I'm calling Autumn." It's a threat that we both know holds merit. Autumn isn't above dumping water on my head to wake me up. She did exactly that freshman year. However, it was a different circumstance. I'd been up late studying, so when I finally fell asleep and Dad called to tell me that Paisley was in labor, I didn't hear my phone. Autumn, on the other hand, did. Apparently, she was having a "good" dream, and trust me, you don't want to know. She was mad she got interrupted and poured a bottle of water I had on my nightstand over my head to wake me up.

"Fine," I grumble. "I'll be there."

"What did you do last night?" she asks.

"Autumn and I met up with some friends at The Outfield."

"You mean the club and not the actual outfield, right?" She laughs.

"The club."

"Sucks you have to be twenty-one to get in," she comments. Peyton is a freshman, and although I know many students who had fake IDs, I'm not going to encourage my baby sister to do so. Besides, I'd never forgive myself if something happened to her because I gave her the access to get it.

"Meh, it's not all that great. I'm sure you and Karina had more fun hanging out in your dorm."

"Are you telling me you didn't have a good time?" she asks.

An image of Holden with his front molded to my back as his hands roamed my body while we were on the dance floor flashes through my mind. "Sure," I finally admit. "We had a good time, but nothing spectacular happened."

"No?" she questions. "Was that your twin I didn't know you had that had Holden Bailey's hands all over her."

Deny. Deny. Deny. "That's crazy." Not much of a denial, but it's the best I've got.

"I saw the picture. There were a few freshmen there with fakes, and they saw you. They knew you were my sister and texted it to me. In fact." I hear a beep, and I don't bother to pull my phone away from my ear. I know she's sent it to me. "I just sent it."

"Yeah, we danced," I confess. I can't really lie my way out of this one with photographic evidence.

"Is that what the kids are calling it these days?" she teases.

"Hush. It was a dance. We got caught up in the moment. It was nothing."

"Looks like something," Peyton retorts.

"I need to shower so I can pick you up. I'll talk to you soon." At this, my sister howls with laughter.

"Fine. Pretend it didn't happen. I'll get it out of you. See you soon, Parker," she says before ending the call.

I fight myself for about two seconds before I open her message and look at the picture she sent. It's of Holden and me on the dance floor. Our bodies are molded together. His hands are resting just above my ass, dangerously low, and my hands are wrapped around his neck. His head is tilted toward mine, and I'm staring at him like he's the best thing since sliced bread. You can see and even feel the chemistry sparking between us in the picture. I might not be willing to be the next notch on his bedpost, but even I can admit that we look hot together.

I stare at the picture for far too long before getting the courage to hit the delete button. After giving Holden Bailey enough of my thoughts since last night, I refuse to give him more.

Tossing my phone on the bed, I huff out a breath and throw off the covers. Time to get my tired ass moving. I spent way too much time not only thinking but dreaming of Holden Bailey last night. He doesn't get my daytime thoughts too.

Thankfully, Peyton was on a call the entire ride to Mom and Dad's. Something about a project for poli-sci, and she's been trying to connect with her partner for a few days. I send up a silent thank-you to whoever happens to be looking out for me. I wasn't ready, and I don't think I will ever be ready to talk about Holden and last night.

"Don't think I'm letting you off the hook," Peyton whispers, just as we're walking into the house.

I ignore her and make my way to the kitchen. My nephew, Jett, spots me right away and gives me a big grin. "Pawker!" he cheers.

"Hey, buddy." I try to take him from Cameron, but he's not having it. He circles his arms around his daddy's neck, and Cameron grins, snuggling him close. "You missed Daddy, huh?" I push his hair back out of his eyes.

"Pey!" Jett exclaims, still holding on to his dad.

"Jettster." Peyton offers him her fist, and he bumps his tiny one into hers.

"Whatever we're eating smells delicious."

"Nothing fancy. Just chicken alfredo, salad, and rolls," Mom says, pulling me into a one-armed hug. "You too." She points at Peyton when she releases me.

"Duchess." Dad opens his arms for me, and I don't hesitate to hug him tight. "You don't come home enough."

"Dad, I'm here once a week. Minimum."

"That's not enough," he says as he shifts his stance and opens his other arm for Peyton. "Lady," he says. I can hear the smile and affection in his voice.

"Let's eat," Mom announces.

"You heard my queen." Dad releases us. Walking to stand behind Mom, he places his hands on her hips and kisses her neck.

You'd think we'd be grossed out by it, but it's the opposite. My sisters and I grew up watching my dad show our mom and us what love is. I'll never settle for anything less. I want that kind of love in my life. A man who looks at me like my father looks at my mother. A man who loves me the way Cameron loves my sister. Soul deep and never-ending. That's what I'm holding out for.

Once we're all seated and have our plates full, Paisley clears her throat. "Since we're all here," she says, smiling at each of us before she turns her eyes to her husband. It's the look they share that tells me I already have a good idea of why she was so insistent we all be here. I watch as Cameron slides his hand behind her neck and places a soft kiss against her lips. "Cam and I have something to say."

"We're pregnant!" Cam announces. Paisley begins to laugh at her husband, and he shrugs. "I couldn't hold it in any longer," he defends himself.

We're all on our feet and congratulating the happy couple. Jett doesn't really know what's going on, but he's smiling and clapping and accepts a hug from each of us. He's soaking up all the love he can get. He's a smart one, my nephew.

For the rest of the night, we talk about the new baby as we all take a guess at the gender. It's the perfect night, and I couldn't be happier for Paisley and Cameron. I also can't help but think that these moments, they're what I crave. Nights like tonight are why I can't risk my heart to a man like Holden Bailey. He's in the game for the play, for a good time, and me, well, I'm the girl who wants what goes beyond the play. I want forever.

CHAPTER 4
Holden

I CAN'T GET HER OUT of my head. The dark-haired beauty who walked away from me without a second glance has dominated my thoughts all week. That's why I'm here, sitting at the bar at the same club, The Outfield, hoping to catch a glimpse of her.

Never in my life have I chased a woman. And I don't even really know if that's what I'm doing tonight. All I know is that I can't stop thinking about her. The way her silky hair slid through my fingers, or the way her body felt pressed against mine. Even more so, I can't forget the way she dismissed me and walked away.

So, here I am, leaning casually against the bar with a drink in my hand, which happens to be club soda, and scanning the crowd. Something tells me that if I do run into her again, I'm going to need a clear head. I want her, and she wants me. I can feel it in the way her body responds to mine. She can't hide the goose bumps that break out across her skin or the way her chest rises and falls faster with each breath when I'm near.

"Holden Bailey," a high-pitched voice says, as a blonde wearing a dress so tight it could be skin tumbles toward me in sky-high heels. "Oh my God, it is you. I'm your biggest fan." She twirls her hair around her index finger and pouts her lips.

News flash, ladies, men don't find that sexy. I debate my identity, but there's no point in lying. Besides, it's not like I'm doing anything to hide my appearance. "That's me," I reply, taking a sip of my club soda and letting my eyes scan the crowd again.

"Huge fan." The blonde steps closer. "How about you buy me a drink?" She tilts her head to the side and licks her lips.

I hate to be a dick, and I can afford it. "Sure." Turning, I signal for the bartender. "The lady needs a drink," I say when he approaches.

"I'll have sex on the beach," she tells him. She's trying out this breathy thing with her voice, but I'm not feeling it. I know it's all for show because her tone was high-pitched a few seconds ago. I have to fight not to roll my eyes at her.

Ignoring her, I go back to scanning the crowd. My mystery girl is nowhere in sight, and I can't help the pang of disappointment that washes over me. This is a big city, and I don't know where to look for her.

"Thanks, handsome," the blonde says, but she's not thanking the guy who just handed her a drink. Her eyes are on me.

"Yep," I say, dismissing her.

"I'm your biggest fan," she coos again, stepping closer and placing her hand on my arm.

"Yeah?" I ask, feigning interest. "You like to see me out on the mound, winding up each pitch?"

She nods. "I love how fast you throw the ball." She moves in a little closer. Now it's not only her hand on my arm but her fake-ass tits as well. Normally, I'd take what she's offering, but not tonight, not after meeting my dark-haired, blue-eyed beauty. This woman standing before me pales in comparison. Everything about her is fake, even her claim to be my biggest fan.

"Funny," I drawl. "I'm a shortstop." She stares at me with a blank expression, and I realize she has no idea what I'm talking about. She doesn't have a clue about the game I love. "I'm not a pitcher."

Her eyes widen. "Oh, I know." She swats at my arm, laughing off her blunder. "I knew you were teasing."

"I see a friend. It was good to see you." With my club soda in hand, I leave her standing there, mouth gaping open. I have no desire to spend another second with her. Instead, I move around the club. I stop and talk shop with a few guys who call out my name and sign a couple of autographs. I have no issue giving my time to my true fans.

I've almost made it full circle. I'm maybe twenty feet from the bar, which is thankfully void of the blonde, and about the same distance from the front door. The same door that my girl is currently walking through. Excitement bubbles through me.

She's here.

The only time I ever feel this kind of rush is when I'm stepping out onto the field. It's the chase. It has to be. On their own accord, my feet carry me to her. I don't stop until I'm standing next to her with my arm slung over her shoulder.

"You missed me, didn't you?" I say, my lips close to her ear.

She stops walking and turns to look at me. I see the desire, and is that confusion in her eyes? "No," she replies and begins to walk again, my arm falling off her shoulders. I rush to catch up with her and her friend.

"Come on now," I say when we reach the bar. "Don't be like that."

"Hi, I'm Autumn." The friend offers me her hand. I open my mouth to tell her my name, but she beats me to it. "Holden, I know." She smiles and turns to raise her hand to get the bartender's attention.

He sees them and rushes over, ignoring all the other assholes of the male variety trying to get their attention. "Ladies," he greets. "What can I get you?"

"Two Long Islands," Autumn orders. She glances over at me. "Holden?" she asks.

"I'm good." I ditched my glass of club soda during my little trek around the club, looking for her.

"I'm Holden." I offer my hand to the woman who I can't stop thinking about. "I think we're way past the time for me to properly introduce myself."

"Parker," she replies but doesn't take my offered hand.

Placing my hand on the small of her back, I lean in close. "Nice to meet you, Parker," I whisper with my lips close to her ear. I see the small shiver that races through her.

"So, Holden, what brings you to town?" Autumn asks.

I'm a little surprised by her question. Usually, it's an autograph or a selfie request. I don't think I've ever had just a casual conversation with a woman, not since before becoming well-known at college and now in the professional league. "Family." It's not a lie. My parents have lived here their entire lives. It was me who moved away to college, and when I was signed in the professional league, it was my career that kept me from home. Well, until now. I'm no longer a Tomahawk. I'm a Blaze, living in my hometown for the first time since graduating high school.

"What about you? Do you ladies live around here?" I ask. I really only want to know about Parker, but her friend is cool. She's keeping me here with them, so there's that.

"Yeah. Born and raised. We're both seniors in college. We live just across town."

"What's your major?" I ask Parker as my hand rubs circles on the small of her back.

"Public relations."

"And you?" I lean in close to Parker to speak to Autumn. I don't miss her slight intake of breath at my nearness.

"Accounting." Autumn shrugs. "I like numbers."

Before I can reply, a guy, one I recognize who was here with them last week, walks up. He drapes his arm over both of their shoulders, and they both have smiles for him. It's awkward because my hand still rests on the small of Parker's back, but I'm not moving it. She's here standing next to me, letting me touch her. No way in hell am I giving that up. Not yet.

"Bailey." The guy nods at me.

I return his nod, and I realize that none of them seem to give one single fuck that I'm a professional baseball player. "You ladies want to dance?" the guy asks.

"What are you doing here, Troy?" Autumn asks him. "I thought we told you it was girls' night?" She raises an eyebrow, and though her gaze isn't even directed at me, I fight the urge to squirm.

"It's guys' night too." He points at a table just off to the right where a group of guys sits with beers. A few have scantily clad women on their laps. I do a double take when I see the blonde from earlier getting felt up by one of them. She doesn't seem to mind as she sips the drink in her hand.

"Poor guy." Parker turns so that she's facing him. This brings her back to my front, and I don't hesitate to move in close, placing my hand on her hip. She doesn't even react other than the way her shoulders slightly stiffen. "Troy boy, we love you, you know that, right?" she asks him.

I don't let the "we love you" part offend me. She's not mine. Not yet. Hell, I don't even really want her to be mine. Not really. That's not how I roll, but I do want her.

"However, Autumn and I are girls. That means we don't have the twig and berries like you do." She reaches out and pats his cheek. Troy tosses his head back in laughter, and I find that I'm biting down on my cheek to keep from laughing as well. Parker's got spunk. I like it.

"Do you need me to show you?" Autumn chimes in.

Troy's eyes heat. "Come on, crazy girl." He laces his fingers with hers and leads her to the dance floor.

"What do you say, Parker? Should we join them?"

The woman who has been monopolizing my thoughts for the past week turns and smiles. "You think you can keep up, Bailey?" she teases.

I lean in close, our lips a breath away. "Let me show you." Just another inch if that, and I could press my lips to hers. I ache to taste her, but it's too soon. She still seems to be unaffected, and that needs to change. It's time for the player to step up his game.

She swallows hard, which pulls my attention from her intoxicating blue eyes to her throat, which leads to my eyes scanning the long slender column of her neck. Her hair is pulled back tonight, giving me a great view of all her creamy skin. My mouth remembers the taste of her as I lick my lips. How is it possible that one night on the dance floor with this woman has me so tied up in knots?

"Come on, gorgeous. Show me what you've got." I take a step back, putting some distance between us. It's not what I want, but I think she needs it, and it wouldn't hurt for me to calm down a little either.

She brings her drink to her lips and drains it before setting the now empty glass back on the bar. "You might be the captain of the infield, but that doesn't mean shit on the dance floor." With that, she walks off, swaying those sexy hips of hers. I follow her like a puppy. When she reaches the edge of the dance floor, she turns to look for me, and I'm there. My hands land on her hips, and I pull her back to my front.

"I think you already know what I can do on the dance floor." With that, I begin to grind my hips, and she pushes her ass against me. Together, we make our way onto the crowded dance floor.

The beat thumps through the speakers, but I couldn't tell you what song or artist it is. All I know is this woman in my arms. We're making music of our own as our bodies sync with every move. It's as if we've been dance partners for years or bed partners. The chemistry is off the charts, and I'm hard as a rock. I need her.

Tonight.

I can't take another week of thinking about her. I need to seal the deal so I can get my life back. The lovely Parker has already taken up way too much space in my head. When she raises her hands in the air and sways her hips, I bend to kiss her neck. She leans into me, letting me hold her weight. She's not fighting this pull between us. Not that I think she could because it's strong as hell.

She turns to face me, and I feel another set of hands behind me. Looking over my shoulder, I see Autumn and Troy behind her. It's like one big cluster of grinding. Hands are everywhere, but only mine are on her. I let it ride for a few minutes before breaking away and moving us to a darkened corner on the back edge of the dance floor.

She's still facing me. Her hands are buried in my hair as I grip her hips. I move us to the wall and slide my hands down to her thighs and lift. She wraps her legs around my waist, locking her ankles.

"You've got me here, Bailey. Now, what are you going to do with me?" she asks.

Gripping her ponytail with one hand, I cover her lips with mine. She's tentative at first, which is something new for me. I can't remember a woman I've kissed in the past five or six years who was hesitant. They're all hoping to change me. To land a payday being connected to a professional athlete.

Not Parker.

"Open for me," I murmur against her lips, then kiss her again. My tongue traces her bottom lip, and finally, her mouth opens. I don't hesitate to kiss her slow and deep. Her tongue battles with mine. Stroke after stroke, I kiss her with everything I have. For the first time in my life, I'm content to stand here in the dark corner of this crowded club with this gorgeous woman wrapped around me and just kiss her.

She's intoxicating.

Song after song blares over the sound system, and we don't move from our secluded spot in the corner. I don't think my cock has ever been this hard. I remove my mouth from hers and trail kisses over her jaw and to her ear. "Let's get out of here," I whisper. My voice is gruff from the need coursing through my veins.

As soon as the words are out of my mouth, she freezes. Her arms drop from my hair to my chest as she unlocks her legs and slides to the floor. Her hands are on my chest, pushing, putting distance that I don't want between us. I don't think she does either. At least it didn't feel like she did a few seconds ago.

"What's going on?" I ask, stepping close again. I tuck a loose strand that's fallen out of her ponytail behind her ear.

"Autumn and I came together."

"We can make sure she gets home safe," I assure her.

"Thanks, but I-I can't. I need to go."

Before I know what's happening, she's slipping away from the wall and rushing onto the dance floor. This time, I follow her. I reach her just in time to hear her yell to Autumn that it's time to go.

"Parker—" I reach for her, but she's fast and steps back.

"I'm sorry, Holden. I just can't." With that, she makes eye contact with Autumn. "I'm going to call an Uber."

This time when she rushes away, I let her. I turn to look at her friend. "What did I do?"

"Nothing," Autumn assures me. "At least not to her. She's just not interested."

I stare at her as I process what she's saying. This is a first for me. I don't know how to handle it. Not interested? "Can I have her number?" I blurt.

"Yeah, no. If you want her number, you have to get it from her."

"How do I find her?" I counter, recalling a similar conversation I had with one of her other friends last week.

"There's a coffee shop not far from the university. She goes there a lot to study. That's as much as you're getting out of me."

"A name? Of the coffee shop, I mean."

"Nope. I've said too much already." She turns to look at Troy, who's dancing all on his own, obviously feeling the alcohol he's consumed tonight.

Autumn steps next to Troy and yells in his ear. I assume she's telling him that she's leaving before turning and walking away. I watch as she links arms with Parker, who is standing on the edge of the dance floor, then they turn and head for the door. I want to rush after her, but I don't know what to say. I need to make sure my next play is the right one. Parker is not only a mystery to me but she's also a challenge, and I never back down from a challenge.

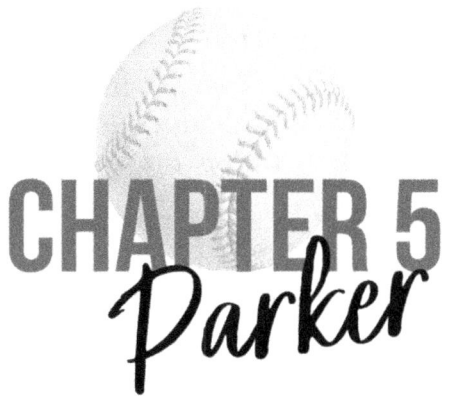

CHAPTER 5
Parker

MY HEART IS RACING. NO, it's thundering in my chest so hard that if I didn't know better, I'd think my chest was cracked wide open. With my arm linked through Autumn's, we move to wait for our Uber outside the club.

"You good?" my best friend asks.

I nod. Forming words isn't something I'm capable of at the moment. I don't know what that was back there. I've never been kissed like that, and I've never felt so consumed by a man in my life. Stepping away from Autumn, I need some space. I can still feel his hands on my body. My shaking fingers move to rest over my lips. I can still taste him.

"Girl," Autumn drawls. I manage to turn my head to look at her. "That was intense, Parker. And hot as hell. I think half the club got off watching the two of you." She fans her face with her hands.

"W-What?" I croak. I swallow hard. "We were in the corner," I defend. It's a poor attempt, but my brain hasn't cleared from the Holden fog he wrapped me up in. Panic sets in. No way if everyone saw us, will this not make its way back to my parents. I'm an adult at twenty-one, but being the daughter of a former professional baseball player has just as many pitfalls as it does perks. Case in point, they find out everything.

My soon-to-be-former best friend grins. "Got ya." She laughs. "But for real, anyone who did happen to be watching couldn't have done so without being turned on."

"I lost my head," I admit.

"Hey, we've all been there," she says, placing her arm around my shoulders as our Uber pulls up to the curb.

"This was different," I whisper once we're headed to our apartment.

"What do you mean? How was it different?" Autumn turns to give me her full attention. I can feel the heavy weight of her stare, but I keep my gaze pointed out the window.

I don't know how to explain this to her. "I can still feel him." I close my eyes, resting my head back against the seat. "I can feel his hands on me. I can taste him, Autumn." Turning my head to face her, I open my eyes. "That's not normal."

"That, my friend, is desire and chemistry. Something the two of you are not lacking."

She's right. There is no shortage of either desire or chemistry between Holden and me. However, there is a lack of a relationship. I'm a steady kind of girl. Hookups are not my thing. I want an emotional connection just as much as I want a physical one.

"Looked pretty emotional to me," Autumn says, reading my mind.

"Get out of my head." I chuckle.

"I know you, Parker. You did nothing wrong. A man like Holden, he's potent, and when he decides to make you the sole target of all that testosterone and swagger, the strongest woman, even those with no experience, wouldn't be able to defend themselves against him."

"He didn't force me," I assure her.

"I'm not saying that. I saw you. I know you were a willing participant. What I'm saying is that it would be hard for a nun to say no to a man like Holden."

When the Uber pulls up to our building, Autumn steps out of the car and holds her hand out for me. I take it, letting her help me stand. I only had two drinks. I'm not drunk, at least not on alcohol. Lust drunk, most definitely.

"Are you going to see him again?" she asks as she pushes open the front door to our apartment.

"No. Both incidents have been a coincidence."

She nods. "Maybe, but it could be fate."

"Come on, Autumn," I say, plopping down on the couch. "You can't really believe that."

"Think about it. With your family's connection to baseball, and your love of the game, you were bound to date a player. Not to mention, I've heard you comment more than once about how hot he is."

"That's not fate. That's genetics. Yes, he's hot. Scorching. I do love the game, and my family does have a strong connection to baseball, but that doesn't mean I'm going to fall in love with a baseball player."

"Paisley did."

"I'm not my sister."

"You're not, but you are attracted to him. Think about it, Parker. He's your hall pass."

"Ugh," I groan. "I was hoping you'd forgotten about that drunken conversation."

"I was tipsy at best, and yes, I remember. I'm your best friend. It's my job to remember."

"So what? He's my hall pass? That's all make-believe. Everyone knows that it never happens in real life."

"It's happening to you."

"No. It's not happening to me. I met him, we danced a few times, and that's that."

"You were practically fucking him on the dance floor, and let's not forget about that kiss." She gives me a pointed look.

"Trust me. I'm not forgetting about the kiss. I'm not forgetting any of it, and I doubt that I ever will."

"Then what's stopping you?"

"Just because I think he's probably the hottest guy I've ever met and kisses like he was made to do nothing but, I know his reputation. I'm not risking my heart. Besides, he's a Tomahawk. I could never date a rival."

Autumn tosses her head back in laughter. "You just keep making excuses, Parker. I'll be here when you come to your senses to say I told you so."

"Well, you're going to be waiting a long time. I'm telling you it's not going to happen. The chances of us being in the same place at the same time again are one in a million."

Autumn holds out her hand, letting it hang in the air, waiting for me to shake. "I'll take those odds, Monroe." She winks.

"Stop." I push her hand away, laughing at her antics.

"Parker, you could be his game changer."

I suck in a breath at her words. Not because I believe them, but because I want to. However, growing up around the game, I've seen it. I know the guys on my dad's team who were unfaithful to their wives, and then some never settled down, always ready and willing to play the field. I'm not sure which category Holden belongs in, but I'm pretty sure he's not in the Easton Monroe category. He's not that man who falls hard and fast and refuses to ever look at another woman. That's the man I want and the one I'll willingly give my time to.

"I'm beat. I'll see you in the morning."

"I'm right behind you." Autumn and I both stand, and after making sure the apartment is locked up, we head to our rooms to crash for the night.

Once I'm in my room, I hesitate on whether I should shower. I *need* a shower. I'm hot and sweaty, but that means washing the smell of him from my skin. I know it was an isolated incident. I know nothing will come out of this, but I kind of want to hang on to the feeling a little longer. He might not be the man I want for my forever, but Autumn was right. Holden Bailey is my hall pass, and he had his hands and his mouth all over me. It's a once-in-a-lifetime, okay, well, twice-in-a-lifetime kind of thing, and I'm not ready to let go of it just yet. Instead, I settle for washing my face before changing into my pajamas and sliding under the covers.

Closing my eyes, I replay every detail of my night. I squirm under the covers, remembering the feel of his strong hands romancing my body. And the kiss, the way he consumed me, it's all I can think about. The need for release is strong, but I refuse. It wouldn't be the same anyway. Besides, Holden is taking up enough space in my head as it is. I don't need him to be what I see when I handle my own pleasure in the dark of night. Instead, I force him out of my mind and roll over, willing myself to fall asleep.

It's Saturday night, and I'm sitting on the couch with my books scattered all around me and my laptop in my lap. This is how I plan to spend my night. I tell myself it's because I want to get ahead. Only a few weeks are left in the semester, and I need to buckle down. The real story, I don't want to risk running into Holden again.

Okay, that's a lie. I'd love nothing more than to have his hands, his mouth, and all his attention, but I know it's a dead-end street, so here I am, secluded in my apartment wearing my ratty sweats and a faded Blaze T-shirt with my hair piled in a messy knot on top of my head. No chance of going out. It's a perfectly executed plan. Now it's just convincing Autumn that I'm set for the night.

"Really, Parker?" Autumn stands at the end of the couch with her hands on her hips, staring me down.

"Is that your mom face?" I point at her scowl. "Your kids are going to be terrified," I tease.

"Why are you not ready?"

"Because I'm not going. I'm going to get caught up on homework. I have a paper due next week."

"I call bullshit."

I open my mouth to defend my excuse, but the look she gives me tells me my best friend is on to me. "Fine. I don't want to see him."

"You're messing with fate, Parker."

I chuckle at her annoyance. "You're crazy."

She huffs out a breath. "You can try to avoid this, but I'm telling you. I have this gut feeling about you and Holden."

"Yeah? What is this gut feeling? That we fall madly in love and have two point five kids, two dogs, and a white picket fence?" It takes all I have in me not to roll my eyes.

"Exactly! Well, I was thinking more of a wrought-iron gate with some brick. You know, to keep the paparazzi out."

"Stop." I smile. "I'm good. I promise. Call me if you need me to come and get you," I say as a knock sounds at the door.

"Come in," Autumn calls out.

Kate and Bridgette walk in. "You ready?" Kate asks, and then her eyes land on me. "Are you sick?"

This time, I do roll my eyes. "No. I just have lots of work to get caught up on. You all have fun. Call me if you need a ride home."

"Parker," Bridgette whines. "You have to come."

"Sorry, B, Duty calls," I say, holding up my laptop.

"Ugh. Buzzkill," she retorts.

"Go. Have fun. You guys are acting like this is the first time any of us have bailed to do homework."

"Well," Kate speaks up, "back then, we didn't get to watch the Holden and Parker show."

"There is no Holden and Parker show. Both incidents were isolated, and it's not happening."

"Well, now we're never going to find out." Kate points at me accusingly. "You're hiding."

"I'm not hiding. I have a paper to write."

What I don't tell them is that the paper is written, and I just need to proofread it. What they don't know won't hurt them, but me running into Holden again, that might hurt me. He's already all that I can think of. Being pulled into his orbit for the third weekend in a row isn't something I need to let happen. I'm not saying that it would, but staying home ensures that it doesn't.

"Come on. He's a Tomahawk." I don't need to explain that I have Blaze blood running through my veins.

"He's a hot as fuck Tomahawk," Bridgette replies, smirking.

"Be gone. Have fun." I wave them off. "Call me if you need a ride." I give them my biggest, widest smile.

"You sure you won't come?" Autumn asks.

"I'm good right here. Promise."

"Fine," she concedes. "I'll see you later." With a wave from the three of them, they walk out the door.

I expel a heavy breath I didn't realize I was holding. Dodged a bullet. I get to work proofreading my paper, and once I'm done, my fingers have a mind of their own as they type Holden Bailey into the search engine. I click on images and carefully study each one. I'm assaulted with memories of his hands, his lips, and his scent.

"You did the right thing, Parker," I tell myself. "Holden has heartbreak written all over him." Closing out of the browser, I pack up all of my books and carry them to my room before making my way back to the kitchen. I grab a bag of chips and a can of Dr Pepper and settle in for some Netflix. I push all thoughts of Holden out of my mind. It's better this way.

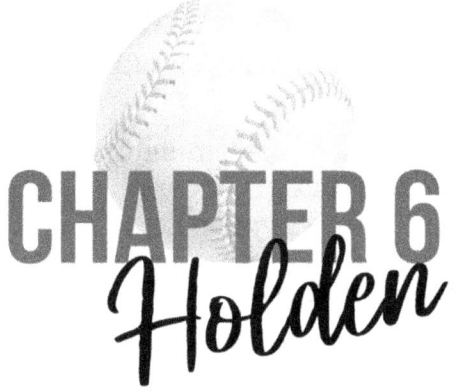

CHAPTER 6
Holden

S ITTING IN MY TRUCK, I stare at the front entrance of The Outfield. The bouncer is checking IDs at the door, and the line is wrapped around the building. My hands grip the wheel as I wage war within myself. There is a 50 percent chance she's in there right now. I'm torn. I want her to be in there. I want to lay eyes on her and feel the softness of her skin beneath the palm of my hands. However, it's after eleven, so chances are if she is there, she's been here for a while. That means there is certainly another man with his hands on her.

The idea of another man's hands on her has me seeing red. I saw her first.

The other part of me hopes she's not there. I don't know how to handle her walking away from me two weeks in a row. It's not something that's ever happened to me, and I can admit, even if it's just to myself, that I don't know what to do with that. I don't know what to do with her.

There's only one way to find out.

Grabbing my keys from the ignition, I climb out of my truck. My feet carry me to the entrance, and I avoid the long line by walking straight up to the bouncer through the VIP lane.

"Bailey, good to see you, man," a tall, burly man greets me. His name tag says his name is Jeff.

"Thanks, Jeff. Looks packed tonight," I comment, making casual conversation. You never know when being tight with the bouncer might be your ace in the hole. For instance, if you have to rip some jackass's head off for dancing with your girl. Sure, she's not mine, but I saw her first. It's my lips that were molded with hers last weekend. If luck is on my side, she'll be kissing my lips again tonight.

"Always is." He nods, raising the rope and motioning for me to walk through.

The music is loud, and the lights are low, just as I suspected. This time instead of going to the bar for a drink, I linger, taking my time walking around the dance floor. My eyes scan the crowd looking for her.

Parker.

It's not until I reach the very back corner do I spot her friends. Autumn is the only name I remember. I stand back against the wall, waiting to see if Parker ever joins them. Much to my disappointment, fifteen minutes later, she's still not with them. Not able to take it any longer, I slide my way through the grinding bodies to stand before Autumn.

She smiles. "Bailey."

I nod. Leaning in close so she can hear me over the blaring music, I ask, "Where's Parker?"

I keep my head bent and turn so she has my ear. "At home."

My heart sinks. I know I said I could go either way, but fuck, I really wanted to see her. She's all I've been able to think about.

I need to. I'm not really sure what I need to be honest. I'm in all-new territory here.

"Where?" I ask.

Autumn shakes her head. "Not a chance," she yells over the music.

I pull my phone out of my back pocket and hold it up for her. "Her number?" I ask, still shouting over the music.

She grabs my hand and pulls me off the dance floor. I follow her like a puppy. She doesn't stop until we're at the farthest corner from the dance floor. The music is still loud, but at least we don't have to shout at one another to be heard.

"Just because we know who you are doesn't mean we know you." Autumn crosses her arms over her chest and stares me down.

"You're right." I nod. "I shouldn't have asked where, but come on. You can give me her number, right?" I'm very aware that I'm for the first time in my life chasing after a woman. I know that I could talk out this club tonight with pretty much anyone of my choosing, anyone but Parker. Not just because she's not here, but because she doesn't want me. At least that's what she's telling herself. Her body, when it's pressed against mine, tells another story.

"Listen, Holden"—she drops her arms to her sides—"as her best friend, I can't give you her number. I already told you where you might be able to find her."

The coffee shop just off-campus. No way am I admitting that I've been there every day this week at varying times and still haven't run into Parker. "The coffee shop." I nod.

"You want my bestie. You're going to have to work for it."

I've never had to work for it a day in my life, and I don't know what to do with this new development. Part of me says I should tell her to fuck off and move on, and the other part of me is excited for the challenge. It's been a long damn time. Hell, I don't think it's even been a challenge. Even in high school, I was destined to go to a D1 school, and the ladies were all over that.

"I'm a professional athlete. Hard work doesn't scare me." It's true. Sure, we get VIP perks and don't have to worry about living paycheck to paycheck to make ends meet, but we also work our asses off.

"I was hoping you might say that." She smiles.

"So let me get this straight. You want me to pursue her, but you won't help me?" I ask.

"I have helped you. I told you where you might be able to find her," she reminds me yet again.

"Well, I've yet to see her there."

My revelation causes her to smirk. "You've been there then?"

"Every day this week," I say, lifting my hat from my head and running my hands through my hair.

"Is that right?" The smile on her face is wide.

"You've gotta give me something."

She studies me for far too long before asking, "Do you believe in fate, Holden?"

"Fate?"

"Yes. Fate. You know things that are beyond your control and are destined to happen."

"I guess. I've never really thought about it."

"Well, I do. I think that you running into Parker two weekends in a row is fate."

"Okay?" I don't really know where she's going with this.

"Holden! I can't interfere with fate. I already did by telling you where she might be. I can't give you more."

I expel a heavy breath. "Fine." I have no choice but to let this go. Obviously, it's not just Parker but also her friend who I can't schmooze with my Bailey charm. "Do you have a ride home?" I ask her. I don't know Parker that well, but I know if she found out I left her best friend stranded or let her drive under the influence, she'd never forgive me. Hell, I'd never forgive myself.

"Oh no you don't, mister." Autumn points her finger at me. "You are not going to use me as an excuse to find out where she lives."

"So you're roommates?" I ask. That wasn't my intention, but I'll soak any amount of intel I can get on Parker. I have a feeling I'm going to need it.

"Yes. And I have a ride."

"Good. Well, I guess... have a good night." I shove my hands in the pockets of my jeans.

"Are you giving up?" she asks.

"I don't know what I'm doing, Autumn." It's the most honest statement I've ever made. I am completely out of my element here.

"Don't give up on her. She's a tough one to crack. She doesn't trust easily, but when she does, she's loyal to a fault. Just... keep trying."

"Yeah," I agree. Although I don't know how much harder I can try. I guess I'll keep hitting up the coffee shop and the club every weekend to see if I can get a glimpse of her. It's a lot of effort for a woman who clearly is telling herself she wants nothing to do with me, regardless of what her body is telling both of us.

"She's worth it." Autumn's voice holds conviction.

Before I can say anything, two other girls who I've seen with them join us. "Oh, damn, Parker's going to be pissed she stayed home to study," the blond-haired one comments.

"That she is," the other one agrees.

"This calls for a selfie." The blonde pulls her cell phone from her back pocket, and the three of them huddle in close. "Smile." I don't smile. Instead, I smolder at the camera.

I know she's going to send this to Parker, and I want her to see the need in my eyes. "You gonna send that to me too?" I ask the blonde.

"Nope. You get my girl to give you the time of day, and I'll reconsider." She winks, but there is nothing flirty about it. She's just like Autumn and has her friend's back. It should piss me off, but instead, I'm relieved she has such great people surrounding her. Good true friends are hard to come by. I have a handful who are ride or die, and I'm happy to know that Parker seems to have that too.

"Come on now."

"Not happening, Bailey."

"I'll guess I'll just have to get it from Parker," I state confidently.

"That remains to be seen," the shorter of the two speaks up.

"Ladies, it's been fun. I think it's time for me to head home."

"Alone?" the shorter one asks.

"Unless you're willing to tell me where Parker lives, then yeah, I'm going home alone." It's none of her business, but pissing off the friends is no way to get in her good graces.

"Fate, Holden." Autumn holds my stare.

"Not sure I'm buying what you're selling." My eyes flash to the short friend. "That remains to be seen," I say, tossing her words back at them. "You ladies, have a good night." With that, I walk away. I've had enough for one night, and that "enough" is basically nothing. I have her friends telling me that we're fated to be together.

I was honest when I said I'm not sure if I believe in fate. I've always been one to follow my gut. My gut is telling me that although I'm putting more work into this than any woman before her, Parker is worth it. It's telling me that she's different. I don't know what it means, but I know that I want to take the time to find out. I owe it to her and to me to explore this. We need to give in to this chemistry that sparks between us. We need to let our bodies succumb to the desire that we feel and work each other out of our systems. Once we've done that, I'm sure this will all fizzle out. It always does.

Sure, when I touch her, it's more intense than anyone before her, but that's the chemistry igniting. Sliding behind the wheel of my truck, I adjust my cock as it hardens at the mere thought of being inside her. If the kiss we shared last weekend is any indication, Parker and I are explosive, and I can't wait to experience more in real life, not just in my mind.

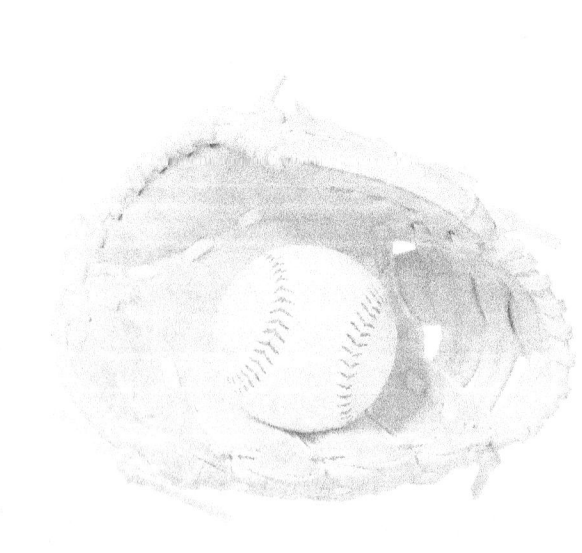

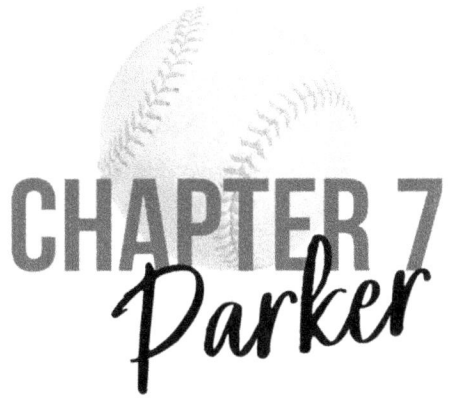

CHAPTER 7
Parker

I'M SITTING AT MY FAVORITE coffee shop just off campus, enjoying my pumpkin spice latte and working on homework when my cell phone vibrates across the table. Reaching for it before it bounces onto the floor, I see I have a new message from Autumn.

Autumn
Where are you?

Cup of Joe.

Autumn
Interesting.

What? How is that interesting?

The little bubbles appear, letting me know she's typing. I reach for my drink and take a generous sip while I wait. The bubbles disappear and then reappear. This happens four times before I begin to get suspicious. Autumn can text a paragraph with one hand in a matter of seconds. Something's not right. Closing out of the messaging app, I pull up her contact and hit call, bringing the phone to my ear. It rings five times before she finally picks up.

"Spill it." She's busted, and we both know it.

"I just didn't know that you were going to be there today."

"I call bullshit. I come here every day. You know this. If I'm anything, I'm a creature of habit, and ever since we discovered this place freshman year, it's been my go-to for a pick-me-up and quiet place to study. So, like I said, I call bullshit."

"Have you seen anyone that you know?" she asks.

"Autumn." Her name is a warning. "What did you do?"

"Nothing. Not really."

"Out with it."

"Fine," she grumbles. "I might have mentioned to Holden that you like to hang out at a coffee shop just off campus. I didn't give him a name or any other specifics."

"What?" I hiss, trying to keep my voice down so that the other patrons at Cup of Joe don't stick their nose into my business. "Why would you do that? *When* did you do that?"

"He was asking for your number and how to reach you that first night. I guided him a little. Just a tiny nudge."

"I can't believe you did that."

"There are like four coffee shops just off campus," she defends. "Besides, it's been two weeks, and you still haven't run into him. He told me that he's been there, but he's never seen you. You two must be missing each other," she muses.

"That might be true, but we both know this is the closest one." She's quiet, which tells me she also gave him this information.

"How am I going to avoid him if you're telling him where to find me?" I pause, letting her words sink in. "And what do you mean he's been here?" I fight the urge to scan the room.

"Maybe you shouldn't avoid him."

"That's not your choice to make." I know she's just trying to play Cupid, but I don't need or want her help.

"He wants you, Parker."

"That's not my problem."

"Fine." She sighs. "If he happens to ever be there when you are, just blow him off like you have been."

"And you think he's just going to give up?" I ask her.

Exhaling, she says, "Probably not. He seems determined to connect with you."

I snort out a laugh. "Yeah, connecting with me is exactly what he wants. Insert part A into slot B. That's the only connection he's worried about."

"Would that be so bad?" she asks, barely containing her laughter at my description.

"Yes. It's not going to happen."

"Grumpy," Autumn mutters, and despite my best effort, I smile.

"Just let it go, Autumn. I love the game, but I'm not out to get played."

"You don't know—" she starts, but I talk over her, cutting her off.

"I don't know. You're right. But I have a good idea, and that's enough for me."

"Fine. I have to get to class."

"It's about time you do something productive," I tell her.

"Oh, hush. I'll see you at our place later?"

"I'll be there, but sleep with one eye open," I warn, with zero heat in my voice. We both know it's an empty threat. Autumn's laughter is the last thing I hear as she ends the call.

Placing my phone back on the table, I let my eyes roam the coffee shop. I don't see Holden, but that could change at any time. He knows where to find me. I grab my pens and shove them in my bag. I'm ready to pack up and head to the campus library, but then I realize I'm being ridiculous.

Holden might have been interested at the club. That's what he does. He goes to clubs, picks up his next fling or whatever, and it's a one and done. He's not going to follow me here to a small coffee shop full of college students. That's not his MO. Not to mention he can have anyone he wants. He doesn't need to be chasing me. I laugh quietly to myself. I can't believe I even considered the possibility.

Grabbing my pens back out of my bag, I take a long, hefty drink of my pumpkin spice latte and get back to work. I lose myself in the business ethics assignment and clear all thoughts of Holden Bailey from my mind.

Two hours later, my assignment is complete, the next week's are started, and my latte is long since gone. Feeling accomplished and knowing I have the rest of the afternoon to myself, I decide to head home and get caught up on laundry. It's been piling up for over a week, and I can't keep ignoring it. Well, I guess I could, but it's bothering the hell out of me to know it's piling up. I hate being behind. Not just on laundry, on anything.

After closing down my laptop, I slide my books, notebooks, and computer into my bag. I gather my pens and highlighters and shove them in the small side pocket, and move to stand, but before I do, a shadow falls over my table.

I don't have to look up to know it's him. I can feel it in the way my body tingles. It's only ever happened around him. There's no denying our chemistry is strong, but I need more than that. That's what I have to keep reminding myself.

Squaring my shoulders, I look up and find him smiling down at me. "Hey, sweet pea." He winks.

"Holden." I try to remain unaffected, but when you're on the receiving end of Holden Bailey winking at you and calling you a sweet nickname, only then can you understand the challenge.

"Planning on going back to college?" I ask.

"College was a good time." He nods. "But that's not why I'm here."

"Well, if you need the table, I was just leaving." I move to stand, but before I can lift my ass out of the booth, he's placing his hand on my shoulder.

"Stay." It's whispered and not at all the cocky version of the man I'm used to.

I don't know why I listen to him. Maybe because I don't want to cause a scene. Maybe it's the sincerity of his voice. Whatever the reason, I find myself relaxing back against the booth, letting my bag slip off my shoulder and tumble onto the seat beside me as Holden slides into the booth across from me.

"Here." He pushes a drink across the table at me. "I asked the barista if she knew what you were drinking. I thought you might need a refill. You've been at it for a while now."

"H-How do you know?"

"I've been here for a while—almost two hours. I saw how focused you were, and I didn't want to interrupt you. I figured that was the last way to convince you to spend time with me."

"You want me to spend time with you?" I ask stupidly. I need to shake out of this Holden daze I seem to be in. Instead, I keep my eyes locked on his and take a drink, knowing it's going to be another pumpkin spice latte. Susie, the barista, is here a lot, and her memory is like a steel trap. It helps that I'm a creature of habit, and Cup of Joe is my local study of choice.

"You know I do," he says, once I've set my drink back on the table. "I've been here every day for weeks. I've even sat in this same booth watching the door, hoping to see you."

I open my mouth to reply, but my mouth is dry. I reach for my drink and take another small sip. "Why?" I finally manage to ask.

He smiles, and I'm glad I'm sitting. I've seen him smile on TV a million times, I've been on the receiving end at the club, but this one, while I'm sitting here across from him, completely sober, it's potent.

"You seem to like running from me. I thought I would level the playing field a little and come to you. A little birdie told me this is your hangout."

"Autumn." I shake my head. "I study here a lot. It's quiet, which is hard to believe as close as it is to campus, but I'm glad that it is. I can disappear into my own world and get my work done."

"It was something to see it. To watch you get lost in what you were doing and block out everything around you. Although, it's not safe." His brow furrows. "You should be more aware of your surroundings, sweet pea."

"This place is perfectly safe. I've been coming here since freshman year."

"And you're a-?"

"Senior." I remind him.

He nods. "I didn't mind college. Most of the work came easy for me."

"What was your major?" I find myself asking. I'm aware that we're actually having a conversation that has nothing to do with him convincing me to jump into bed with him.

"Sports medicine. I figured if the pro gig doesn't work out, I can still be around the sport and be a trainer."

"My sister, she's a trainer." I almost messed up and told him her name and that she used to work for the Blaze but gave it up to be home with her son, Jett, and be able to build a home for him while her husband, Cameron, is on the road all season. They also travel to the away games when they can.

"Nice." He nods. "Where does she work?"

"Um... she's a stay-at-home mom right now. Her little boy, he's three, and she's having another. Her husband, he does well for himself, so she's raising their family." Not a lie, but not very forthcoming as to who my sister and my brother-in-law are, but that's okay. I don't like to divulge that information. Everyone knows who we are or who our dad is. Paisley had already graduated when she met Cameron, and my little sister, Peyton, is now on campus. Most people treat us just like anyone else, but a few fans of my dad or Cam's will ask for autographs. Sometimes, Peyton and I oblige them. Other times, we give them a polite he's just Dad, or he's just Cam, and leave it at that.

"That's good." He nods. "What about you? What's your major?"

"Do you really care?" I ask. It's rude, and by his flinch, I know he feels the heat of my words. "Sorry," I mutter. I don't know why I'm so rude and short-fused when it comes to him. He's trying to be nice, making polite conversation, and he even bought me a latte. The least I can do is be civil. I have no reason not to be. The fact he lights my body on fire anytime he's near isn't an excuse. That's my issue. Not his.

He reaches across the table and links his fingers with mine. "I wouldn't have asked if I didn't want to know."

I nod. Swallowing hard, I answer, "Public relations."

He grins. "So you graduate in a year, right?"

"Yeah, next spring."

He nods. "I'll be your first client."

"I— What?" Did he just say what I think he did? He wants me to represent him? I couldn't have heard that right.

He runs his thumb over the palm of my hand. "Yeah. I'm a professional baseball player, and we all have a PR person backing us."

"Do you have one now?"

"Yeah, and the entire company, as well as the agent who is assigned to me, are complete shit. They let the press think and say whatever they want about me."

"Do you deny the claims?"

"No. They advised me not to during my first year pro. Some bullshit about any press is good press, and here I am with the playboy player title that I never wanted."

"Are you telling me you're not the player the press portrays you to be?" I pause, giving him an "I call bullshit" look. "Come on, Holden, you don't have to pretend to get to me. I already told you this"—I point with the hand he's not holding to him and then back to me—"isn't happening."

"Didn't your momma ever teach you not to believe everything you hear? Or in my case, everything you read?"

"Yes, actually she did. But I don't need to hear or read anything to see you with a different woman on your arm every other week." I give him a pointed look.

"I have events that I'm required to attend. I'm a single guy, and I take a plus-one."

"It's a good cover," I say, trying to pull my hand away. He holds tight, not letting me go.

"It's not a cover." His blue eyes hold mine, willing me to believe him.

"I should be going."

"Have dinner with me?"

I close my eyes and pull in a deep breath. When I open them, he's watching me intently. "Thank you for the offer," I say, remembering my manners. "However, I have to pass."

"Who is he?" he blurts.

"Who is who?"

"The man in your life that's keeping you from having dinner with me?"

"There isn't a man in my life. My dad, my nephew, and my brother-in-law." I almost said his name.

"Then why won't you have dinner with me?"

"Holden." I sigh. "I don't want to be portrayed as one of the many who've been lucky enough to be on your arm. I'm single for a reason."

"What reason is that?"

"I'm waiting for a love like my parents have. I've had enough dead-end relationships to know that it's not worth the effort if he's not who I want."

"Who do you want?"

"I want to fall in love with a man who loves me like my father loves my mother."

He nods. "I'm not giving up, Parker."

"You're wasting your time, Bailey."

"Something tells me that's not true," he says, tilting his head to the side.

"Tell me something?" I ask. This time when I pull my hand back, he lets me go. I grab my bag and place it over my shoulder, prepared to make my escape.

"What?"

"How many women have told you no in your life?"

He swallows hard, and my eyes follow the bob of his Adam's apple in his throat. "None that I can ever remember."

"There you have it," I say, sliding out of the booth.

"What are you talking about?"

"It's the chase, Holden."

"Sure." He shrugs. "That's part of it."

"And the other part?"

"We have chemistry."

I nod. "I won't deny that, but that's not enough."

"Why are women so complicated?" he grumbles under his breath.

"Thank you for the latte. I'll see you around, Bailey." With that, I walk as fast as my feet can carry me, without looking like I'm running away, and push out the door. As soon as I'm outside, I suck in a full breath of the fall air. Next week is Thanksgiving, and the fall air feels more like the winter air today. Ignoring the bitter cold, I rush to my car and don't even wait for the engine to warm up before I'm speeding away.

My hands grip the steering wheel, and it does nothing to remove the memory of his hand laced with mine and the lazy circles he drew on my palm. As I pull into the lot of my apartment complex, it hits me that after four years of using Cup of Joe as my personal study venue, I'm going to have to change things up. I don't know if I'm strong enough to keep pushing him away, so desperate times call for desperate measures.

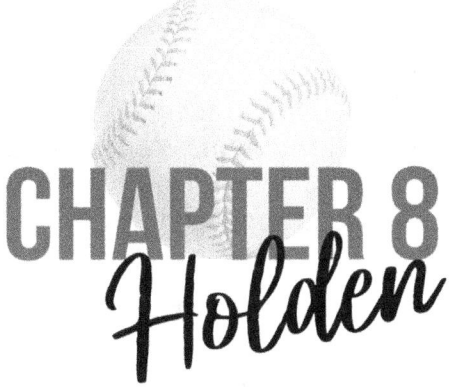

CHAPTER 8
Holden

I WAS DREADING COMING HERE today. I know I need to meet my new team, but I'm still coming to terms with the fact that I'm now a Blaze and not a Tomahawk. However, as I sit here in the players' lot staring at the stadium, it's not dread I feel, but peace. It sounds crazy, but that's what it is. I'm suddenly calm and, dare I admit, eager to meet everyone and start this next chapter of my career.

Grabbing my keys and my cell, I climb out of my truck and make my way inside. I flash my badge that arrived in the mail last week to the security guy.

"Glad to have you on board, Bailey," the big burly guy says, slapping a hand on my shoulder as I walk by.

"Thanks." I nod and smile. There's no point in being a broody asshole. This is my new family, at least for the next year. The

Blaze bought out the remainder of my contract, of which I only had a year left to play. Hopefully, all goes well, and I can make this my permanent home, my permanent extended family. The thought of jumping from team to team until my career is over doesn't sit well with me. I just want to… settle down in one place. I shake my head, the words sounding foreign even in my own head.

I follow the instructions included with my badge and take the elevator to the top floor for the meeting that will be down the hallway, the last door on the right. Walking onto the elevator, I push the button to take me to the top floor when I hear "hold up" being called out. My hand reaches out and holds the door as Cameron Taylor steps onto the elevator.

"When Daddy gets home, we're going to Grandma and Grandpa's for dinner," he says into the phone. I stare at the numbers, trying not to listen to his conversation. "We can toss the ball there. Maybe you can get Aunt Parker and Aunt Peyton to toss with us," he suggests.

At the sound of the name Parker, my mind drifts to my Parker. Well, she's not mine, but you know what I mean. I haven't seen her since that day at the coffee shop. Not for lack of trying. I've been there every day, and sometimes multiple times a day, just trying to get a glimpse of her. Something tells me that she's been avoiding her favorite hangout to evade me. I don't know what to do with that knowledge. I've never had a girl who clearly wants me to push me away like she does. Is it the chase? She said that's what it was for me, but maybe, just maybe, that's what it is for her as well. Maybe she enjoys the attention and the fact that she has me losing my damn mind thinking about her all the time. That's not me.

She's consuming my thoughts and my body. I went to a place called Shorty's with a few of the guys a couple of days ago. The four of us were all traded to the Blaze, and we had a few beers and talked about our new team. Oddly enough, all four of us have come to terms with the trade and hope to work here for the remainder of our careers. Anyway, Shorty's is a place where Blaze players can go and not get accosted by fans. There was a woman there at the bar, making eyes at me, but I couldn't find it in me to give her the time of day. She knew she wasn't allowed to approach me. We learned that from the owner himself when he came over to introduce himself. If she approaches us, she gets tossed on her ass.

At first, I thought it was crazy and that he was talking out of his ass. However, as the night wore on and she kept glancing my way but didn't approach me, I was shocked and relieved. It's not her blond hair that I imagined splayed out on my pillow. Instead, it's a brunette, the same one, in fact, who has had me in knots since the first night I laid eyes on her. I considered that I just needed to get laid, but as I took in the woman with long blond hair and the tight little body, I felt nothing. No stirring of desire below the belt, and that's when I realized that Parker had broken me. I need to get her out of my system so I can move on.

"You coming, Bailey?" Cameron asks.

Shaking out of my Parker-induced fog, I see he's now standing outside of the elevator holding the door for me. "Yeah. Zoned out there for a minute."

"I get it. New team, new teammates, but we're a chill group," he assures me. "Coach Drummond is damn good at what he does."

"Helps to have the talent to back that up." I nod in agreement as we make our way down the hall.

"That it does." He turns to face me, pushing the door open with his back. "Welcome to the Blaze, Bailey," he says, before turning and walking into the room.

I catch the door with my hand as my eyes scan the room. I immediately spot Sonny, Wade, and Tucker, my fellow Tomahawks, or should I say former Tomahawks who were traded with me. There's a seat left next to Wade, who is a third baseman. Sonny and Tucker are a part of the farm team and are both outfielders. I'm surprised they're here today, but maybe Coach Drummond wanted to give them an official welcome. The farm team is just as important as the Blaze professional team. If one of us gets hurt, they're our backup. I like that he included them. It says a lot about him as a coach.

"Hey," I say to Wade. I look past him to nod at Sonny and Tucker. They're both twenty-one and right out of college. That's just two years younger than me, but it seems like a lifetime ago after two years in the majors. Their eyes are wide as they take in the room. I can remember being them. I was one of the lucky ones who went straight to the professional team, but that didn't make it any less overwhelming. I was rubbing elbows with some of my favorite players because I was suddenly one of them. Talk about dreams coming true. It's a moment I will never forget, and part of the reason I was so upset when I was traded. However, the Blaze is a solid team, and if I was going to be traded, I'm glad it was to here.

Coach Drummond stands in front of the room, and we all go quiet. "Welcome. We have some new faces and plenty of old," he greets us. "I'm not going to bore you with strategies. Today is informal and a way for everyone to meet the new members of the Blaze. When I call out your name, stand up."

I feel like I'm back in high school, and I'm the new kid. However, I can admit that bringing the new people into the fold, making them feel as if they are a part of this team is a good move on Coach's part. Hell, he even included Sonny and Tucker, knowing they're on the farm team. Something inside me eases just a little more. I love the Tomahawks, but maybe this move is going to be what I needed.

Parker pops into my head, and I shake off the thought. The last thing I need is to get lost in my thoughts of that woman while I'm surrounded by my new teammates. Turning my focus back to Coach, he ends his pep talk, and Drew Milton, the Blaze General Manager, steps up.

"Welcome." He smiles. "I'll leave all the pep talks to Coach Drummond. I'll start by saying I'm glad that you're here, and I'm looking forward to an amazing season." Everyone in the room cheers and claps, including me. Drew raises his hand, telling us to pipe down, and as soon as we do, the door opens with a loud clink, and all heads turn.

My mouth falls open when I see it's her. It's Parker. She's dressed in a pair of leggings and a sweater that falls just above her knee, and her hair is cascading in curls down her back. What in the hell is she doing here?

"Ah, there she is." Drew smiles at her. She hands him a stack of papers. "Most of you know my niece Parker," Drew introduces.

"My sister-in-law!" is called out, and I turn in time to see Cameron Taylor smile and wink at her.

His sister-in-law?

"What's up with you?" Wade Hoffman, my fellow Tomahawk that was a part of my multiplayer trade, asks.

"That's the girl."

"What?" He turns to look at Parker.

"The girl who keeps turning me down at every turn. That's her." I nod toward where Parker still stands at the front of the room, talking to Drew and Coach Drummond. I'd told the guys about her when we were at Shorty's the other night. I had a few beers and ended up spilling my beans about the beauty who continues to baffle me.

"Hold on. Drew Milton's niece is the girl you've been chasing?" Wade asks.

"I haven't been chasing her." *Lies. Lies. Lies.* I have been chasing her, and I don't understand why I can't just let it go. She clearly isn't willing to give in to what her body wants, so I should move on. However, no matter how many times I tell myself this exact thing, I keep going back to that coffee shop to hopefully get a glimpse of her.

Today is the first time I've seen her since that day at Cup of Joe, and like a jolt to my system, she's as beautiful as ever. I wish I could explain this intense pull I have toward her. And the chemistry we have, it's palpable.

"Dude, she's out of your league," Sonny chimes in.

"Fuck off," I grumble. "I could have her if I wanted her." More lies. She's resisting me.

"Keep telling yourself that, buddy." Sonny laughs.

"You're just pissed off someone finally told you no," Tucker taunts.

He's not wrong. "She will be mine." The words are out of my mouth without thought. The truth is, that's not the truth. It's a lie. I do want her. I'm finding that I want her more than even I first realized, but she's not budging. Hell, she's been avoiding one of her favorite spots just to keep from seeing me. Sure, I don't know that for certain, but I've spent a hell of a lot of time at Cup of Joe, and I've only seen her the one time.

"I call bullshit," Tucker fires back.

"Boys, I sense a wager," Sonny says, rubbing his hands together.

"No wager. It will be satisfaction enough to prove you assholes wrong." Not only that, but if I end up failing, I'm not at the losing end of a bet. Besides, I can't help but think that Parker deserves better than some bet. "I wrote the playbook, boys. Trust me, Parker will be screaming my name before opening day."

"He's afraid he's going to lose," Sonny quips.

"Fuck off," I say, my eyes going to the front of the room, once again landing on Parker.

"You've got it bad, Bailey," Wade says.

I don't bother to reply. We both know I don't chase, and I barely know this woman. I've had my hands all over her and my tongue in her mouth, but I don't even know her last name. Wait. Cameron said she was his sister-in-law. Pulling my phone out of my pocket, I google Cameron Taylor and his wife. I click on the first article, and my mouth drops open. Parker is Parker Monroe. As in Easton Monroe's middle daughter, according to this article. My girl, well, she's not mine, but you know what I mean. She's baseball royalty.

That actually explains so much to me. She's not impressed by my career or my position on the team. Why would she be? Her pseudo uncle is the general manager, and her dad, one of the best first basemen to ever step on the field. I should let this newfound information deter me. I should back away while I can. The waters are too muddy already. However, as I watch her turn to walk out of the room, I know I'm not giving up. When her eyes find mine, her step falters. She squares her shoulders and rushes out of the room.

This chase has turned into something more. Something that I can't define, but I'm going to. I'm not going to stop until I know what this is and why I'm so drawn to her. It's more than chemistry. Of that, I'm certain.

"What do you think, Bailey? Think you can execute the play?" Tucker asks.

"I'm not only going to execute it but I'm also going to fucking excel at it. Watch and learn, boys. Watch and learn."

Sitting back in my chair, I zone out the rest of the meeting. My mind is racing as to what my next steps should be. Parker Monroe thinks she can run, but I've got other plans. I might be new to this chasing a woman plan, but I never fail. I fight for what I want, and I want Parker Monroe.

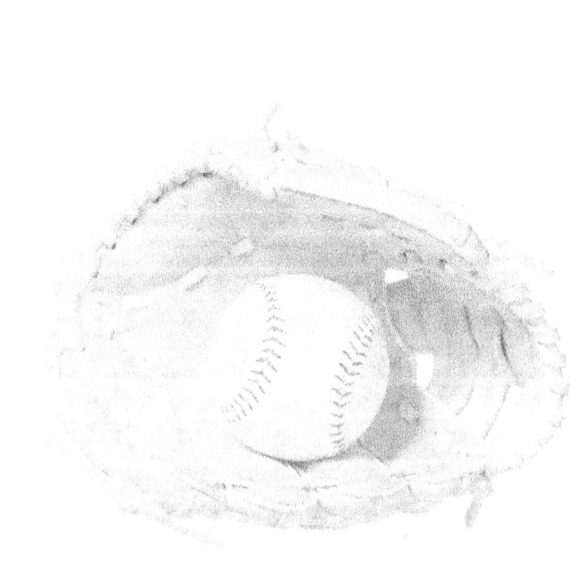

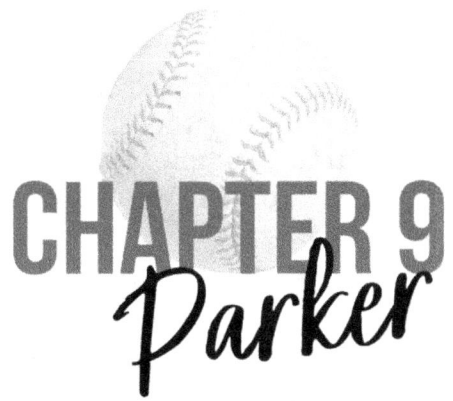

CHAPTER 9
Parker

I PULL INTO THE PARKING lot of Cup of Joe and heave a sigh of relief. I've been avoiding my favorite spot like the plague, but today, I couldn't stay away. My booth in the back corner of Cup of Joe has been my go-to study destination the last four years, and with finals looming, I need my coffee fix and the quiet to get some studying done.

It's not just the quiet atmosphere, but I need all the madness in my head to quiet down as well. I've been helping Uncle Drew. Well, he's not really my uncle, but my dad's best friend. Anyway, I help out in the front office of the Blaze sometimes. When the regular staff are on vacation or just overwhelmed, I give them a hand. It's extra spending money for me, and it looks good on job applications.

When Uncle Drew called and asked me to fill in to make some copies and assemble some packets for the team, I readily agreed.

It is the holiday season, after all, and I still have some Christmas shopping to do. Never in my wildest dreams did I imagine I'd see Holden Bailey sitting in that room full of Blaze players.

I rushed out of the meeting room and straight to the copy room, pulling out my phone and searching his name. Sure enough, a ton of articles popped up about his trade to the Blaze. I'd been going out of my way to avoid him and missed that sliver of information. I sent Uncle Drew a text that I had a test I forgot to study for and hightailed it out of there. Of course, I knew there were new players and a trade. I admit I love the sport, but I don't follow the team as much as I used to when my dad played. Hence the shock of seeing Holden.

Back to the present, I missed my regular study location and their coffee, and I have a ton of studying to do, so today, I'm taking my chances and risk that he might stop and see me. My plan is to hide here in the corner, keep my head down and my nose buried in my books and ignore the world around me. Sure, it's naïve, and I know there is a pretty good chance he's going to catch me here, but I can't focus at our apartment, and the library is always too crowded. I needed my familiar space, so here I am. Risking it for the greater good of my education. I'm one semester away from graduation. I'm not going to let my GPA slip now.

Pulling open the door to Cup of Joe, I'm assaulted with the familiar scent and instantly feel my shoulders relax. Quickly I get in line, and when it's my turn, I order the largest pumpkin spice latte they offer. My usual booth in the back is open, and I rush to settle in. I unpack my laptop, books, notebooks, pens, and highlighters and get to work. I lose myself in my studies, feeling more relaxed and controlled in regards to classes and upcoming finals than I have in a couple of weeks.

I've refilled my drink once and opted for a bottle of water instead of a third latte. Four hours later, and I feel like I have a handle on my course load, and although I still have studying to do, I'm not as stressed as I was before I walked in here today. Slowly, I pack everything back into my bag and stand from the booth, tossing my trash in the can next to the door. As I walk to my car, I can't help but feel relieved that Holden didn't show up.

Maybe this means that he's given up. Hopefully, he's realized I'm not worth the effort of the chase. I'm not falling into bed with him like a jersey chaser. I have higher standards not only for myself but for the man I'm falling into bed with. Tossing my bag into the passenger seat, I buckle up and point my car toward home.

It's Friday, and next week is finals. I've been to Cup of Joe every single day and studied my ass off. I feel good about next week. I'm prepared. What's even better is that not once have I run into Holden. A part of me is disappointed that I was right. He was after the chase, and once he realized I wasn't giving in, he gave up. The other part of me is mad at myself. Holden Bailey is hands down the sexiest man I've ever laid eyes on, and he wanted me. I wish that I could be that person, the one who can just live carelessly and take the one night he was offering. That's just not who I am or who I will ever be.

Resting back against the booth, I exhale. I'm ready. Bring on finals and my last semester of college. The last four years have flown by. Closing my laptop, I begin to pack up my things. I turn to grab my bag, and when I spin back around, a surprised squeak flies out of my mouth when I see Holden standing beside my booth.

"Hey," he says quietly.

"Holden." I breathe his name.

"Can I sit?" he asks.

This is unusual for him. He's never asked for permission before, and it catches me off guard. "Sure," I finally say. He slides into the booth and pushes a small bag and a bottle of water my way. "What's this?"

"You've been at this for hours. You need to eat."

"H-How do you know?"

"I've been here every day this week. I've sat over there." He points at a booth at the other end of the café. I have to lean out of my booth to see it, which explains why I never saw him. I was so lost in my studying and worrying about him being here that I actually missed him.

"You've been following me?"

"No. Well, yes." He pulls his hat off his head and runs his fingers through his hair. "I came Monday to see you. I've been coming here every day to see you, and when I saw how focused you were, I decided not to bother you."

"So, what? You decided to sit and watch me instead?" My palms are sweaty.

He shrugs. "You looked like you were deep in it." He taps his fingers against my closed laptop.

"Have you really been here every day while I've been here?" My heart flutters as I wait for his reply. It might sound creepy, but the thought of Holden Bailey just hanging out so he can see me, even though he didn't talk to me, is kind of thrilling.

"Yeah."

"Why?" I can't figure him out. It if was just the chase, why would he sit and watch me study and not come and talk to me? Is he trying to get into my head? Make me think it's more than that? He has to be.

"I'm not sure," he replies. The tilt to his head and the tone of his voice tell me he really isn't sure why he did it.

"And today? Why did you come to see me today?"

"Today, you seem less stressed, I guess. Almost as if a weight has been lifted from your shoulders." He shrugs.

"Yeah, that's pretty accurate, actually. I've been cramming for finals."

"You're ready." He nods.

I can't help but chuckle. "What's in the bag, Bailey?" I ask him.

"Just a sandwich from the deli across the street."

"They have food here."

"Pastries, which I know are delicious, but you need more than that. You're going to wither away or get sick if you don't eat."

"I eat."

"Well, you need fuel to study."

"I'm done for the day. I'm as prepared as I can be."

"Parker." He sighs. "Just eat the damn sandwich." He hesitates, then says, "Please."

"Are you eating with me?"

"No. I wasn't sure you'd let me stay."

"You mean you'd actually give me a choice?" I'm starving, and the deli bag taunts me. I'm trying to reconcile this nice version of Holden. Not that he's ever been mean to me. He's just usually all bossy and whatnot.

"I'm trying to." A small smile pulls at his lips.

Reaching for the bag, I pull out the deli sandwich and the small bag of chips. "You really have nothing better to do than hang out here all day?" I ask before taking a bite of the sandwich. I moan. It's a turkey club, which is my favorite. When he doesn't reply, I look up to find his heated stare. "What?" I ask, reaching for a napkin to wipe my mouth.

"Did anyone ever tell you your sexy as fuck when you eat?" He licks his lips, and I shift in my seat.

I can't help the nervous laugh that sputters out of me. "No. Can't say that they have." Embarrassment heats my cheeks. It's not every day a girl gets a compliment from a man like Holden.

"Dumbasses," he mumbles under his breath.

"So, what are your plans for today?" I ask before taking another bite.

"I need to do some last-minute Christmas shopping."

"Procrastinator, huh?" I tease.

"Nah, there's this girl I met. I've been trying to get her to give me a chance, so that's been taking a lot of my time." His lip curls in a smile, and if I were standing, it would have made my knees weak.

"Sounds like maybe she's not interested." I manage to keep my voice steady as I say the words. I'm interested. Anyone on the receiving end of Holden Bailey's attention is interested. However, interest does not outweigh common sense. I mean, the point of dating is to find your forever, and Holden doesn't do forever.

"Nah, she's interested." He leans forward, resting his elbows on the table.

"You sure about that?" I ask, popping a chip in my mouth.

"I'm sure."

"Cocky much?" My tone is teasing.

His deep blue eyes hold my own. "It's not being cocky when it's facts. You see, this girl, she wants me, but she's fighting it. Our chemistry is off the charts." He pauses, waiting for me to reply, but I've got nothing. No words come to mind. "Every time I'm near her, her breathing accelerates. I can see the rapid beat of her pulse in her neck." Before I know what's happening, his long arm reaches across the table, and he slips his hand around my neck. We're both leaning close. "Right here," he says softly. "I feel it right here." Slowly, his hand slides down to rest over my chest. "And here. Her chest rises and falls rapidly with each breath every time I'm near her."

I shift in my seat. I should break his stare, but it's as if he has me hypnotized, and I can't look away. It's times like this I wish I could just throw caution to the wind and give him what he wants, what we both want.

"I want you, Parker," he says huskily.

"I want you too," I confess. My words seem to break open something inside him. It's not just me who's breathing rapidly. His calm and cool demeanor has shifted.

"Have dinner with me?"

"No."

He tilts his head to the side and studies me. "Why not?"

"I won't deny the chemistry. It's almost electric, but that's not enough."

"Trust me. I'll take care of you," he says, his heated stare causing my girly bits to stand up and take notice. Who am I kidding? They always notice when Holden is involved.

"Probably," I say, sitting back, causing his hand to drop from my chest.

"There is no probably about it, Parker."

"We'll never get to find out."

"Why? You feel this, you admitted it, and you said you want me. I don't understand."

"I need more. I can't do meaningless. It's not in me. I won't say that you don't commit because I don't really know you. I do know what I've seen and read about you in the past two years since you came on the pro scene, and you've never been seen with the same woman twice. I'm not that girl. I'm not going to jump into bed with you no matter how bad I might want to just to say that I did. I want meaning and more than one night."

"Giving you more than one night isn't going to be a hardship for me."

"I want more than sex, Holden. I'm flattered you've put in this much effort to pursue me, but trust me, I'm not the fun-loving party girl you're after. I like quiet nights in and spending time with my family and friends. I'm not about trying to grow my celebrity status."

"That's what all of those women are. Most of those dates are arranged by my agent. I don't sleep with all of them, and I can guarantee you I never had this kind of chemistry with any of them."

"I'm sorry, Holden." I wrap up the rest of my sandwich and the bag of chips, placing them back in the deli bag. My stomach is in knots, and I can't eat another bite. I'll save it for later for when I'm not in his orbit.

"I've never done committed, but I can."

"I'm sure you can. When you're ready."

"What if I'm ready now?"

"Come on, Holden. We both know that's not the case."

"Dude! You're Holden Bailey," a guy I've seen on campus says, walking up to our table. "My buddy said he heard you were hanging out here. Can I have your autograph?" he asks, digging into his backpack for a notebook and pen.

"Nice to meet you," Holden says, smiling up at him. "However, I'm spending time with my girl right now. We're just about to leave, so give me five and keep the crowd away, and I'll take care of that for you."

The guy is all too eager, and the crowd, well, his loud-ass declaration of who is sitting across from me is the reason there's a crowd.

Holden turns his attention back to me. "Let me prove it to you."

"Prove what?"

"That I can be committed."

"That's not necessary. Besides, that's not how this works. You commit to someone when you care about them."

"Then let me show you I can get to know you. That I can keep my dick in my pants."

"Do you hear yourself right now? Is this really worth the effort of me falling into bed with you?"

"You said it yourself. You don't know me. You're judging me from what you've seen in the media. You of all people should know that the media exaggerates."

I nod because he's right. I do know that. My parents have dealt with it over the years, and my sister and her husband have as well. Hell, both of them still do at times. The media is always looking for something to twist in their favor to sell magazines and get more subscribers.

"Come on, sweet pea. Let me prove it to you."

"I don't want to play this game, Holden."

"No games." He holds his hands up in the air. "Just me and you. Getting to know one another. If that leads to more, then it leads to more."

"I-I don't know." I'm torn. Part of me wants to hold strong, and the other part wants to see if the player is finally going beyond the play.

"Give me your number." He pulls his phone out of his pocket and unlocks the screen before handing it to me. "We can keep in touch. You can take some time to think about it. I don't want you to avoid your favorite place because you're afraid of running into me, and I don't want to not communicate with you for weeks on end. We can start with calls and texts. You control the pace. Just promise that when we walk out of here, you're not going to ghost me."

I bite down on my bottom lip. I know that if I agree to this, I'm setting myself up for heartbreak. Any time spent with this man sitting across from me will only have me falling for him. I know that. I know I won't be able to keep my heart out of the equation. However, as long as I don't sleep with him, maybe I can keep the damage to my heart to a simple crack and not have it blown to a million tiny pieces when this ends or backfires on me.

Taking his phone from his hands, I open his contacts and type in my number before handing it back to him. "I reserve the right to say if this is too much. If I tell you that this"—I wave between us—"whatever it turns out to be is over, it's over."

"I don't know if I can agree to that."

"Then the deal of taking it slow and getting to know each other is off the table. You can delete my number."

"What if you fall in love with me?" he asks. He's not being cocky this time. His tone and his facial expression tell me he's serious. "I can't just let you walk away if that's the case."

"What if you fall in love with me?" I toss his words back at him.

"Never been in love." He shrugs. "Probably won't be an issue, but I already know that if you do fall for me, like that, it would be hard for me to let you walk away."

"Slow, Bailey."

I watch as his fingers fly across the screen of his phone before he puts it into his pocket. My phone vibrates on the table. "You better check that." He smiles softly.

Unknown:

We'll take it slow, sweet pea. You hold all the control here.

I stare at my phone, not sure I can believe the words he's sent me, but wanting to. I really want to believe him. I quickly add his number to my contacts and type out a reply.

Slow

"I should get going," I say, slipping my phone into my purse and packing up the rest of my things.

"You want to come shopping with me?"

I smile at him. "You should look up the definition of slow."

"Fine." He returns my smile. "I'll walk you to your car." He grabs my bag and throws it over his shoulder as we both slide out of the booth.

With his hand on the small of my back, we make our way out of the café. His fans are waiting for us and swarm him before the door to the café is even closed. He holds up his hands to stop them. "Hold up. It's freezing cold out here. Let me get my girl in her car, and then I'll sign whatever you want me to."

Shouts of "thanks" and "is she your girlfriend?" follow us as he walks me with his hand on the small of my back to my car. I quickly unlock the door and climb inside. He hands me my bag and bends down so that we're face-to-face.

"Drive safe."

"Always."

"Text me when you get home."

It's on the tip of my tongue to argue that I'm a big girl, but he appears to be sincere, so I nod. He reaches in and taps my nose with his index finger before stepping back and closing the door.

CHAPTER 10
Holden

F INALLY, I'M ABLE TO BREAK away from the crowd and make my way to my truck. I must have signed a hundred autographs and taken just as many pictures. I don't mind it as the fans keep me in a job, but today, I just wanted to be with her. I had to field questions of who she was to me. I left it at "she's my girl." I know that they read more into it than what this currently is between us, but no way was I telling them she was available. I don't need the competition. Not when it comes to Parker. Waiting for my truck to warm, I check my phone for a message from her, and sure enough, she sent one three minutes ago.

Parker

Made it home.

Dinner?

She replies with a string of laughing emojis, which makes me smile. I admit it's nice that she calls me out and doesn't just fall at my feet. At first, I hated it, but it's growing on me. *She's growing on me.*

Parker:

You have to eat to live.

S.L.O.W.

Repeat that over and over, Bailey.

I toss my head back in laughter. This girl is full of sass, and I love it. I knew she was going to turn me down. Hell, I'm surprised she gave me her number. It's not in my nature to give up, though, and I figure regardless of her wanting to go slow, I'm not going to stop asking for more time with her. There is just something about her that pulls me in. My conversation with the guys comes to mind, and I'm glad I didn't make that bet. Parker is worth more than that. One afternoon in her presence where we're not grinding against each other or tossing out constant barbs is enough to know that.

Fine. Can I at least call you?

Parker:

You just saw me.

Not long enough.

Parker:

Autumn and I are making dinner.

Great. What can I bring?

I laugh as I hit send. I can see her rolling those pretty blue eyes of hers and probably biting down on her bottom lip. Fuck me, but I want to kiss her. I don't think I've ever craved a kiss in my life, but I do with her.

Parker

> You're not invited.

> You wound me, sweet pea.

Her reply is an eye roll emoji. I don't have to look in the mirror to see the smile lighting up my face. She knows how to keep me on my toes. That should worry me, but it just intrigues me more.

> Can we talk later?

I'm trying not to sound desperate for little scraps of her time, but that's what it's starting to feel like. It's almost as if my time watching her work this week has switched something inside me. She's dedicated, and her sass... fuck me, do I love her sass. I watched her that first day, and she looked stressed, so I decided to let her be. I didn't want to be responsible for her missing out on study. She was already there by the time I got to the café on Tuesday, and she was deep into her studies, and I chose to let her be again. Wednesday and Thursday were the same way. Today, however, I needed to talk to her. I watched her work for hours and knew she had to be hungry. She needed more sustenance than just the caffeine she seemed to be living on while she was here. I slipped out and went across the street to grab her something, and well, here we are. I have her number and the challenge for us to get to know each other slowly.

Challenge accepted.

Parker

> I'll see what I can do.

> That's not a no.

I see the bubbles that she's responding pop up and then disappear. Finally, her reply comes through.

Parker:

It's not a no.

I don't reply, knowing she's with her roommate, and I've pressed my luck pretty far today. I'm not going to keep texting and piss her off. I know I have to have limits when it comes to her, and that's a struggle for me. I'm one of those people who knows what I want, and I don't stop until I achieve it. Parker Monroe is on my list of wants. However, I think it might be more than that. Pushing that thought out of my head, I put my truck in drive and head home.

I've spent the past four hours in my room at my parents' house on my laptop looking for my own place. The team offered to put me up in a condo, but I knew that would break my mother's heart. So here I am in my childhood bedroom. Thankfully it has been redecorated. I love my parents, but I'm twenty-three, and I have a multimillion-dollar contract. I need my own place. It's time to make that happen.

I've searched through a ton of listings and contacted a local real estate agent for showings. I'd like to be in my own place before we start off-season workouts in late January. I have about a month to make that happen.

There's a knock on my door just as I'm closing my computer. "Come in," I call out.

"Hey." Mom smiles as she comes in carrying a plate. "I brought you some dinner."

"Thank you. I would have come downstairs."

"Meh, it was nothing. It's just leftover pot roast from last night."

"I'm starving," I confess.

"What have you been doing locked away up here all evening?"

"House hunting," I say, reaching for the bowl and taking a hearty bite. My mother is the best cook in the state of Tennessee. Hands down.

"You know you can stay here."

"I know that. But I need my own space." Thoughts of Parker flash through my mind. I want her, and I don't want her in my childhood bedroom. Sure, that was always a fantasy, and I snuck girls up here in high school, but I'm going to need to take my time with Parker, and I want her screaming my name. Yeah, not here. Not her.

"A mom can dream." She laughs.

"I'm local now. You'll be seeing so much of me you'll be sick of me."

"That could never happen. Besides, once the season starts, we'll never see you."

"Yeah, but on my days off, we can visit, whereas we didn't before. So regardless, you're going to still be seeing a lot more of me."

"Perfect."

I smile and shake my head before taking another bite. Man, this is good. "Where's Dad?"

"Asleep in the chair." She smiles fondly, just like she always does when she's talking about my dad or me. He does the same. My parents were high school sweethearts, and they're still madly in love. I was lucky growing up. So many of my friends had parents who split up or, worse, fought all the time. Stephen and Ashley Bailey are the poster couple for a happy marriage.

"I wish you both would just let me take care of you and quit your jobs."

"You know that's not going to happen. That's your money, Holden. We both love our jobs."

"Come on, Mom. You wipe noses for a living."

Her laughter rings out through the room. "I'm a teacher. Sure, I'm still reminding them to wipe their noses in third grade, but it's more than that. I love my students."

"I know you do."

"And your dad, he's been working at the feed mill since he was in high school. He's running the show and loves every minute. He's content, and so am I. We do well for ourselves. You don't have to worry about us."

She can ask me not to worry all she wants, but we both know it's not going to happen. My parents busted their asses when I was growing up to provide for me. I played select baseball, and we traveled all over. They never once complained, and I always had the best equipment. Sure, I put in the hard work, but they got me involved when I was young and supported me every step of the way. I owe them my career.

"Houses," Mom says, smiling. "You found some options?"

"I found a few. I messaged a real estate agent, and I'm going to look at them tomorrow."

"Well, let us know if you want us to go with you."

"Thanks, Mom."

"Love you, Holden."

"Love you too." She smiles softly before turning and leaving the room.

I scarf down the rest of my dinner and set the empty bowl on the nightstand. Phone in hand, I pull up her contact and hit call.

"Hello." I smile at the sound of her voice.

"Hey, sweet pea. What are you doing tomorrow?"

"Um, this feels like a setup." She chuckles.

"You'd be right. I have three appointments to look at houses tomorrow, and I wanted to see if you'd come with me. I could pick you up, and we can go get breakfast before we have to be at the first showing."

"That's not very slow of you, Bailey," she says. I can hear the humor in her voice.

"I'll eat really slow and promise to drive under the speed limit," I joke.

"You're too much." She laughs.

"What do you say? Breakfast and touring a couple of houses?" I'm keeping it light, but I really want her to go with me.

"I don't know."

"You can meet me at the restaurant. That way, I don't get to find out where you live yet. You can leave your car there, and I'll drop you back off when we're done. Come on, Parker. You know you want to. How are you supposed to get to know me and see if the media is right unless you spend time with me?"

"We said slow. You've asked me to dinner and now inviting me to breakfast and house showings, and it's been what, five hours?" she asks.

"Five hours is a long time," I counter.

"I'm pretty picky about my breakfast."

"Lucky for you, I have the perfect place." She's quiet, and I know she's thinking. It's time to seal this deal. "Come on, sweet pea, please?" I ask. My voice is soft. When she sighs, I know I have her.

"What time?"

"Nine. My first appointment is at ten thirty. That gives us plenty of time to eat and drive to the first showing."

"No funny business, Bailey. I'm going as a friend. That's it."

"Friend. Got it." I agree, keeping my fingers crossed. This girl is going to be more than just my friend. What exactly is yet to be determined, but I can feel it in my bones.

"Send me the address of where we're meeting."

"I'll do it now." Pulling my phone away from my face, I put the call on speakerphone and google the address. I copy the address and text it to her. "Done."

"Momma's Grill. I love that place."

"Yeah?"

"You have good taste, Bailey."

"Of course I do. I picked you, didn't I?"

"I'm going to regret this, aren't I?"

"Nope. I'll be on my best behavior. Promise."

"Fine.

"So, what are you wearing?" I ask, barely able to contain my laughter.

"Stop!" She laughs. "We are not going there."

"Party pooper."

"What are you wearing?" she fires back.

"Same thing you saw me in earlier. I came home and started looking for houses, and now I'm talking to you."

"Such an exciting life for a playboy."

"Yes, I've dated—a lot. I'm young and single. Dating isn't a crime."

"Is that what the kids are calling it these days?" she asks.

"I don't sleep with all of them, Parker." My tone is serious as I will her to believe me.

"It's none of my business either way."

"Maybe not, but you're refusing to spend time with me because of it. Tomorrow and even today is the first step in me proving to you I'm not the player you think I am."

"You've got your work cut out for you."

"Nah. I know me, and soon you will too."

"You excited to start off-season workouts?" she asks, changing the subject.

I know what she's doing, and that's okay. I'm not giving up, and eventually, she'll see she's been running for no reason. I like women. I like sex, but I can refrain. I'm not an animal. I don't stick my dick in anything that walks. However, the thought of Parker and my dick, well, that's definitely something I can get behind.

"Yeah. I was angry at first, but I'm starting to think this trade to the Blaze might be exactly what I needed."

"They're a great team."

"You might be a little biased."

"Maybe," she says, and I can almost hear the smile in her voice. "I should probably go. I told Autumn I'd watch a movie with her."

"I'll see you in the morning?"

"Yeah," she whispers. "I'll be there."

"Good night, Parker."

"Good night, Holden."

I end the call and toss my phone on the bed. My heart is beating a little faster, and something that feels a lot like excitement flows through my veins. What is she doing to me?

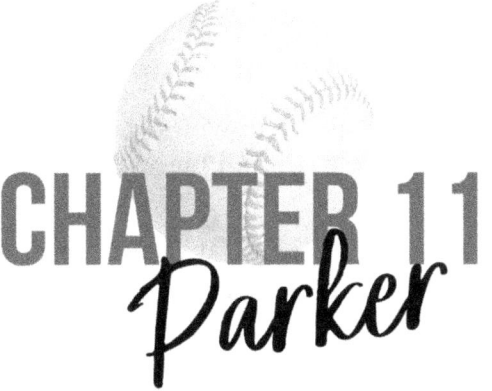

CHAPTER 11
Parker

P HONE IN HAND, I MAKE my way to the living room. I told
Autumn I was going to change. I didn't know Holden was
going to call, but I should have guessed. I can't believe I let him
talk me into going to house showings with him tomorrow. I set
parameters today, and I'm already bursting through them. I
should probably cancel, but I won't. I'll just have to make sure
he understands that I'm doing this for him as a friend.

"I was getting ready to send a search party," Autumn teases
when I take a seat on the couch next to her.

"Sorry, I got a phone call."

"That's cryptic," she says, turning to face me.

Here goes nothing. "Holden called."

"What? Holden? Holden Bailey?" She barely contains her excitement.

"Yep."

"How did he get your number?"

"Funny story." I tell her about earlier today and how Holden said he's been there watching me all week. "It's creepy, right?" I ask.

"It's sweet, is what it is. Who would have thought the player had it in him? Why didn't you tell me when you got home?" she questions.

"I was still processing it all. I didn't expect him to call, although I should have. If that man is anything, he's persistent."

"So what did he want?"

"He asked me to come to a couple of house showings tomorrow."

"Parker! You have to go," she says, moving to sit on her knees. "He's into you. You'd be crazy not to see where this goes."

"I know where it goes, Autumn. Straight to his bed to carve another notch."

"I think you're wrong."

"Come on. This is Holden Bailey we're talking about."

"I get it. He's hot as sin, and he can have anyone he wants, and he's... indulged, or so that's what it seems. You know as well as I do the media can exaggerate things."

"That's what he said."

"You have to admit he's been pursuing you pretty diligently."

"Whose side are you on anyway? Grinding up on me at the club and stalking me at my favorite coffee shop is hardly anything to be happy about."

"It is when he can have anyone he wants."

"That's why he's doing this. He's enjoying the chase."

"I think you're wrong. He agreed to go slow and prove it to you."

"And now here I am, hours away from going house hunting with him."

She grins. "He's wearing you down."

"I should cancel."

"No!" she shouts, placing her hand over my arm before I can reach for my phone. "You need to let this play out. See what happens."

"We both know all that's going to do is crush my heart. I can't detach. It's not in me. Not when he's all sexy and being sweet. He bought me a latte, and then today, he brought me lunch. He's being sweet regardless of his sexy broodiness. It's a lethal combination. Let's not forget he's my hall pass. I was already crushing on him. I'm doomed."

"I'm glad to see that you're finally admitting it. Now we're getting somewhere."

"What are you talking about?"

"Parker, he's into you. I've seen him at the club looking for you. I saw the two of you together. I see the sparks, and I can see the way he looks at you. This isn't just a game to him."

"He's a player, Autumn. He's perfected the act." I say the words, but deep down, I don't want them to be true. I want Holden to be everything she says he is, and I want this... whatever this is between us... to be real. I already know I'm going to fall for him and that I'm going to get my heart broken, yet here I am, willingly allowing it to happen.

"All it takes is for him to find the right one."

"This is a bad idea."

"Maybe, but you're going anyway."

"Yeah, I'm still going." Regardless of knowing he's all about the game, I'm still going because I want to spend time with him.

I want to see the house he chooses to make a home. I don't know what'll happen, but I agreed to go, and I'm not backing out.

"You know, you should be less worried about his intentions and more about how your dad is going to react." Autumn laughs.

"Oh God. He was so awful to Cam."

"I remember you telling me."

"It won't get that far."

"Never say never, my friend. Let's watch this movie," she says, ending the conversation.

I'm thankful for the reprieve. I need to just push Holden and tomorrow out of my mind and focus on time with my best friend.

I'm twenty minutes early, but I was ready and pacing the floors of the apartment. I needed to get out of there before I called Holden to bail, so here I am. Pulling into a spot next to the building, I put my car in park and reach for my phone. I'll scroll through social media and check my email until he gets here. I barely have the screen unlocked when a knock sounds on my window, scaring me half to death. Holden waves and smiles.

Here goes nothing. Grabbing my keys, my purse, and sliding my phone inside, I climb out of the car. "You're early," I tell him.

"So are you." He leans in and hugs me. "Thanks for coming, Parker," he says softly before pulling away. This sweet, softer side is new, and if he keeps this up, it's going to make it harder for me to pretend I don't want him. He laces his fingers through mine and leads me into the diner. My hand tingles from the contact as the warmth of his skin soaks into mine.

He moves past the patrons, nodding when they call out to him, but he doesn't stop until we reach a booth in the very back corner. He releases me, and I drop onto the bench.

"I'm starving," he says as if his hug and hand holding didn't just light my entire body on fire.

"How long have you been here?" I ask, finding my voice.

"About a half an hour or so. I didn't want to miss you."

"We said nine."

"Yet here we are, sitting across from one another before nine." He winks. "I hate to be late. It bothers me."

"I don't like to be late either. I hate to think that I'm holding someone up. And with college, I hate to be the last to enter class, with all eyes trained on me. Yeah, I'll pass."

He nods. "I get a lot of attention because of my career. I've found that if I'm one of the first to arrive at an event, there is less hoopla that comes my way, and instead, it's shined on my teammates."

"You don't like the hoopla?" I ask.

"Nah, not really. Sure, I go with it. It comes with the job. I just wanted to play ball, you know? I wanted to make it my career, and it doesn't feel like work. I get to play and train for the game I love."

"You love to train?"

"It's more like it's a part of me. I started playing T-ball, and my coach then was adamant about physical fitness. My dad says he made us run at that age to wear us out so we would focus, you know, get rid of all of the excess energy." He smiles. The look on his face tells me it's a fond memory for him. "It just stuck with me. Even when the coach didn't require it, I put in the work. In high school, I doubled my efforts. Going pro was my dream. One I wasn't sure would happen, but I knew I was going to give it all that I had. I would know if I didn't make it to the professional league that I gave all that I am to the sport and to my efforts to make my dreams come true."

"That's some serious dedication."

"Nothing new to you. Your dad was one of the best first basemen in the league. And your brother-in-law is damn good too."

"I see you've done your homework."

"You made it easy when you showed up at our meeting last week. The guys talk. It helped that Cameron called out that you were his sister-in-law." He laughs.

"Cam is a great guy. He loves my sister and my nephew something fierce."

"As he should."

"Yeah." I nod. "I've seen a mix when it comes to professional athletes. There are guys like my dad and Cam, and then there are guys like Travis Henderson who openly sleeps with every cleat chaser who so much as looks at him. He brags about it. Did you know he was married for a while? He cheated on her, and she stayed with him for so long. Finally, she got smart and divorced his cheating ass."

"What a dick."

I tilt my head to the side to study him. "Cheating is a deal breaker. I don't care how much I love someone. No excuse can back up the act." I might as well make my thoughts on the subject clear. Not that I think that whatever this is will get to where I need to worry about being cheated on, but it's good to be clear about what you want. To be clear about what you expect.

"I agree with you."

"Well, I'll be. Two of my favorites who haven't been to see me in far too long," Hattie says. She's the owner of Momma's Grill. Her great-grandmother opened the diner many, many years ago, and it's been passed down from generation to generation.

I open my mouth to say hello, but I immediately clamp it shut when Holden stands from the booth and gently wraps his arms around the older woman. "Missed you too, Hat," he tells her.

"It's been too long," I agree when he takes his seat.

"What can I get you kids?"

Holden nods for me to order. "Big breakfast for me. Bacon, wheat toast, over easy, and milk to drink." I ask for my go-to breakfast order.

"And for you?" Hattie asks Holden.

"I'll do the same." Holden hands her back the menu without even looking at it.

"Coming right up." Hattie gives us her signature friendly smile and rushes to put in our order.

"You want to see the houses?" he asks. There's a sparkle in his eyes, and I admit his excitement is contagious.

"Yes." I offer him a smile at the same time that he lifts his phone and snaps a picture of me. "What are you doing?"

"I wanted to capture your smile." He taps the screen and turns his phone so I can see the picture. My eyes are bright, brighter than they should be after my sleepless night wondering how today would play out.

"House, Bailey," I remind him.

"Right." He slides out of his side of the booth and moves to sit next to me. I want to protest, but it does make it easier for both of us to look at his phone at the same time, so instead, I scoot over, giving him more room. "This is the first one." He shows me a two-story monstrosity.

"That's huge for one person," I comment.

"They're all big. They have a decent amount of land and privacy fences and gates."

"My parents and my sister have the same at their places. It's still a big place for just you."

"Well, when you come to visit me, it won't be just me." He winks.

"I'm buying you a dictionary."

"Perfect. I can put it in my new office once I choose a house."

"You're terrible." I chuckle.

"Here we go, kids," Hattie says. She places our plates overflowing with food in front of us, as well as two tall glasses of milk. "I'll be right back with some jelly for the toast and syrup for your pancakes." With that, she scurries away.

"Good choice, sweet pea," Holden says, squeezing my thigh under the table.

My breath hitches in my chest, and I pray he doesn't notice, but I should have known better.

He leans over, placing his lips right next to my ear. "You're beautiful." He turns back around and dives into his food. His hand is no longer on my thigh, but his leg is pressed against mine, and I can still feel his hot breath against my skin. My body can't seem to get the memo that we're taking this slow. Holden's touch is electric, and I can see myself easily craving his touch, craving his warmth.

"Something wrong, sweetheart?" Hattie asks when she returns with the jelly and syrup and a refill for Holden since his glass of milk is already half empty.

"No. I'm good." I smile at her, hoping it comes off genuine. I'm hoping she can't see what the man sitting next to me does to my hormones.

"All right. You let me know if you need anything else. I'll be back to check on you."

"Thanks, Hat," Holden tells her. Once she walks away, he turns to me. "Everything okay?"

"We're going slow."

He nods. "I made you a promise."

"You're sitting next to me."

"Is that not allowed?" he asks, raising his eyebrows. There's humor in his voice, and I want to yell at him for it, but I'm the one who's being ridiculous.

"It's allowed. Just... unexpected."

"You want me to move?"

I want to say yes. I want him to move back to the other side, but then I think about losing his warmth and the swirls in my chest from being this close to him. I want to take things slow, so being next to him like this is going to be a rare moment. We're just sharing a meal. I can do this. "No. It's fine," I finally answer.

Another nod from him, and he turns back to his plate. I pull my fork out of my napkin and begin to do the same. With each bite, I relax further. The food is delicious as always, and it's been forever, so I'm quickly lost in the meal. We eat in comfortable silence, and when it's time to go, Holden insists on paying since he invited me today. I don't put up a fight, deciding to choose my battles.

Instead, I let him lead me out of the diner with his hand on the small of my back. He ushers me to the passenger side of his truck, and I climb up. He waits like a gentleman until I'm settled to shut the door. I'm an hour in and already seeing sides of Holden Bailey I didn't think existed.

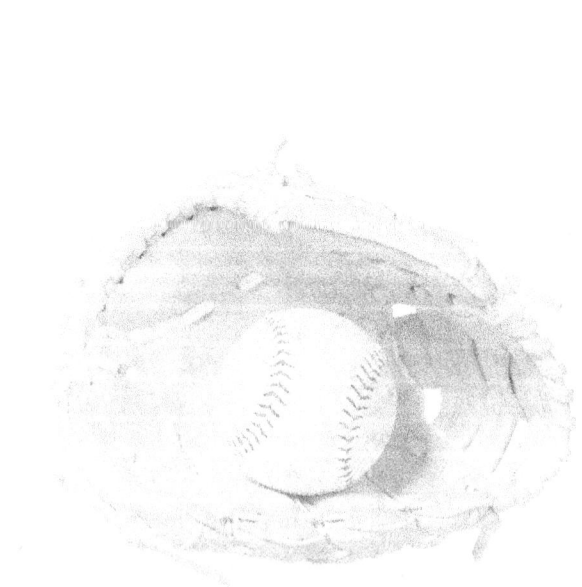

CHAPTER 12
Holden

S TRUGGLING WITH THE URGE TO reach over and place my hand on her thigh, I grip the wheel. It would be so easy, so effortless, but I fight it. I promised her we would go slow. I want her to form her own opinion of me, not one she's gained from the media, and the best way to do that is to follow her rules.

"Are you excited?" she asks, breaking our silence.

"I am. I love my parents, but I miss having my own space."

"I couldn't imagine moving back home with my parents. They're empty nesters as of a few months ago when my little sister, Peyton, started college. She's living in the dorms."

"I'm sure that's taking some getting used to. I know it was rough on my parents. Hell, I'm twenty-three, and just last night, my mom told me I could stay as long as I needed. I read between the lines, and like I said, I love them, but no." She laughs. The sound filling the cab of my truck is better than any song on the radio.

"Yeah, but I'm sure my dad is taking advantage of them having the house to themselves," she says, making a gagging sound.

"How do you think you got here?" I ask.

"The stork, obviously."

"Obviously." I chuckle. "We're here," I say, pulling up to the gate of the first house. It's open, so I drive on through and up to the house.

"Wow."

"Yeah. The pictures don't do this place justice."

"It looks much bigger in person."

It's on the tip of my tongue to reply with "that's what she said," but I bite my tongue. I'm on my best behavior to win this girl over. Instead, I park the car, unbuckle my seat belt, and turn to look at her. "Ready?"

"Yes." She smiles, takes off her belt, and hops out of the truck.

Grabbing the keys and my phone, I do the same.

"Mr. Bailey," the young real estate agent greets me. She's wearing a skintight dress that's way too short and too low cut to be professional. Her heels are a mile high, and by the looks of it, you'd have to scrape her makeup off her face with a chisel because it's caked on so thick.

"Tosha, nice to meet you." I reach my hand out for hers.

"The pleasure is all mine," she purrs, batting her eyelashes.

I move to stand beside Parker, sliding my hand around her shoulders. "Help me out here, Parker. Just go with it, please," I whisper in her ear. "Tosha, this is my girl, Parker."

Surprise crosses the real estate agent's face. "Nice to meet you." She smiles, but it's forced.

"You as well," Parker says kindly.

"Right, well, this way." Tosha shakes her ass as we follow her up the front steps and through the front door. As soon as we're inside and our coats are off, she pulls out a sheet of paper and begins to read. "Six bedrooms, eight bathrooms," she starts, but I interrupt her.

"Can I just read that?" I ask her, holding my hand out for the paper. Her voice is already grating on my nerves.

"Of course." She winks and hands it over.

I'm a man. I appreciate beautiful women. Hell, I'm secure enough with my masculinity to even comment when a guy is good-looking. I've been hit on more times than I can count, and yes, I usually eat that shit up. However, for Tosha to be flirting with me openly with Parker standing next to me just pisses me the hell off. What's worse is that I know for certain other women have done the same thing when I was out with someone else, and not once did it bother me.

Today it does.

"Can we just look around?" I ask, not bothering to keep the irritation out of my voice.

"Oh, well, yes, you can do that. I thought I'd show you around." Tosha sticks her lip out in a pout. Literally, the woman is acting like a toddler.

"We're fine. In fact, we prefer to do it on our own." I lace my fingers through Parker's, making a statement to this woman, and lead her upstairs.

"She's... something," Parker comments when we reach the landing.

"Can you believe that she was hitting on me? Right in front of you?" Removing my hat from my head, I run my fingers through my hair.

"You are Holden Bailey," Parker teases.

"She doesn't know you're not my girlfriend."

Parker shrugs, pulling her hand from mine, and moves toward the first door we come to. "She doesn't seem to care."

"I care."

"Have you in the past?" she asks, calling me out.

"No." The confession feels like sandpaper on my tongue. I hate admitting that to her, the woman I'm trying to impress, but I'm not a liar. I'm not about to start now. Honesty is always the best policy. My eyes find hers, and I will her to believe me. "No. I never cared before."

"I'm sure that's why she thinks it's okay."

"It's not okay." I'm frustrated as hell over this.

"She assumes this time is not any different to any others."

"I've never met her before," I defend.

"Maybe not, but you're a professional athlete, a gorgeous one, and you get a lot of media attention. We've all seen you on the red carpet of a gala flirting with the female interviewer, with a beautiful woman on your arm."

"Fuck," I mutter in frustration. A sudden panic rises in my chest. I'm fearful that she's never going to see past all of that. How can I make her see that this is different? That me spending time with her is different. Sure, it didn't start that way, but well, now it is. It takes one long stride to be standing toe-to-toe with her. My hands cup her face, and I angle her head so that she's looking at me.

"This is different, Parker. *You're* different." Something flashes in her eyes, but it's gone before I can get a read on what it was.

"This isn't slow," she whispers. She swallows hard, and I want to press my lips against her pulse—anything that connects me to her on a deeper level. I crave that connection with her.

"Trust me. *This* is slow. If it wasn't, I'd already have had my lips on yours. I'm not going to stand here and spout bullshit that I don't understand. All I know is that this started out as less. You shot me down, and I wanted you. It's as simple as that. However, things aren't that simple anymore. You're all I think about, and I crave the moments I get to spend with you. I can't see anyone but you, and that should scare me, but it doesn't. So, yeah, this is definitely different." She's staring up at me with what looks like hope in her eyes. She's hoping that I'm not feeding her a line of shit, I'm sure. I'm going to prove to her that I'm a man of my word.

I want to kiss her. I want to bend my head just a little farther and press my lips to hers. I want to taste her. I want to know if her lips are as soft as they look. I run through the ramifications in my head. I told her we'd go slow, but dammit, the need to kiss her is strong.

"How's it going?" Tosha says from behind us, effectively ruining the moment.

Closing my eyes, I push down the anger of being interrupted. Did I not ask her to give us some time? Dropping my hands from my girl's face, I turn to look at the woman over my shoulder. "We've been up here maybe five minutes. I asked you to give us some time."

"Do you have any questions?" she pushes.

I've had enough of this woman. "No. We're done here." I reach for Parker's hand, and surprisingly, she's there, ready and willing to lace her fingers with mine.

"Oh, okay, well, off to the next house," Tosha purrs.

"Actually, we're done here. I'll be calling your agency and getting a new agent assigned to us, and we can look at the houses then." Tosha's face pales. "You've blatantly flirted with me, and she's right here. My hand is locked in hers, and you damn well know it."

"I-I'm sorry, Hold—" she starts, but I cut her off.

"It's Mr. Bailey. I will be talking to your supervisor." This isn't me. I'm pretty even-keeled with this kind of thing, but Parker makes every situation mean more. She deserves respect, and I refuse to work with someone who won't give it to her. It's eye-opening and different for me, but it feels right, and I know that it is, so I'm going with it.

"Mr. Bailey," she quickly corrects. "What can I do?"

"You can go sit in your car and let us have time to explore this place. You can apologize to my girl, and you will treat her with respect."

Tosha turns to look at Parker. "I'm sorry. I'll be outside if you need me." She turns and rushes down the stairs as fast as her skyscraper heels will take her.

"I'm sorry," I say, pulling Parker into a hug. Fuck me, but it feels good to have her wrapped up in my arms like this. I don't know what's happening here, but I do know that whatever it is, I don't want it to stop.

She pulls out of my embrace. "Come on, let's have a look around." With a small smile, she steps into the room, and we do just that.

All the bedrooms have their own bathroom. The master suite is huge, and the bathroom is bigger than my room at my parents' place. "We could definitely play baseball in here."

"I'm not sure if you're channeling your inner Nickelback or if it's just your love of the game," Parker teases as she steps into the shower, turning in circles with her arms stretched out beside her.

"Can it not be both?" I fire back.

"Yeah," she agrees, "it can be both." She takes a seat on the bench in the shower. "This would be great if they had a wand here, so when your significant other is shaving her legs, she can rinse off." She points at the wall. "Or you know, after a game when you're exhausted, and you want to shower, but you're too damn tired. You could just sit here and do your thing."

"I could always have one installed." I don't tell her that I'm picturing her with a different kind of wand. You know, the one otherwise known as my cock.

"You could, but Holden, this is a lot of money. If it's not everything you could ever want it to be, then pass until you find what you've always wanted."

It's not lost on me that when I try to think about what I've always wanted, it's her face that comes to mind. Is it possible to want something, to want someone so bad, even when you never knew it's what or who you wanted?

"Let's go check out the downstairs." She steps out of the shower and moves past me.

I want to reach out and lace her fingers with mine, but I know I've already pushed my luck today. My actions have not reflected our agreement of going slow. I blame her. She's too damn sexy and intoxicating for me to keep a level head when she's close.

Forty minutes later, we've walked through the entire first floor and the finished basement. Parker was right when she said this place was huge.

"So, tell me, does this place feel like home to you?" she asks as we slip back into our coats.

"Not really."

She nods. "You didn't seem to be feeling it."

"It's a beautiful home, but I want to see the others."

"Well, Mr. Bailey, what are we waiting for?" She pulls open the front door and steps outside. I hit the remote start on my truck to get the cab warmed up before stepping up to Tosha's car.

"We're ready for house number two." The real estate agent nods, and I turn away, not sparing her another glance. How could I when I have Parker sitting in my truck waiting for me?

"I'm starving," I announce when we reach the truck. We just left the third house, and it's late afternoon, closer to dinnertime than lunch.

"Where are you taking me?" she asks.

"What sounds good?"

"Anything. I'm withering away over here, Bailey," she teases.

"I should have stopped before this house," I admit.

"It's fine. I'm just messing with you, but food is our next stop."

"Yes, ma'am." I chuckle. I've noticed I've been doing a lot of that today. Parker is so much fun to be around. She's real and honest. She gave me her thoughts on each house as we toured them. I'm not used to women not throwing themselves at me. To have an actual meaningful conversation is new and welcome. Most of the women in my orbit just want the status that comes with being seen with me. Parker doesn't want or need that, and it's refreshing.

She's refreshing.

My phone rings, and *Mom* flashes across the screen in my truck. I glance over at Parker and grin. I hit the button to accept the call. "Hey, Mom. You're on speaker," I warn her.

She laughs. "Thanks for the warning. I just wanted to tell you that Dad and I are going to a movie. I made baked spaghetti. It's in the fridge."

"You spoil me."

"I enjoy it. How was house hunting?"

"Good. Looked at all three."

"And?"

"And I'm processing," I admit.

"Well, take all the time you need. You know that Dad and I are happy to have you home with us."

"Ash, you ready?" my dad says in the background.

"Your dad's impatient. I'll see you when we get home. Love you." The call ends before I can tell her that I love her too.

"Your mom is sweet."

"She's the best. Both of them are. I got lucky in the parentals department."

"You and me both. My dad is one of a kind. He adopted my older sister," she says.

I glance over at her, and her eyes are wide. "I'm sorry. I don't know why I just told you that. Please don't say anything. I mean, it's public knowledge, and they didn't hide it, but that was years ago."

This time, I don't fight it. I reach over and place my hand on her thigh. "I promise I won't say anything. He's a good man."

"The best," she agrees.

"How about we head to my parents' place? I promise you my mom's baked spaghetti is not something you want to miss."

"Are you sure that's okay?"

"I'm positive. We'll stop there and eat, and I'll have you back at your car before they get home. You don't have to worry about meeting the parents," I tease.

"It's not that. We just said we would go slow."

"Friends can't meet friend's parents?" I ask.

"Is that what this is?"

I love how she calls me out. "No. Not even a little."

"It was supposed to be," she reminds me.

"It will be whatever you want it to be."

"But to you?"

"It took one day, hell, not even all day for me to know that it's more than that."

"Spaghetti sounds great." She turns to look out the window, ending the conversation.

That's fine with me. Our time together isn't over quite yet, and I was open and honest with her. Something I will always be. Too many times I've seen relationships fail with my teammates over lack of communication. That won't be Parker and me. We're not technically in a dating relationship yet, but we will be.

I wait for the shock factor of my thoughts to sink in, but it never comes. That's how I know I'm in deep with this woman. The thought of her being mine doesn't scare me. In fact, it only makes me want to work harder to make it happen.

"So, which house did you like best?" I ask, breaking the silence.

"The last one. It's still huge, but I love that it has an in-law's suite. The master bath was excellent. They thought of everything, and that kitchen... Two islands, Holden. *Two.* One to cook and one to serve or to eat at. The backyard is already set up for entertaining with a pool and hot tub. There's plenty of space for you to build your own ball field for your kids. My dad did that with us, and we loved it. A four-car garage that this monstrosity will fit in." She laughs. "And a huge man cave outbuilding that's heated and cooled."

"Is that all?" I joke.

"I can keep going."

I'm not looking at her, but I can hear the smile in her voice. "That was my favorite too. It just felt like home, or like it could be."

"Right?" she agrees. "And honestly, you wouldn't even need to paint. The colors they chose are perfect, and they had it touched up before putting it on the market. It's move-in ready."

I hit my signal to turn into Mom and Dad's driveway. "I want it."

"Then call her and make an offer."

Grabbing my phone out of my pocket, I dial Tosha, and the call rings out through the cab of the truck. "Mr. Bailey," she greets. Her tone is nothing but professional.

My eyes find Parker's, and she slaps her hand over her mouth to keep from laughing. "The last house, the one on Hillcrest Lane. I want it. Full asking. Let's get this done."

"Yes, sir. I'll email the paperwork for you to sign and send back to me within the hour."

"Perfect. Thank you." I hit end, not bothering with further pleasantries. "Come on, sweet pea, let's get you fed." We climb out of my truck and head inside. A part of me wishes my parents were here so they could meet her, but I know we're not there yet. I've never wanted my parents to meet a woman, not until Parker.

CHAPTER 13
Parker

AUTUMN WAS GONE LAST NIGHT when I got home. I was grateful. Not because I didn't want to tell her about my day with Holden, I did. I just needed some time to process it myself before I could retell it.

He was... unexpected. He was sweet and attentive, and the way he stood up for me, well, let's just say I was turned on. He was honest with me about his past, and I'm still floored that he thinks that this, whatever it is between us, is different. He thinks that *I'm* different.

I'm trying really hard not to let myself fall for him, but in one day, he's managed to start tearing down the walls I thought I had thoroughly constructed to keep him at a distance. One look into his sparkling blue eyes, and it's as if my body forgot everything we had decided.

That we're not going to fall for Holden Bailey.

It took forever for me to fall asleep last night, so why I'm up at the ass crack of dawn on a Sunday is beyond me. I should probably get up and get moving. I need to do laundry, and I want to read over my notes for finals one more time this week. Reluctantly, I climb out of bed and head to the shower.

When I make it back to my room, I'm not surprised to see Autumn curled up in my comforter, eyes still heavy with sleep, waiting on me. "Morning, sunshine," I greet.

"Ugh, why are you up so early?"

"Time to get started on laundry and get some studying in."

"I can't wait for finals to be over." She groans.

"You and me both."

"So, I need the details from yesterday, but first you have a message. It must be important for it to be going off at this hour."

"It's seven thirty." I laugh at her.

"Too early to be up. We sleep in on Sundays, remember?" she asks as she burrows deeper into my covers.

Grabbing my phone from the nightstand, I unplug it from the charger and swipe at the screen. I see Holden's name, and my heart rate spikes.

Holden:
Good morning, sweet pea.
Can I see you today?

Lots of laundry and notes to review for finals next week.

Holden:
I can help you study.

You really think I'll get any studying done?

> **Holden:**
>
> Parker Monroe! Get your mind out of the gutter.

> You know what I mean.

> **Holden:**
>
> Dinner?

> Let's see how the day goes.

> **Holden:**
>
> That's not a no.

I smile. This conversation sounds very familiar. I can imagine him smiling too. He's too charming for his own good. The worst part is I don't think he even tries to be. That's just who he is.

> That's not a no.

"That's him, isn't it? That's Holden?" Autumn asks. She's now sitting up with her back leaning against the headboard.

"Yeah, it's Holden."

"Tell me everything." Autumn squeals, suddenly very awake.

"We had a good day. He took me to Momma's Grill for breakfast, and we looked at three different houses. We had dinner, and he took me back to my car."

"Nope. Not good enough. I want details, Parker. Spill."

"Really, there's not much to tell. I mean, the real estate agent was blatantly flirting with him even though he introduced me as his girl, and his hand was on the small of my back. He pretty much told her off and told her I was to be treated with respect."

"Damn. It sounds like Bailey has a little alpha in him," she teases.

"It was sweet, really. We're not together. We're not dating or anything. We agreed to take whatever this is one day at a time. This is slow, but he still stood up for me."

"You think he's just trying to impress you?"

Our conversation in the hallway of the first house flashes through my mind. "No. I really don't think so. I pointed out that he's been recorded during several red carpet events with a woman on his arm and the reporter openly flirting, and he never seemed to mind."

"And what did he say?" she prompts.

"He said that yesterday was the first time it ever bothered him."

Autumn squeals and does a weird shimmy dance. "I told you!" She points a manicured finger at me. "I told you that he was into you. You're going for it, right? You're going to see where this goes?"

"We're taking it slow."

"To hell with slow." She waves her hand in the air, making me laugh. "What did he want?"

"He said good morning and wanted to know what I was getting into today. I told him I had to do laundry and study."

"And what was his reply?"

I try really hard not to smile, but I can't seem to stop it. "He offered to help me study."

"Holden Bailey offering to help his girl study." She places her hand over her heart dramatically.

"Stop." I shake my head at her theatrics.

"For real, though, you said yes, right?"

"No. I told him I didn't think it was a good idea, and he asked about dinner. I told him I'd think about it."

"Text him back and give him our address. Tell him you thought about it and you'd love the help and dinner. I'll go hang out with Bridgette or go see my parents. You can have the place to yourselves." She wags her eyebrows.

"We don't need the place to ourselves, and I'm not sure I want him to know where we live."

"He's not a stalker, Parker."

"I know, but he already knows about my escape to Cup of Joe. This is the only other place I can hide from him."

"Why do you want to hide from him?"

"Because he makes me want... more. So much more."

"That's not a bad thing."

"That's just it. I'm starting to think you might be right. But I don't know. I wanted to go slow, get to know him, and form my own opinion."

"You can still do that. Hiding from him isn't going to make that happen. You can still have him come help you study and eat dinner together. That's not jumping into bed with him. Take things slow in that aspect, but you have to open yourself up to him if you expect the same in return."

"I know you're right."

She picks my phone up off the bed and hands it to me. "Call him. I'm going to grab a shower and go hang out with my parents. Besides, Mom always sends me home with leftovers and yummy snacks." Her laughter follows her out of my room.

Sitting on my bed, I stare down at my phone as if it has all the answers. Autumn is right. I can't expect him to let me see who he really is and hold back on him. I like him. I like spending time with him, and I already know falling for him through all of this is inevitable. He admitted that it's more to him, and I pretty much did too. I didn't tell Autumn that. Not because I didn't want her to know, but those thoughts that we openly shared with one another felt intimate.

Lifting my phone, I dial his number and place it to my ear. If I'm doing this, I'm going to go all in. I know I'll have my friends and family here to pick up the pieces, but there's a part of me deep inside that says I won't need them to. That my pieces are going to remain firmly intact.

"Parker?"

"Hey, Holden." I hear an audible sigh. "Everything okay?" I ask, concerned.

"Yeah. I just didn't realize how bad I wanted to hear your voice until I did. You know?"

My heart does this fluttering thing that's never happened before in my chest. "Have you made plans yet for today?" I ask him.

"None. Well, other than waiting on the real estate agent to call about my offer on the house. I was hoping to hear from you."

"You still feel like helping me study?"

"Yes." There is no hesitation in his reply.

"Okay, well, I'd really like that," I admit.

"Tell me when and where."

"My place." I pause. "Whenever. I just finished my shower, and I'm going to grab something for breakfast."

"I'll bring breakfast. Is Autumn home?"

"Yeah, she's still here, but she's going to her parents."

"Tell her to wait. I'll bring breakfast for all of us. Just send me where I need to be. I'm putting my shoes on now."

"You don't have to come now." I chuckle.

"I do. I need to get there before you change your mind. Send me the address, sweet pea. I'm on my way." The line goes dead, and my smile is so wide I fear my face might crack. I text our address and rush to make my bed and do a quick sweep of the apartment.

"Whoa, where's the fire?" Autumn asks when I run into her as she's coming out of the bathroom.

"I did it. I called him. He's on his way over. He said not to leave. He's bringing us breakfast, and I'm rushing to do a quick pick up of the apartment."

"Relax, Parker. We keep this place on point. We're both neat freaks. Besides, you need to be yourself. You want the real Holden. Give him the real Parker."

"You're right." I nod as I pull in a deep breath, trying to calm myself.

"Grab your books and get set up. He's coming to help you study."

"Right. Good idea." Turning, I walk back into my room, grab what I need, haul them to our small kitchen table and get set up. I have study guides and can have Holden quiz me. I feel good about the material, but I want to use today as a refresher. However, I'm not really sure how much information I'll retain with Holden being here. Good thing I'm ready.

To keep from pacing, I unload the dishwasher. I've set out plates, but I have no idea what he's bringing for breakfast. I didn't ask, and to be honest, I don't care. Neither Autumn nor I am picky eaters. I'm just nervous. It's not like Holden is the first guy to come see me at our place. I've dated, hell, I've had boyfriends. Sure it's been a while for both, but the point is this isn't a first for me, but it sure does feel like it.

I wipe my sweaty hands on my leggings and glance at the clock on the wall. His parents don't live far, so he should be here anytime. Just as I think the thought, there's a knock on the door. I glance down the hall, hoping Autumn heard and is ready to come out and help break some of the tension, but her bedroom door is shut.

"You can do this, Parker," I whisper to myself. With careful steps to hopefully calm my racing heart, I make my way to the door. I check the peephole just to make sure it's him and pull the door open. "Hey." My voice is breathy, and I inwardly curse myself. He's just a man, Parker. A very sexy man.

"Beautiful," he greets. With a large bag of whatever he brought in one hand, he leans in close and gives me a one-armed hug with the other. "I hope you're hungry."

"What are we having?" I step back and let him in before closing the door.

"Homemade biscuits and gravy, with sausage patties."

"You cooked?"

"I did." He smiles. "I made my parents breakfast, and this was left over. I always made too much when I was living on my own, so I could go a few days without cooking. It's a habit." He shrugs, and this sexy man actually manages to look adorable.

"What smells so good?" Autumn asks, joining us.

"Holden made breakfast." I widen my eyes just for her, and she grins.

"It smells great. Thank you."

"You're welcome." He gets to work sitting out a container of biscuits, another of gravy, and another of sausage patties. "Eat up, ladies." He winks at me as I hand him a plate. "I already ate," he reminds me.

"Come on, Bailey," Autumn goads him. "You're a growing boy, and this is the off-season. Enjoy it while you can."

"Trust me. I have been. Parker and I had spaghetti and garlic bread for dinner last night, and I had two helpings."

"Oh, did you?" Autumn asks.

"Mom's baked spaghetti doesn't last long in our house," he replies.

"It was really good," I agree.

"Sounds like it." Autumn gives me a look that lets me know she knows I held some information from her and that she'll be grilling me about it later. That's fine. At this point, I'm in this, and my bestie is great at giving advice and keeping me out of my head. I'll tell her everything. I told her we had dinner. I just failed to mention it was at his parents' place. There's not much to report. He was the perfect gentleman. But he is Holden Bailey, and I was in the inner workings of his home, so yeah, there's that.

We make small talk while we eat, and when we're finished, Holden insists we keep the leftovers and helps us clean up the kitchen. Something else I could never really imagine him doing.

"Well, I'm out of here. You kids have fun. I'm going to visit with my parents and disappear in their basement to get some studying done too."

"You can join us," Holden offers.

"Thank you, but I do better closed off on my own. I'm too easily distracted. I could never study at Cup of Joe like Parker does. Later." She waves, grabs her bag, and rushes out the door.

"You ready?" Holden asks.

"Let's do this." We move from the small kitchen island to the table, and I hand him my first study sheet.

CHAPTER 14
Holden

"**I** CAN'T DO IT. I'M done." Parker leans her head back and groans. The sound does things to me that it shouldn't. "This chair is hurting my ass. I'm tired, my brain is on overload, and I'm hungry."

"Do you want to go out or order in?" I don't give her the option not to have dinner with me. We've been sitting here for hours going over her study guides, and I'm not ready to end this day yet. If you'd have asked me six months ago if I would have been happy to spend the day studying, I would have told you that you'd lost your damn mind. Yet here I am. I have a feeling I'd do just about anything this girl asked of me. It's a scary thought, but not scary enough to walk away.

"I don't want to go out. I want pizza." Lifting her head, she grabs her phone from the table and looks at me. "What do you want?"

"I'll eat anything." I bite down on my cheek to keep from smiling. The fact she's including me instead of trying to get me to leave says I'm growing on her.

"Meat lovers it is." I watch as she dials the phone and places it to her ear. "Hi, I need to place an order for delivery." She pauses. "I need a large meat lover, an order of breadsticks with cheese, and twenty boneless wings, mild." She rattles off her address and hangs up. "It'll be here in thirty minutes."

"Come on." I stand from the hard-ass chair and offer her my hand. She places hers in mine and allows me to pull her to her feet. I lead her to the living room and sit on the couch, taking the spot next to her. "Turn toward the kitchen." She does as I ask without complaint. My hands settle on her shoulders as I begin to knead her muscles.

"Oh God." She groans, and the sound goes straight to my dick. Two words and a moan from her, and I'm hard as steel and ready to go.

"Feel good?" I ask, my voice gruff. It's a dumb question as questions go. Her moan is proof enough that it feels good.

"Mmm," she replies.

Every noise that comes out of this gorgeous girl does it for me. Hell, she could cough, and my dick would stand up and salute her. I've never had this kind of reaction to a woman before, never been turned on just because she's breathing.

Removing my hands from her, I move to rest my back against the couch, spreading my legs wide.

"Wait, why did you stop?" She looks at me from over her shoulder.

"Come here." I pat the spot between my spread legs. "I can get a better angle this way."

She hesitates for maybe a second before she moves to sit between my legs. Her ass is pressed up against my dick, and I realize this was a bad idea. No way is she going to miss what she does to me. Not in these sweats. I knew we were having a day of just hanging at her place, so sweats and a long-sleeve T-shirt are what I'm wearing.

"Oh," she says and moves to stand.

I pull her back into my chest, wrapping my arms around her waist. "Stay. Please. Let me help you." My voice is low and gruff. I'm so fucking turned on my vision starts to blur.

Her shoulders relax, and I continue her massage, ignoring my throbbing cock. "You're ready, Parker. You know the material," I say to distract myself from the sounds she's making and the raging hard-on in my pants.

"I know. I just want to finish strong, you know? This is it. I have one more semester, and I'm a college graduate." I can hear the pride in her voice.

I lean in close, my breath caressing her cheek. "You're going to do great, babe."

I watch as goose bumps break out across her skin. I'm glad she can't see my face, so I don't have to try to hide my grin. It's nice to know I'm not the only one affected by us being this close to one another. Instead of continuing our conversation, I keep quiet and rub her shoulders. With each caress of my hands, I can feel her muscles relax

"I told you we should have moved to the couch."

"The couch is... too tempting," she confesses.

"The couch or me?" I put the question out there.

"Both." She laughs softly. "We both know what happens when we get too close."

"I'm close to you now," I remind her, digging my fingers into the base of her neck.

"You are, and trust me, it's not easy to just sit like this. I can feel how much you want me, and your hands are on me. It's taking extreme effort to be good."

"Who said I wanted you to be good?" I don't want her to be good. She should be bad, very, very bad. In fact, we can be bad together.

"Holden—" she starts, but the knock on the door stops her. "That was fast," she says, standing. She moves to the kitchen to grab her purse. I don't wait on her. Instead, I make my way to the door, my wallet already in hand, ready to pay for our dinner.

"Thanks, man. My girl was starving," I say, looking down to pull some cash from my wallet. When I look up to hand it to him, I'm taken aback when I see Cameron Taylor and his wife, Parker's sister Paisley, standing before me.

"Who's dat?" the little man in Cameron's arms asks.

"Holden, I've got it. You helped me study, and the mas—" Her voice cuts off when she stops to stand next to me and sees who's standing at her door.

"Pawker!" the little guy exclaims and leans over for her to take him.

"Hey, buddy." She smiles and pulls him from Cameron's arms to her own. "I missed you," she says, snuggling him close. She presses kisses to his cheeks, and he laughs as if it's the funniest thing to ever happen to him.

I step back from the door and hold it open for them. Cameron watches me intently while Paisley grins and pats my chest as she enters her sister's apartment. As soon as I get the door closed, there's another knock. I take a deep breath and hope it's not another member of her family. Not that I want to hide, but I don't know how she's going to handle this. And as selfish as this sounds, this was our night.

Pulling open the door for the second time, I sigh in relief that it's the delivery girl. I quickly hand her a wad of cash, way more than the cost of the food, and shut the door. "I'll just put this in the kitchen," I say when I turn to find all eyes on me.

I place the box on the small island and rummage to find paper plates and napkins. I set it all up like this is my place and her family are my guests. After it's done, I brace my hands on the island and bow my head. Parker and I were having a great day. I felt like I was actually getting somewhere with her, and now, I don't know if all of that's going to be washed away.

"What's up, man?" Cameron says.

I look up to find him standing in the doorway. "Hey. Hungry?" I ask.

He shakes his head. "No, but I heard you say your girl was." He gives me a look that tells me I need to explain.

The thing is, I don't need to explain shit to him. I open my mouth to tell him that exact thing, but then I think about Parker. This is her family, and although I'm not sure what we are, I know I want to be more with her than I've ever been with anyone else. So, instead of barking off with some sarcastic comment, I go with the truth. "She is. We've been studying for her exams all day." I point at where her books and laptop are covering every inch of the small kitchen table.

"So you were helping her study?" he asks, crossing his arms over his chest.

"Yep," I say, popping the *p*. I want to tell him to fuck off, but again, he's her family.

"She's my sister."

"Sister-in-law," I correct. He narrows his eyes but doesn't get to reply before Parker and Paisley join us.

I grab a plate and open the pizza box. I add a slice, a breadstick, and three wings and hand it to Parker, who's still holding her nephew. Parker takes the plate, and I reach for the little guy.

"Hey, little man," I greet him. He comes to me easily. "Are you hungry?" I ask him.

"What's your name?" he asks.

"My name is Holden. What's your name?"

"I'm Jett."

"Nice to meet you, Jett." I offer him my hand to shake, and he giggles because it's the wrong hand for a proper handshake. "You want something?" I point at the food on the counter.

"I wuv chicken," he tells me. "Papaw eats dem wif me when we watch baseball."

I look up at Paisley. "They're mild. Can he have one?" I ask her.

"He'll eat them hot." She laughs.

"All right, buddy. Let's sit you next to Aunt Parker, and I'll make you a plate." I carry him to the table, and with one hand, I help Parker move her study materials to a pile and push them off to the back of the table.

"I sit wif you, Pawker." Jett smiles at her like she hung the moon. I know the feeling.

"I'll be right back." I sit him in the chair next to her and make sure she has him before going to grab him two wings and a stack of napkins. I have a feeling they're going to need them.

"Tank you, Holden," Jett says, grabbing a wing and putting it to his mouth.

"What do you want to drink?" I ask Parker.

"Uh... water's fine."

"And what about you?" I ask Jett.

"I want milk."

My eyes find Parker's. "He has a sippy cup in the cabinet. I can get it." She starts to rise.

I place my hand on her shoulder. "I got it, babe. You're hungry. Eat." She smiles up at me, and my chest tightens. It happens every damn time she gives me that smile. I move around the kitchen like I own the place. I get lucky, and the first cabinet I look in holds the sippy cup. I pour my man Jett some milk and grab Parker a bottle of water.

"You want something to drink?" I ask Paisley and Cameron as I deliver drinks.

"No, thank you. We've actually already had dinner, but this one won't pass up food." Paisley smiles, taking the seat next to Jett at the table.

"Not that you're not welcome, but what are you guys doing here?" Parker asks.

"We were just out for a drive looking at Christmas lights."

"All the wights, Pawker." Jett nods.

"I love Christmas lights," she tells her nephew.

"Anyway, Jett recognized your apartment complex and wanted to stop and say hi."

"Aw, did you miss me, Jett?" Parker asks.

He bobs his little head. "And you have chicken." The four of us laugh at his antics.

"Are you not going to eat?" Parker asks me.

"I will. You ready for more?" I ask, seeing she's almost finished her slice of pizza.

"Not yet. Make a plate."

I nod, doing as I'm told, and grab a water from the fridge for myself. I don't sit at the table. Instead, I choose to lean back against the counter and observe.

"So, how long has this been going on?" Cameron asks.

"By this, you mean me studying for finals?" Parker glances over at me. "You got here at what, a little after eight?" she asks me.

"About that," I answer her.

"Holden made breakfast, Autumn left for her parents, and we've been at it ever since. Hence the reason we're starving."

"I'm starving too," Jett chimes in, making her smile.

"You made breakfast?" Cameron asks me.

"She needed fuel to study." Neither one of us mentions that I didn't cook here, but I don't think it really matters. I made her breakfast, and she's telling her family all about it. That tightening feeling in my chest is back. Then again, I'm not sure it's left since the day I first met her.

"You ready for your exams?" Paisley asks her.

"I am." She looks over at me.

"She's ready," I tell her sister. "She knows the material like the back of her hand. And now I do too." I laugh.

"I'm so full," Jett says, popping the last bite of his second boneless wing into his mouth.

Paisley wipes his hands and mouth and grabs his trash, standing to throw it away. "Jett, give Aunt Parker a hug. We need to get home and give you a bath."

"Wove you, Aunt Pawker," Jett says, hugging her tight.

"I love you too. We need to have a sleepover soon."

"Yay! Can Holden come?" he asks in all of his innocence.

"Maybe." Parker smiles at him.

Maybe? Hell yes. I need to remember to spoil this kid rotten anytime he's with us.

Jett surprises me when he runs to me and wraps his arms around my legs. "Bye, Holden," he says, smiling up at me.

I ruffle his hair. "It was nice meeting you," I tell him.

He nods and runs to his mom, who lifts him into her arms. "Paisley, let me carry him," Cameron says with concern in his voice.

"I'm pregnant, Holden, not handicapped. The doctor said now that I'm in the second trimester, I can lift him."

"But you don't need to if I'm here. Come to Daddy," Cameron tells his son. He pulls Jett from her arms and snuggles them both close.

Paisley looks at her sister. "We're going to go. Good luck next week." She turns to me. "Holden, it was nice to meet you." She gives me a kind smile.

Technically, we were never introduced, but she did watch me introduce myself to her son, and it's obvious she already knows who I am. Then there's her husband, my new teammate. He doesn't seem happy to see me, but that's fine. He's just going to have to get over it. The more time I spend with his sister-in-law, the more of her I crave.

"Thanks for helping me today," Parker says as we pack up the leftovers and place them in the fridge. She called Autumn to see if she wanted us to leave it out for her, but she said she was eating with her parents.

"Thanks for letting me," I say, pulling her into a hug. It's not the actions of a man who is supposed to be taking things slow, but I just needed to feel her against me for a minute.

She pulls back, just enough to look up at me. "What are you doing now?" she asks.

"Holding you."

"I mean, do you need to go?"

"No."

She nods. "You want to watch a movie?"

"Yes." Hell fucking yes, I do. She steps out of my embrace and moves to the couch. I hit the light switch on the wall, and the kitchen goes dark. I don't pretend I don't want her in my arms when I take the spot next to her on the couch and put my arm around her.

"What do you want to watch?" she asks, pointing the remote at the TV.

"You."

"Come on." She laughs.

"I'll always be honest with you, Parker."

"Then tell me what you want to watch."

"I just did."

She rolls her beautiful blue eyes. "Fine. But I don't want any grumbling if you don't like what I choose."

"Deal."

She scrolls through the channels and lands on Hallmark. "You good with Christmas movies?"

"Sure. I grew up watching them with my mom."

"Aw, you're such a good son." She snuggles into my chest, and that ends our conversation. Parker focuses on the movie, and me, well, I focus on her. I run my fingers through her hair and just enjoy being here with her like this. It's simple and more than I expected when she called me this morning.

I'm so enthralled with her, and just being close to her, I don't even notice that the movie is over until the front door opens. I turn to see Autumn walking in, holding a bag of what looks like laundry, a backpack, and a reusable grocery bag. I move to help her, and she shakes her head.

"No. You'll wake her." I look down, and sure enough, Parker is sound asleep. I knew her body was completely relaxed against mine, and I thought maybe she was, but I didn't want to speak and break the spell we were both under. Well, that I was under since apparently, she was asleep.

I nod and sit back. She places the bags on the floor and comes to stand next to me. "Glad to see you're still here, Bailey," she whispers.

"She's hard to leave," I confess. "What time is it?"

"After ten."

I look down at Parker. "I should get her to bed." I nod toward the bags she placed on the floor. "You need help with that?"

"No. I can get it. You know which room is hers?"

"No."

"First door on the right."

"Thank you." I move Parker into my arms and lift her effortlessly.

"Where are we going?" she asks, placing her arms around my neck.

"I'm taking you to bed."

"That's not very slow of you, Bailey," she says, her voice laced with sleep and sounding sexy as fuck.

"I'm going as slow as I can, sweet pea. You don't make this easy on me." Her bedroom door is open, which makes things easier for me as I move to place her on her bed. She wiggles around until she's under the covers.

"Thank you, Holden. For today, for breakfast, for helping me study, for being so great when my family showed up. For putting me to bed. All of it."

I sit on the edge of the bed and push her hair back from her eyes. "It's been a long damn time since I've had a day as good as this one. In fact, I'm not sure I ever have."

"Come on now. You're a professional baseball player. The world is at your fingertips."

"The world might be, but you haven't been. Not until today."

"Who knew Holden Bailey could be sweet?" she teases, a little more awake.

"Only for you, Parker. Only for you." I lean down and place a kiss on the corner of her mouth. "Sweet dreams, beautiful. Good luck with your exams this week. Text me and let me know how you did." I expect her to argue that I've done enough, so her reply surprises me.

"Okay. I'll talk to you tomorrow?" she asks softly.

I lean close again. "Yes. And every day after that," I assure her. This time, I kiss her lips. It's a soft, quick press, but it lights me on fire just as our kiss at the club did that night.

I stand and walk away. I have to, or I won't leave. When I reach the door, she calls out my name. I turn to look at her. My hand grips the door handle so hard I fear I might rip it off. I want to climb in that bed beside her and hold her all night long. Something I've never done, but I want to with her. "Yeah?"

"Text me when you get home. So I know you're safe. It's late."

"It's just after ten, and I don't want to wake you."

"Please?"

I never had a chance of not doing what she asked. "Okay." With that final word, I release my hold on the door handle and walk out of her room, pulling the door closed. Autumn isn't in the living room, so I turn off the lights, make sure the door is locked, checking it again once I'm in the hallway, and force my feet to carry me to my truck.

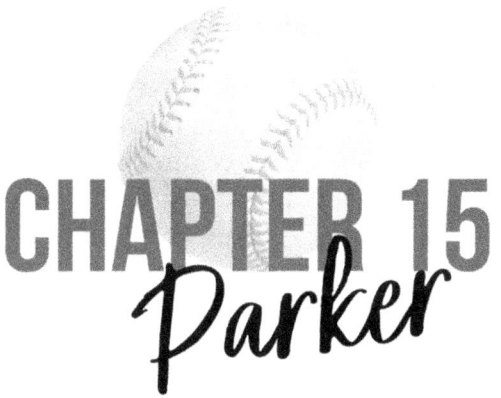

CHAPTER 15
Parker

"TIME'S UP," PROFESSOR HAWKINS SAYS from his spot in front of the class.

I set my pencil down and smile. I had enough time to review my answers twice, so I feel good. Confident. It's been that with each final I've taken this week, and this is the last one. I'm officially free for winter break, and I'm not the least bit worried about my grades. I'm confident I passed. I owe that to Holden. Every question throughout the week reminded me of him and our study session. I wonder if I can convince him to be my study partner next semester too.

I'm one semester away from being a college graduate. The past four years have flown by, and now I'm ready for whatever comes next. Uncle Drew offered me a position with the Blaze PR team, and although I don't want a handout, Paisley reminded me that Uncle Drew wouldn't do that. He did the same for her, and she earned her spot. Although, he might change his mind when he finds out I've been hanging out with one of his players. From what I remember, he was cool with Cam and Paisley being together, so maybe it will be okay. Besides, Holden and I aren't together. Not really. We're friends at best. Friends who apparently kiss each other good night and text all day, every day.

This week has been more than I ever could have expected. Monday morning, as I was stepping out of our apartment to go to my first class, Holden was there waiting for me. He had coffee and a muffin in hand. When I asked him what he was doing there, his reply was simple. He said he wanted to see me and to wish me luck. He walked me to my car with his hand on the small of my back and my bag thrown over his shoulder. He didn't try to kiss me again when I climbed behind the wheel. He handed me my goodies, told me to kick ass, and stepped back, watching me drive away.

I haven't seen him since then, but every morning I've had a text from him wishing me luck and then more throughout the day. I'm definitely seeing a side of Holden Bailey I never knew existed. I feel bad for judging him, and at some point soon, I need to apologize for that.

Slipping into my coat, I grab my purse and my bag and head to the front of the room to turn in my final. Professor Hawkins stands vigil over the room, his thinning hair sticking up haphazardly all over his head and his tiny reading glasses perched at the end of his nose. He makes me smile. Hell, everything this week makes me smile. I'm refusing to think about why. He consumes enough of my thoughts as it is.

Pushing on the metal door, the chilly December air slices through me immediately. I pick up my pace as I head toward my car. I'm officially finished with this semester. Pulling my coat up around my neck to try to ward off some of the cold, I keep my head down, hoping that helps. When I get to my car, I see two boot-covered feet. Very big feet. I stop and look up to find Holden leaning against my car with his feet crossed at his ankles.

"You were supposed to text me," he says in greeting.

"I was going to once I got in the car. It's freezing-ass cold out here."

"Come on, my truck's running, and I'm taking you to lunch." He reaches for my hand, and I let him lead me to his truck that's parked beside my car that I didn't even notice. He pulls open the passenger door, and the heat surrounds me. "Buckle up," he says before closing the door and rushing to the driver's side.

I place my hands over the vents to warm them up. "I don't remember it being this cold in December," I tell him when he slides behind the wheel, bringing a gust of cold wind with him.

"Yeah, the news said we're having lower than normal temperatures right now." He reaches over and takes my hands in his, brings them to his lips, and blows. "How was your final?" he asks.

I smile at him. "Good. I finished early and read over my answers twice. I knew the material."

"Of course you did."

"What are you doing here?" I ask him.

"Well, I drove around campus until I saw your car and just so happened to find a spot right next to you. Luck is on my side today." He winks.

"Who did you have to sign an autograph for?" I ask him.

He laughs. "Some guy. He recognized me right away, and apparently, he's my biggest fan. A little chitchat and a signed notebook later, he gave me his spot."

"I bet he was curious as to why you wanted this particular parking spot. You better be careful, Bailey. Rumors are going to fly."

"Yeah?" he asks as he leans over the console. "Too bad these windows are tinted. We could really give them something to talk about." He winks, closing the distance and dropping a kiss to my cheek before falling back into his seat. "He was curious. I told him I was waiting for my girl." His words make me warm and tingly all over, and the cold outside is long forgotten.

"So, where are we going?"

"I wanted to take you to celebrate. I thought we could grab a late lunch. Besides, I was having Parker withdrawals. I haven't seen you since Monday. That's far too long, sweet pea. Far too long."

"Where are you taking me?" I ask, reaching for my seat belt.

"Wherever you want to go."

I pretend to think about it when I already know what I want. "How about Mexican? I think this deserves a margarita or two." I smile. Before he can answer, my phone rings. I dig it out of my purse and show him it's Autumn calling. "Hey," I greet her.

"We're done!" she yells, making me laugh and pull the phone away from my ear. "It's time to celebrate. Where are you?"

"I'm sitting in the parking lot just outside of Margaret Hall in Holden's truck."

"Well, you two are late. Meet us at the Tasty Quesadilla."

"I'll let you know." I don't really know if Holden is going to be up to hang out with my friends. I don't know if I'm up for Holden hanging out with my friends.

"Parker," Autumn whines. "Put Holden on the phone."

"I'll text you." I ignore her request.

"I'm going to keep blowing up your phone," she tells me.

That's fine. I can turn it off if I need to. "I'll let you know." I don't wait for a reply before ending the call.

"What's up?"

"That was Autumn. She and some of our friends are actually going to Mexican, so we can pick somewhere else."

"What?" He furrows his brow. "Why would we do that?"

"I'm sure you don't want to spend the afternoon hanging out with my friends."

"I don't care who's there as long as you are, and you're sitting next to me. Everything else doesn't matter to me."

My heart races at his confession. How am I supposed to keep from falling for him when he says things like that? What's worse is that I believe him. He's looking at me, staring into my eyes, and this isn't just a ploy to get me into his bed. If it is, he's a damn good actor. He really just wants to hang out with me.

I place my hand over my heart. "You make my heart race, Holden Bailey," I confess.

He places his hand over mine and entwines our fingers. "Good race or bad race?"

"Good race."

He nods. "Text Autumn and tell her we're on our way." He pulls his hand from mine and buckles his seat belt.

"We really don't have to."

"Sure we do. They're your friends, and you've all worked hard, putting another semester of college behind you. I was there just a couple of years ago. I know the relief. We're going to celebrate." He reaches over and pats my thigh. "Let's do this."

I do as he says, too stunned that he's willing to hang out with my friends and me to argue. Once I'm strapped in, he backs out of the space and follows my directions to the Tasty Quesadilla. It's maybe a five-minute drive from campus, and they're cheap, which means it's always packed full of college students.

"Holden, we don't have to do this," I say, my anxiety starting to rise. "We won't be able to hide in the corner here. People will sure recognize you."

"Are you embarrassed to be seen with me?" he asks. His voice is soft, and if I didn't know better, I'd say my words hurt his feelings.

"No. That's not it at all. You know people are going to talk. They're going to see us arrive and leave together. Although I could get a ride with Autumn."

"Are we hiding this, Parker?"

"What is this?" I question. "I don't even know what we're doing. I mean, I know it started out that we were going to take things slow and get to know one another on our own merit and not the media, but—" I stop talking. I almost said too much.

"But what?"

I shake my head.

"No secrets, sweet pea. Not between us. Tell me what you were going to say." He removes his seat belt and turns to face me. Thankfully we're in the back of the parking lot, and I don't think my friends know what he drives. Then again, this is Holden Bailey. They probably do.

"It feels like it's more," I say softly, staring down at my hands that are gripping the strap of my purse like my life depends on it.

"Parker." He pauses. When I don't look at him, his index fingers rest under my chin, and he lifts my eyes to his. "This is more. It didn't start that way, but here we are." He smiles, and I swear this man has a direct line to my heart as the organ squeezes in my chest every time he turns that smile on me.

"Here we are," I repeat.

"We don't have to figure it all out right now. We're going to go inside and celebrate the end of the semester with your friends. Then I'll take you anywhere you want to go, and we can talk about this. About us, or we can just hang out. I don't care as long as I get to spend time with you. Five minutes with you on Monday morning is not enough time with you this week. So, now that classes are over, we'll be fixing that."

"Okay." I nod. Then panic hits me. "Wait. They're going to ask what's going on with us."

"Then we tell them the truth. We're dating."

"But what about the others?"

"What others?"

"The women."

This time, it's his hand that cradles my cheek as he leans impossibly close. His blue eyes bore into mine, willing me to believe every word he's about to speak. "Baby, there is no one but you. You're all I see."

"So we're dating. Exclusively?" I ask. I just need to be sure before I walk in there with all of my friends. I don't want to be the laughingstock.

"We're dating exclusively. As an only child, I've never been much of a sharer, and I sure as fuck don't want to share you."

"Well, I'm not an only child, but I-I don't want to share you either." It's a huge confession coming from me, and we both know it.

"You'll never have to. I promise you. I'm a man of my word, Parker. If this ever feels as though it's not working, I'll talk to you about it, and we can go from there."

"You don't do relationships," I remind him.

"I didn't."

"You do now?" I don't know why I keep harping on this, and in the parking lot of the Tasty Quesadilla at that.

"I do now." He moves forward and presses his lips softly against mine. "We can talk all you want after this. For now, we're dating. Only each other. That's all they need to know. You and I can figure the rest out as we go."

"This isn't very slow." I smile at him.

"Baby, we had no chance of ever going slow." He taps my nose with his index finger, turns off the engine, and climbs out of the truck.

I fumble with my seat belt but manage to finally push open the door, and he's there waiting for me. His strong hands grip my hips as he lifts me from the truck, kisses me quickly, and then places me on my feet. I step back so he can close the door.

"Ready?" he asks, offering me his hand.

"Let's do this."

He grins and links his fingers with mine. He leads me inside, and the door is barely closed behind us before Autumn is calling out for us. "It's about time," she yells, waving her hands in the air like a fool to get our attention.

Holden leads us to the long table and takes my coat, placing it on the back of my chair before pulling my chair out for me. "Damn, Holden Bailey has game," Autumn comments.

"How many has she had?" I ask Kate.

"That's her first," she answers with a laugh.

Holden takes off his coat, places it on the back of his chair, and sits beside me. He places his arm on the back of my chair.

"Bailey, what are your intentions with our girl here?" Troy asks him.

"She's *my* girl," Holden replies. No one at the table misses the emphasis he puts on the word "my."

"And your intentions?" Troy asks, crossing his arms over his chest.

"Come on, Troy." Autumn places her hand on his arm. "Their relationship is none of our business."

"I'm just looking out for her."

"I'm a big girl, Troy," I remind him. "Besides, he doesn't have to answer to you."

I feel lips press against my temple. "I've got this," Holden says, his voice low only for me to hear. "My intentions are to keep her my girl as long as I can."

"So you want to hold her hostage?" Troy questions, and the entire table laughs at his take on the conversation.

"No. Well, yes, but I won't." Holden winks at me.

"Enough," Bridgett chimes in.

"Yeah, lay off, man. It's not our business." Garrett lifts his beer and nods at Holden.

Holden returns his nod. The server appears next to us, and we order our food. I get my margarita, but Holden declines and orders a Dr Pepper instead. "You're not drinking?" I ask him.

"No. I try to limit myself even in the off-season, but this is your day, sweet pea. You drink as much as you want, and I'll be sure to get you home safe."

Kate, Bridgette, and Autumn all sigh.

"Bailey definitely has game," Garrett comments.

"Dude, you're making us look bad," Troy complains, again making us all laugh at his antics. That's just Troy. He's always all over the place with his conversations. There is never a dull moment when he's around.

The guys launch into baseball talk with Holden, and he indulges them. They seem to be hitting it off after Troy's little overprotective questions. As for the girls and me, we're content to drink our margaritas and listen to them. We chime in here and there, but for the most part, the four of us are just relieved finals are over and are enjoying a little downtime. We have one semester left, and times like this will become few and far between.

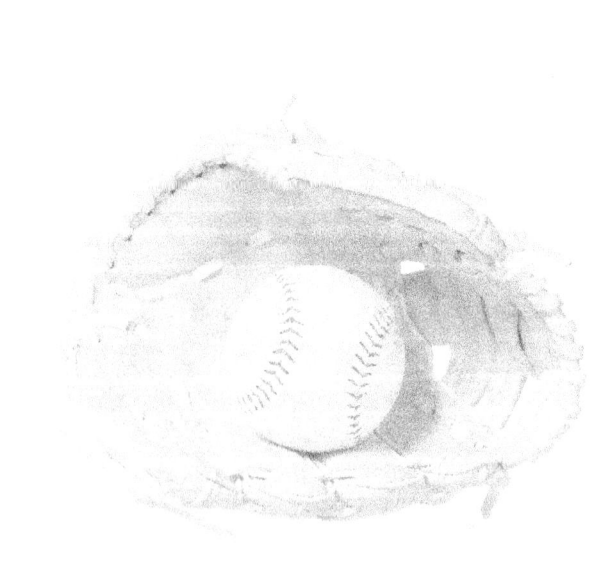

CHAPTER 16
Holden

"THANK YOU FOR COMING," PARKER says once we're back in my truck and headed toward her place. She's had two margaritas. I promised I'd bring her to get her car later.

"It was a good time. I like your friends, even when they're grilling me."

"Sorry about that. Troy has a thing for Autumn, but we've all been close since freshman year."

"You have nothing to apologize for. I'm glad you have them in your corner. What are your plans for the rest of the day?" I ask her.

"I've got nothing. Not one single thing, and it's glorious." She laughs. "I can't believe I have one more semester, and I'm a college graduate!"

Her enthusiasm is contagious. "Will you go somewhere with me?" I ask her. I'm at the stoplight. I need to turn left to take her home and right to where I want to take her.

"You know, I think I'd go anywhere with you, Holden Bailey." Her head is resting back against the seat, and a lazy, happy grin pulls at her lips.

I ignore the way my heart squeezes at her confession. She's been drinking, so I can't ravish her. Not tonight anyway. "Perfect." I hit my signal to turn right, and when the light turns green, I make the turn. I'm nervous and excited to bring her here. I don't know if it's because I signed the papers this morning or if it's her. Probably both.

"Hey, this is the way to your house. What's going on with that? I know they accepted your offer and were doing the title search."

"I signed the papers this morning."

"Wow. That's fast."

"We didn't need to involve the bank since I paid cash."

She nods. She's Easton Monroe's daughter, so she's not new to the kind of money our contracts and endorsements bring in. I spend wisely, and I've got a great financial planner who has helped me invest, and I've made a pretty good nest egg from those investments. In fact, the money I used for the house is from those investments. My place in Northern Tennessee, where I lived when I played for the Tomahawks, is also for sale, so I'll be able to put that money back once it does.

"You're taking me there? To your new place?"

"I am."

"It's all yours?" she asks.

Reaching into the cupholder, I hold up the set of keys I got today at the closing. "All mine."

"Holden! I'm so excited for you." Her hand lands on my arm, and sparks flow through my veins. It happens every time she touches me and every time I touch her. The chemistry between us is like nothing I've ever felt before.

"You felt it, too, didn't you?" I ask. I can see it in the way she just looked at her hand before placing it back on her lap.

"Did you?"

"Yeah, sweet pea. I felt it too." I don't want to have this conversation with her while she has alcohol in her system. This feeling, it's also something that's completely foreign to me. I've never felt the flash of desire from just the brush of skin against mine. I've never craved time with a woman. I've craved the release that comes with sex, but that's not what this is. She's all I think about, and any sliver of time she gives me is like winning the lottery.

"It's weird, right?" she asks. "It only happens with you."

Internally I'm fist-bumping and screaming hell yeah. On the outside, I try to remain calm and cool, when I'm anything but.

I turn into the driveway of my new house, stopping at the gate to enter the security code. I called the company and had it changed as soon as I signed the papers today. Driving up the long driveway, I hit the button for the garage door opener and pull inside. That's another thing I love about this house. The attached garage is big enough for my truck. Leaving the garage door open and the engine running, I remove my seat belt, then reach over and do the same to hers. Moving my seat back as far as it will go, I pat my lap.

"Come here, Parker."

She smiles softly and climbs over the console. "My shoes are in your seat." She giggles.

Drunk Parker is fucking adorable. "I don't care," I tell her. "I just want to hold you, and I couldn't wait until we got inside." Not to mention I have zero furniture in the house. I need to drive to my old place and arrange for movers to bring it all here. This is my home now.

"This isn't something that I'm used to either," I tell her, wrapping my arms around her. "It's only ever happened with you. I think you've bewitched me somehow," I tease.

"Right," she scoffs. "Like I could bewitch the sexy Holden Bailey."

Drunk Parker is also apparently an open-book Parker. "You think I'm sexy?" I ask. I don't bother to pretend her comment doesn't make me smile.

"You know you are." She runs her hands over my chest.

My cock twitches in my jeans, and her little ass wiggling on my lap tells me she knows what she's doing to me. "That's all you," I tell her.

Her eyes widen. "For me?" She tilts her head to the side, a coy smile playing her lips.

"You know it is," I say, pressing a kiss to her forehead.

"Holden?"

"Yeah?"

"Why are we sitting in your truck in your new garage?"

"There's no furniture inside, and I wanted to hold you."

"We need to go get you some furniture."

"I need to drive to my old place and get movers organized."

She looks up at me. Her bottom lip pushed out in a pout. "You're leaving? It's Christmas in three days. You can't leave."

"I'll just be gone overnight. I need to pack up personal items and organize movers for the rest of it. I won't leave until after Christmas."

"Okay, good."

"You going to miss me, sweet pea?"

"I always miss you when you're gone."

Her words grip my heart like a fucking vise. Whatever this magnetism is between us, it's growing fast. If it were anyone but

Parker, I'd probably be scared as hell as to what it meant, but it's Parker, and I can't find it in me to fight it. I don't want to fight it. I want to see where this crazy connection leads us.

My arms tighten around her. "I always miss you too," I confess.

"I didn't want to, though. I didn't want to miss you. I didn't want to let you in because I knew it would happen."

"You knew what would happen?"

"I knew my heart would get tangled up in you."

Another tight squeeze in the center of my chest. "Is that what's happening? Your heart's tangled up in me?"

"You know it is."

She's wrong. I didn't know that, but knowing that she's falling just as fast as I am is a huge relief. It's good to know that I'm not jumping in feet first, and she's nowhere near the water.

"You wanna know a secret?" I ask. I know she's buzzed, but not so much she's not going to remember this conversation tomorrow.

"I'm good with secrets."

I laugh at her goofy smile. "My heart's tangled up in you too."

She sucks in a breath. "Does that mean you'll kiss me?"

Reaching up, I run the pad of my thumb over her lips. "I'll kiss you anytime you want, but not tonight."

"Then you lied."

"Tonight, you've been drinking, and I refuse to let you make a decision about us while you're intoxicated." No matter how badly my lips ache to taste hers.

She sits up straighter. "I know what I'm doing."

"Okay," I reply, tucking her hair behind her ear. I know she's not tanked, but she's different. Sure, I've been drinking and picked up a woman who was also drinking, and we've hooked up. That was me in the past. This is me with Parker, and everything about this woman sitting in my lap is different. I could kiss her, and we'd both enjoy it, but I'm trying to show her I'm not the playboy she thinks I am, especially now that she's wormed her way inside my chest.

"You're really not going to kiss me?"

Is that hurt in her voice? "Oh, baby, I'm going to kiss you." My eyes flash to her lips. "Ask me again tomorrow and see what happens."

"So, what? You're never going to kiss me if I'm drinking? You had no issue with it at the club." Her blue eyes turn darker with not only hurt but anger.

"Things are different now."

"Explain that." She moves like she's going to crawl out of my lap, but I lock my arms around her.

"I admit, I wanted you then. But Parker, what you don't realize is that want is more now. It's need. It's waking up next to you each morning and falling asleep next to you each night. It's calling you first when something good happens and leaning on you when it's bad. What we are is more than a hookup in a club. That might be how we started, but baby, this is beyond the play."

"You play, Holden. That's what you do."

"Not with you." I press my forehead to hers. "Trust me on this. Please. I don't ever want you to think that you're not different. Tomorrow, I'll spend the entire day kissing your sweet lips if that's what you want."

"What do *you* want?" she asks.

"I want you, Parker Monroe, anyway I can have you. Once you decide completely sober that I'm what you want."

"I can decide that now," she says, leaning in and pressing her lips to mine. She pulls back, and her eyes find mine. "I wanted to do that, and tomorrow when I'm sober"—she rolls her pretty blue eyes—"I'll remind you of this very moment."

"I hope so," I admit. I really hope she has no regrets come the light of day. "Now, how about a tour of the house?"

"I've already seen it."

"I know, but now it's mine." I grin and wink.

"You're just a boy in a sexy man's body," she teases. She moves to crawl off my lap, and this time, I let her. She's right. I feel like a randy teenager where she's concerned, and to be honest, I'm almost afraid to take things further with her, just like I would have been as an inexperienced teenager.

With a smile on my face, I turn off the truck and hit the button to close the garage door. "Go on in," I tell her when she turns to look at me over her shoulder where she's standing next to the door. The same giddy smile on my face graces hers as she turns the handle and walks inside with me hot on her heels.

"I think you made the right choice," she says, linking her arm through mine. We casually stroll through the kitchen once we step out of the mudroom. "This kitchen is perfect for get-togethers and holidays. You're going to have so much fun entertaining here," she says.

I don't reply, and I don't need to. Besides, I'm afraid if I do, it will be something along the lines of we can have get-togethers here. Together. We're not there yet.

"Can you imagine a Christmas tree here in front of this window?" She stops walking and smiles up at me. "This place will be gorgeous. All decked out for the holidays."

"You think so?"

"Absolutely."

"Well, let's do it then."

"What?"

"Let's decorate. I admit I don't have a lot of decorations for the holidays at my old place."

"What's not a lot?" she asks.

"None."

"What? How is that possible? This is your off-season, and you're home to enjoy it. How could you not decorate?"

"Well, I usually spend the month of December here with my parents, so I never really bothered to buy decorations. I've only lived there for two years. It was my first purchase when I signed my contract with the Tomahawks, and it's much smaller than this place."

"Walmart is smaller than this place," she jokes.

"Ha-ha," I say, tickling her side and making her shriek with laughter.

"Christmas is three days away."

"I'm going to need it anyway."

"But all that decorating for three days?"

"Come on, Parker. You know you want to."

"You're right! I do want to." She claps her hands. "Can we go now?" she asks.

Glancing down at my watch, I see it's just after seven. "I think the stores are open a couple more hours."

"Come on, Bailey. What are you waiting for? We have shopping to do."

"I've created a monster." I laugh as she grabs my hand and pulls me back to the garage. I open the door for her, and she climbs in, the happiness still on full display on her face.

"Where are we headed?" I ask once I'm behind the wheel. I hit the button to open the garage door and start the truck that's still warm, and back out of the garage.

"Just follow my directions," she tells me. "And what we don't get today, we can get tomorrow."

"Oh, well, I've got plans tomorrow."

"What?" She turns to face me. "What plans? You can't dangle decorating this blank canvas"—she points over her shoulder at the house as we're pulling out of the drive—"like a carrot. You said we could decorate."

I pull up to the stop sign at the end of my road. "I did say that, and we will, but I promised you I'd spend all day tomorrow kissing you."

"Oh. Well, yeah, we're going to have to work that into decorating. Make a right," she says, patting my cheek.

"Yes, ma'am."

She points me to the nearest Hobby Lobby and tells me we're both going to need a cart. I don't argue and grab a cart, following along behind her. Everything she oohs and aahs over, I put into the cart. It's a big-ass house, and if it puts this kind of smile on her face, it's worth whatever this little shopping trip is going to cost me.

CHAPTER 17
Parker

"Maybe we went a little overboard," I say to Holden. We're sitting on the island in his massive kitchen eating burgers and fries we picked up from the drive-thru on the way back to his place.

"There is no we in this equation, sweet pea," he teases.

I smile at the use of the nickname he's given me. I love the play on the fact that my first name begins with *P*. Clever one he is. "What do you mean?" I ask, pretending to be appalled.

"You loved it all."

"Of course I did. That doesn't mean we had to buy it all."

He shrugs, popping a fry in his mouth. "It's a big house."

"You're crazy." I shake my head at him, grabbing the chocolate shake sitting next to me on the counter and taking a drink.

"Crazy about you."

His confession hits me right between the thighs. Sure, my heart flutters in my chest, but it's the heat that rushes to my core that has me squirming on the counter. Holden cocks a brow, and without a doubt, he knows exactly what I'm thinking and why I can't sit still.

"Are you still on this no-kissing-me kick?" I ask, my face flaming. I'm not usually this bold, but something about Holden brings it out in me. I sobered up hours ago. Sure, I might have been a little looser-lipped than normal, but I knew exactly what I was asking for. Him and his lips on mine. It's a simple request, really.

"Parker."

I turn to look at him, and his lips press to mine. It's a peck, just a quick press of our lips, but to me, it's more than that. It's him and me sitting here together in his empty house, our legs swinging from the kitchen island with the bag of takeout between us, and his living room floor full of Christmas decorations and his new Christmas tree. It's more than a kiss. It feels like a promise—a promise of more.

"We've got work to do."

"Slave driver," I complain, shoving the last bite of my burger into my mouth. Jumping off the counter, I wad up my trash and place it in the bag. "Ready?" I can barely contain my excitement, and I know my smile must be splitting my cheeks wide open. I love Christmas, and the fact I know he's doing this for me, well, that warms every part of my soul.

He hops down from the island and places his trash in the takeout bag. "What's first, boss lady?" he asks.

"This is your house."

"Maybe." He shrugs. "But this is your project." He sweeps his hand out in front of us as if offering up the entire house to me. "Blank canvas, sweet pea, and it's all yours."

Tilting my head back, I smile up at him. "We might need more decorations," I tease.

"That will have to wait until tomorrow. Let's start with what we have."

His easy acceptance of my claim is not what I expected. "Let's put the tree up first and go from there."

"Let's do it."

We get to work on pulling the pieces of the huge pre-lit artificial tree out of the box and arrange it in front of the window. I was right. The tree with just the lights is gorgeous. I can't wait to see what it looks like once we get it decorated.

"Well?" I ask a few hours later.

"It looks great, Parker. It makes this place feel more like home."

"It really does." We're lying on the floor in the living room surrounded by opened packages.

"I don't have enough furniture to fill this place," he tells me. "I'm going to need to buy some more."

"Well, you have Christmas taken care of."

"I don't know. I think I'd like to put up some lights outside next year."

"Yeah?"

"Maybe Cameron and Paisley can drive Jett and the new baby by to see the lights."

It's a good thing I'm lying down. Who knew Holden had such a way with words? I admit it wasn't overly sweet or mushy, but he's including my family. *Next year.* As in twelve whole months from now. "I'm not sure they'll really be able to see them from the road."

He links his pinky with mine and turns his head to look at me instead of the ceiling that he's been staring up at. I know because

I've been staring at him. "Then they'll just have to come to visit to see them."

My chest rises and falls with each breath as I try to keep my cool. It's not working if the thundering of my heart is any indication. "Yeah. I'm sure they'd love that."

"What about you, Parker?"

"What about me?"

"You going to come and visit me next year? Maybe even help me put all this stuff up again?"

"Is that what you want?" Can he hear my heart? My hand that's not linked with his rests over my heart.

Holden turns to his side, resting his head on his elbow, and stares down at me. "I'm pretty certain that I'm going to want as much time with you as you're willing to give me."

"That's a year from now. Things change."

He nods. "I agree with you, but this…" He drops my hand and cups my cheek instead. "This feels bigger than anything before it."

"One day at a time."

"Slow." He smiles before angling to kiss me. Reaching for his hat, I toss it to the floor beside us and bury my hands in his hair. His hand slides behind my neck, and he deepens the kiss, his tongue slipping past my lips. With slow, leisurely strokes, his tongue glides against mine.

It's the slowest, most sensual kiss of my life. I know what he's doing. He's trying to prove to me that he can go slow. That is what we decided just mere days ago, but he should know that he can't kiss me like this and expect the same old rules to apply.

He pulls back and rests his head against my chest. We're both breathing heavily. I continue to run my hands through his hair, memorizing the feel of the silky strands through my fingers. We stay in this position for so long I lose track of time. Hell, it could be mere seconds, but it still feels as if a lifetime has passed. When he raises his head to look at me, his blue eyes are swirling with desire.

For me.

"I'm sorry."

All the happiness I was just feeling settles like lead in my stomach. "What are you sorry for."

"I promised you no kisses until tomorrow." The corner of his mouth lifts into a smile, and the happiness is back.

"Can you do me a favor?"

"Name it."

"Never apologize for kissing me again."

"I should probably do something to make up for that, huh?"

He doesn't give me the chance to answer before his lips are on mine once again. He moves closer, his body molding to the length of mine, and I toss my leg over his. I can't get close enough.

He kisses me slowly, as if we have all the time in the world, and although my body craves more, I'm okay with this speed. As long as his hands and his lips are on my body like they are now, I can handle the pace. Besides, I know that we need to slow this down. My head is telling me I gave in way too easy. My heart tells me this is the right thing. That there are no set standards for the timeline of a relationship.

"You're thinking too much," he says against my lips.

"I'm sorry. Sometimes I get lost in my head."

"What are you thinking about?"

I debate on blowing him off, but I want this to work. I want this to be more for both of us, and I know hiding what I'm thinking isn't the way for that to happen. "My head's telling me we need to stop."

"Okay." He eases back, but I grab onto his shirt and pull him back to me.

"My heart and my body, they're telling me that this feels right." I brush his shaggy brown hair back from his eyes. "That you and I feel right."

"That's because we are."

"This is really soon."

"I've been trying to get you to give me the time of day for weeks."

"But the time we've spent together, it hasn't really been all that much."

He nods. "We do this your way, Parker."

"You know, my grandma has this saying. It's something my parents said to us a lot growing up, and me and my sisters, we try to live by it."

"What's the saying?"

"Always speak from your heart."

He rests his hand over my heart. "What does your heart want to say, sweet pea?" he whispers.

"That it's falling for you. That it's scared because everything I thought I knew about you seems to be opposite of who you are." I pause, collecting my thoughts. Holden stays quiet, sensing I have more to say. "I'm scared. I know you can't believe the media. I grew up with it, so I understand the gossip of the business. I watched it with my parents and still with my sister. Every moment that I spend with you has me craving that many more. I want to let my heart take over, but I don't want it to be shattered when this, whatever we label it to be, ends."

"We said we were exclusive," he reminds me. His voice is soft, almost as if he's afraid I'm going to jump up and run out of the house. That's the thing. I probably should keep running, but I just don't want to. Not from him.

"I know."

"Then why did you say whatever we label it to be? We're us."

"I know," I say. "I don't know what I'm trying to say. Everything is all jumbled in my head. I guess my head is looking for a guarantee that my heart is not going to be broken, while my heart is all in, regardless of the outcome."

"I don't want to hurt you."

"I know that too."

"And why do you think this is going to end?"

I smile up at him. His blue eyes are dark with concern and maybe worry. "Because you're too good to be true, Holden Bailey."

He moves closer, his lips hovering over mine. "I've never been a romantic man, Parker. I never gave myself the time to get to know someone to fall for them. I never wanted to. With you, everything is different. It's more than want at this point. Do I want you? Hell yes, I do. With the passion of a thousand fucking suns. But I also have this... need. I can't explain it. I've never thought about a woman this much before in my life. I've never thought ahead to what I could do to make her mine. I've never wanted to whisper to a woman that she's my everything. You're not the only one wondering what the hell is going on. This isn't me. It's not who I am. However, it turns out it's who I am with you. You're changing me."

"I don't want to change you, Holden."

"I know that. But that doesn't change the fact that you are. Before you, it was all physical. I couldn't care less about hanging out, grabbing takeout, and just spending the evening lying on the floor in an empty house surrounded by empty packages." He grins. "But here we are, and there is no place I'd rather be."

I roll to my side and face him. "I want to be here too. And by here, I mean wherever you are."

This time it's his heart that his hand is covering. "Your words do some crazy shit right there," he says, tapping his chest. His voice is low, and dare I say, laced with a tad bit of vulnerability.

I smile. "Good. Now you know how it feels." I lean forward and press my lips to his.

"Let's recap this," he says when I pull away. "We're together, you and me. As in, I'm going to call you my girlfriend. You good with that?"

"Do I get to call you my boyfriend?" I ask. "Why do I feel like I'm in middle school with this conversation?" I laugh.

"Yes. You do. And those titles they seem insignificant for what this feels like, but I think it's a good place for us to start."

"Agreed."

"Come here, beautiful." His arms snake around me, and he pulls me close, and then his lips capture mine.

We spend hours on his living room floor, making out like teenagers. It's fitting because this giddy feeling he gives me makes me feel like a girl with her first crush. By the time he drops me off at my place, it's well past midnight. I almost invite him in to stay but decide it's best if I don't. Instead, I let him kiss me good night and close the door behind me.

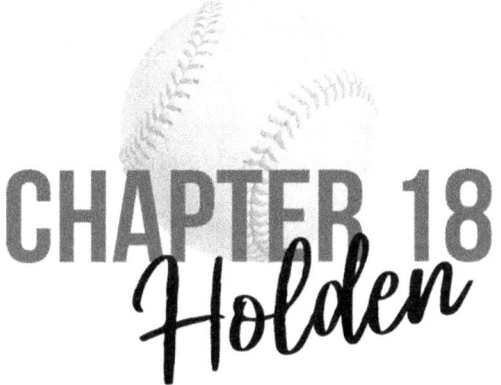

CHAPTER 18
Holden

I T'S TWO DAYS BEFORE CHRISTMAS, and I find myself in an unusual predicament. For the first time since high school, I have a girlfriend. A girlfriend I don't have a gift for. I need to do something about that.

Rushing through a shower, I make my way to the kitchen, where my parents sit having breakfast. "Morning, son," Dad greets.

"Morning."

"I came to wake you, but you were in the shower," Mom tells me.

"Yeah. I have some errands to run today."

"We were hoping to come by and see the new house."

I smile when I think about the mess that Parker and I left last night with our decorating adventure. "Yeah, it's a mess right now. Give me a few hours to get it cleaned up."

"Why on earth is it a mess? I thought you said it was move-in ready?" she asks.

"You should talk with the real estate agent," Dad chimes in. "They should have taken care of that for you."

"Yeah, well, I kind of made the mess."

"You made the mess?" Mom asks, confused.

"Yeah. I took Parker, this girl I'm seeing, over there last night to see it again, now that it's mine. She was talking about how pretty a tree would be in front of the huge windows in the living room, so I suggested she go with me to buy one. That led to more decorations, and we went back and set it all up last night."

"Oh, tell me more about this Parker," Mom says.

"Honey, leave him alone. You know he's not ready to settle down." Dad comes to my defense.

Usually, I would agree with him. My parents know I've not been a saint. They know that my typical response is "I'm young and playing the field." Today, however, my answer is going to be different.

"She's special," I confess. My parents both stop eating and give me their full attention. "We actually made it official last night."

"I'm going to need a little more than that, Holden." Mom gives me a look that tells me she's completely shocked by my confession.

"I don't know how else to explain it. Parker and I are dating. Officially. As in, she's my girlfriend."

"Damn," Dad mutters. "I never thought I'd see the day."

"Sorry to disappoint, old man," I tease.

"No. It's just I thought you would forever be in this 'wild, sow your oats' stage. Your mother and I both worried that being on the road all the time with the, uh, possibilities thrown your way, that you would be a forever bachelor."

"It was a good possibility," I agree. In my freshman year of college, I started on the baseball team. Word spread fast about my talent on the field, and all the girls wanted to be with me. I was their meal ticket, or so they hoped. I used them like they used me. Well, used is a strong word. I was honest with each and every woman I've ever been with. They knew it was one night of fun and that it would never be anything more. I mean, come on. When a woman walks up to you and offers to blow you in the middle of a frat party, she's not exactly in the running for taking her home to meet your momma.

"When do we get to meet her?" Mom asks.

"I'm not sure. I know she's really close with her family, so I assume she'll be with them for Christmas."

"Well, you let me know, and I can make us dinner. We have dinner Christmas Day at Aunt Lottie's at five, but if she can't make that, we will do something small with just the four of us."

"I don't want to scare her away, Mom. I just got her."

"I'll be on my best behavior," she replies, making Dad and me crack up laughing.

"Sure you will," I say, shoving a piece of bacon into my mouth. "Anyway, I need to go out and grab her something for Christmas."

"Holden! You should have done that already," Mom scolds.

"We were dating at best, and it seemed like I was doing more chasing than dating. I had planned to pick up something small, but now she's mine, and well, it needs to be more than that."

"You know this girl doesn't sound like monetary gifts are her thing," Dad comments.

"You're right. She's not, but at the same time, she's the first woman I've ever wanted to spoil."

"Aw." Mom sighs, clutching her hands over her heart.

"So, yeah, let me get the place cleaned up, and I'll shoot you a text. We didn't have a trash can last night, and I didn't even think about it."

"We'll be there," Dad assures me.

"Thanks." I finish off my breakfast and stand to help clear the table.

"You go on. You've got shopping to do, and the last-minute crowds are going to be awful." Mom waves her hand at me, basically telling me to get out of her way and get moving.

"Thanks, Mom. You're the best." I kiss her cheek and head to my room to grab my wallet and my keys. Walking to the window, I hit the button for remote start on my truck to let the cab warm. Soon, I'll be parking inside, and the snow and ice will no longer be an issue. While I wait, I pull up Parker's name and hit call.

"Good morning," she says.

"Morning. You sound happy."

"I had a good night last night. I guess that just flows over to my morning."

"Oh really? Anything you want to tell me?" I tease.

"Yeah, this guy I've been running from finally caught me."

"Is that so?"

"It is. He's not at all who I thought he was."

"I'm glad to see that you haven't changed your mind with the light of day."

"No. Have you?"

"Never," I assure her. "What are your plans today?"

"I have some gifts to wrap and a few last-minute things to pick up, but other than that, I'm a free woman."

"No, you're not. You have a boyfriend, remember?" I know that's not what she's referring to. She's free from college for three weeks, but I'm still going to take every opportunity to remind her she's now attached to me. She's mine, and I want everyone to know it.

"So bossy," she jokes.

"When it comes to you and you being mine, you're damn right I am."

"So, caveman, what's on your agenda today?"

"I'm going to buy a trash can, and I have some last-minute shopping that I need to do as well."

"Anything I can help with?"

"I think I've got it. Do I get to see you today?"

"Do you want to see me today?"

"Yes. Actually, I've been meaning to ask you. What are your plans for Christmas?"

"Well, we usually get together and have Christmas morning breakfast, which is actually brunch since Jett came along. Paisley and Cameron like to have him wake up and open his gifts from Santa before heading to Grandma and Grandpa's."

"When do you all do Christmas dinner?"

"Usually that evening. It's an all-day event at the Monroe household. What about you? When does your family get together?"

"Christmas Day Usually, we all meet at my aunt Lottie's house for dinner around five." There's silence. "I want you to meet my parents." The words feel foreign because they are. I've never introduced them to a woman, not since high school.

"Are we doing this?"

"Yeah, sweet pea, we're doing this."

"Maybe we should hold off. This is so new..." Her voice trails off.

"Kicking me to the curb already?" I tease.

"No. That's not it at all." She's quick to defend. "We literally just started dating. Officially."

"What can I say? When you know, you know. I'm not hiding this, Parker. I don't care who knows that you're mine. In fact, I prefer that everyone knows."

"Okay. Well, we can't be in two places at once," she says, shocking me.

"We can't. My mom has already said she'd make dinner for the four of us some other time when you were available."

"You can't miss your family's Christmas."

"We're a couple now, so we're going to have to start compromising sooner or later. What if we have dinner with your family and then leave in time to stop in and say hello to mine?" I'm aware that I just invited myself to her family Christmas, but we're a unit now. Where she goes, I go, and vice versa. I might have never had a relationship in my adult life, but I do know that I want to be where she is.

"Can you let me process this a little? We can talk about it when I see you tonight?"

"Sure, but don't think I'll forget," I say, my tone teasing.

"Oh, I know." She chuckles. "Do you need anything while I'm out? Something you've been looking for but can't find."

"I already found it, Parker. You."

"Holden Bailey and his silver tongue."

I almost tell her what this silver tongue of mine can do to her, but I keep that comment to myself. She's already worried this is just about sex. Well, she used to be. I'd like to think that I've convinced her it's more than that. And it is. It's more, but that doesn't mean I don't want to strip her bare and show her what my tongue can do. And my cock. We can't forget my cock. The two together can give her an out-of-body experience, but that will come, and so will we.

"What time are we getting together tonight?" she asks.

"Call me when you're done with everything that you need to do, and we'll see where we are."

"Sounds like a plan."

"Be safe, Parker."

"Always. You too."

"I'll see you soon."

"Bye." She ends the call, and it dawns on me that I'm one of those guys. You know the ones who say "you hang up first?" I want all her time, even if it's on the phone. What is this woman doing to me?

Three hours later, I have furniture bought and scheduled for delivery later today. I have a couple of gifts for Parker that are really more for me, but also for her. Now all I need is a few gifts just for her, a trip to the store to grab some food, and the essentials like blankets and sheets, and a trash can and trash bags.

With my hat pulled low to try to hide my identity, I pull open the doors to the mall and set out to finish my shopping. My parents were easy. I bought them a vacation like I have the past two years. They've done so much for me, and they work hard. I want to spoil them. In March, they will be married for twenty-five years. I bought them a trip to Italy. It's prepaid through a travel agent, and all they have to do is call and schedule it. The agent knows to spare no expense and to give them what they want, and I'll pay whatever the difference might be.

"Holden?" I turn to see Autumn walking toward me.

"Hey. Where's my girl?" I ask, looking behind her.

"She's here. We split up. Not going so well?" she asks.

"Actually, it's going great. This is my final stop to grab Parker a few more things."

"Need some ideas?"

"I have a feeling you're going to give me some anyway." I laugh.

"Actually, no. Not unless you need them. I'm kind of interested to see what you come up with on your own."

"I've got this," I assure her.

"I'm sure you do."

"Fancy seeing you here." I turn to look at the person who owns the voice who is always in my head.

I don't say a word. Instead, I bend and capture her lips with mine. "Hey, sweet pea," I finally say, pulling out of the kiss.

"You're going to draw a crowd," she whispers.

"Don't care," I say, wrapping my arm around her shoulders and pulling her close.

"Did you buy it?" Autumn asks.

"Nah, I don't need it."

"Need what?"

"Oh, nothing. I was just looking at a coat."

"Show me."

"No."

"Come on, show me."

"Not happening, Bailey. I was just admiring it. I have way too many coats, and I don't need it."

"But you want it."

"I was admiring," she says again, shaking her head.

"Fine," I grumble. I kiss her again softly. "I need to go get my shopping done so I can spend some time with you."

"We're done here and headed back to our place."

"Damn," I mutter. "I still have to go grab some groceries, a trash can, trash bags, that kind of shit."

"I can do that for you."

"Are you sure?"

"I don't have anything else going on until you're done anyway."

"I thought you had presents to wrap?"

"I finished."

"Are you sure you don't mind?" I ask, already reaching into my pocket for a credit card. I hand it to her. "Take this. We need pretty much everything."

"What about what you're moving here from your old place?"

"Hand-me-downs from my mom when I moved in." I shrug. "So, yeah, dishes, pots and pans, spices, all that shit, including food. We need it all."

"We?" Autumn asks.

I turn to look at my girl. "Me and Parker." I kiss her again. "There's no limit on the card, baby. You've seen the house, so go crazy. Oh, and I need king bedsheets and a comforter set too."

"Gee, is that all? Holden, I can't pick out everything in your house."

"You're not. I ordered furniture today that's being delivered later, so you're actually helping me so I can get this done and be there for the delivery. I was going to have to go back out to get what you're picking up for me." One more quick kiss and I force myself to step back.

"Are you sure about this?" she asks.

Another step back. "Positive. Thank you, sweet pea, you're doing me a solid. Take your time. I have a couple of hours left of shopping before I have to meet the furniture delivery." With a wave, I turn on my heel and let my feet carry me in the opposite direction. I have to wrap this up and get home. Hopefully, I can get this all set up before she gets there. Hopefully, she takes my little "take your time" to heart.

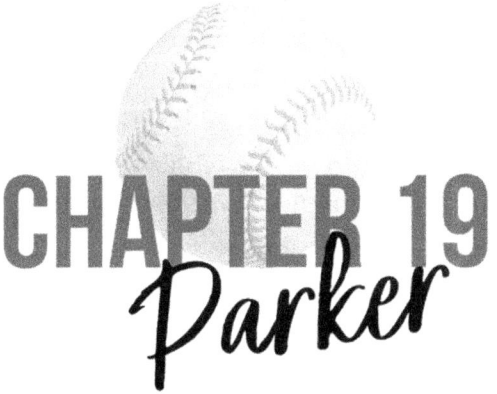

CHAPTER 19
Parker

"**D**ID THAT JUST HAPPEN?" I ask Autumn.

"Yep."

"Okay. Well, I guess I have some more shopping to do. Do you want me to take you home and come back?"

"Are you kidding me? I want to be here for this."

"Be here for what?" a deep voice asks, and I know without turning around, it's my dad. My face heats because I have yet to tell my parents about Holden. Sure, Paisley knows, but I know my big sister, and she didn't tell them. They both would have been blowing up my phone if that were the case.

"Duchess?" Dad says.

Schooling my features, I turn to face him. "Hey, Daddy." I smile and wrap my arms around him in a hug. "What are you doing here?" I ask, stepping back.

"Last-minute shopping. What are you doing here?" His lips quirk up in a grin. We're at a mall two days before Christmas. Of course, he's here shopping. "Hi, Autumn."

"Hey, Mr. M." My best friend turns on the charm.

"So, what are you here for?" Dad asks Autumn.

I give her a warning look, but she's not looking at me. "Oh, Parker and I are helping Holden with some shopping."

"Holden?" Dad turns to look at me. "Do I know this Holden?" He turns back to Autumn. "Is this your new beau?" he teases.

"Um, no. Not mine."

And she just threw me under the bus. I glare at her, and she mouths that she's sorry. I know what it's like to be on the receiving end of my father's intense gaze. I don't blame her. Besides, I should have at least mentioned him by now and called them to let them know I was seeing someone. This is on me. I was going to call Mom and ask her about inviting him on Christmas Day. I knew she would be fine with it, and I was hoping she could soften the blow to Dad.

"Holden's my boyfriend," I say, squaring my shoulders and meeting my father's stare.

"Boyfriend?" Dad's eyes widen. "Since when do you have a boyfriend, duchess?" he asks, his voice tight.

"Since last night."

Her shoulders relax only slightly. "Who is he?"

Here goes nothing. "Holden Bailey." I wait for the name to register. It takes him no time at all, and his eyes narrow.

"He was just traded to the Blaze."

"He was." I nod.

"And how did the two of you meet?"

Great. I'm twenty-one, so it's not like hanging out at The Outfield is illegal, but I know Dad won't like it. He's protective of us. "We met several weeks ago at The Outfield."

"I see," he says, his voice tight. "Well, when do we get to meet him?"

"About that," I say slowly. "I was going to talk to you and Mom later today about him coming over for Christmas."

"You just started dating."

"But we've been seeing each other." It's not a complete lie, but where Dad's concerned, it's better this way. "I'm meeting his family."

"This is serious?"

"He's my boyfriend, Dad."

"A boyfriend I've never met," he counters.

"You'll meet him."

He nods. "So, what? He doesn't have time to buy his own gifts for his family and has you doing it? What's he doing today? Do you know where this boyfriend of yours is?" he asks.

I don't dare tell him that he's here at this very mall. I can only hope that Dad and Holden don't run into one another. "He's actually doing some last-minute shopping."

"So, what are you doing shopping for him?"

"He bought a new house. He has to rush home for a furniture delivery this afternoon, and he needs, well, everything." I open my hand where his credit card is still clutched. "He gave me this and told me to do my worst."

"He gave you his card?"

"He did."

"And what? You're going off a list or something?" Dad's trying really hard to find something wrong with this scenario, but he's not going to find what he's looking for.

"No. He rattled off a few things he needs and told me to buy whatever."

Dad looks at Autumn, and she nods. "It was really sweet, Mr. M. Holden was all 'I trust you' and 'I need it all.'"

"Right." Dad runs his hand that's not holding his purchases down his face. "You need to call your mother."

That's his go-to when he doesn't know what to do with my sisters and me. I imagine it's hard for a man's man like Easton Monroe to raise three headstrong daughters and have a wife just like us. He's a man in a woman's world. We know he loves us, but oftentimes, especially as we all get older and develop our own lives outside of their home, he struggles with how to handle us. When it was my older sister, Paisley, I found it amusing. Now that that weariness is because of me, not so much. It's not enough to make me give up Holden, but it still makes me feel bad.

"I will," I assure him. "Are you headed home now?" I ask. Partly, so I can have him tell Mom I'll call her, and the other part is worried about him running into Holden without me being with him. At least not until I get Mom up to speed and can be the buffer for their first official meeting with Holden being introduced as my boyfriend.

"I just finished up and was heading home."

"Well, tell Mom that I'll call her when we're done here."

"She's not going to be happy hearing about Holden from me." He tries to lay on the guilt, but it's not working. I know my mom, and as long as her girls are happy, she's happy. Dad's deflecting, and we both know it.

"I'm sure it will be fine." I step up and wrap my arms around him for another hug. "Love you, Daddy."

"Love you too, duchess. Autumn, it was good to see you."

"You too, Mr. M."

With a nod, he turns and walks away. I stand there in the middle of the busy mall and watch until I see him exit the building. Luckily, we're close to the doors, or I would have been forced to stalk my own father. Don't judge. Desperate times call for desperate measures.

I turn to face my soon-to-be-ex best friend. "Really, Autumn?"

"I'm sorry," she says. "I panicked. I'm not a good liar. You know that."

"You could have lied by omission."

"I know. I'm sorry." She places her arm around my shoulders. "I'll buy you some lunch to make up for it. Please don't be mad."

I sigh. "I'm not mad. I should have told them. I was just waiting to talk to Mom first. Holden and I just discussed Christmas with our families this morning."

"He's all in, isn't he?"

"He says he is."

"And you don't believe him?"

"No, I do. It's just... not at all what I expected from him."

"I'm happy for you."

"Thank you." I bite down on my cheek to fight my grin. Sure, this isn't how I wanted my dad to find out about Holden, but Autumn's right. He's all in, and as his girlfriend, I've chosen to believe him, and the possibilities of what the future might hold have me giddy.

"Come on, let's grab some lunch at the food court, and then spend some of your man's money."

"I'm not with him for his money." It's important to me that she knows that and that Holden knows it as well. He could be working at one of these stores here at the mall, and I'll still feel the same way about him. I'd still be falling for him.

"I know that. You're Easton Monroe's daughter. Hell, you don't even have to work if you didn't want to." She gives my shoulders a tight squeeze. "Now, come on and let me feed you."

"Okay, so we have a comforter set, sheets, towels, dishes, and cookware. You think that's enough to get him started?" I ask Autumn as we take our second load to my car.

"He said he needed everything."

"Yeah, but surely he wants to pick some of that out himself."

"He's a man."

"Men choose things for their homes."

"Not if they don't have to." She laughs. "I say we head to Walmart to get groceries, and we can pick up things like mixing bowls, cookie sheets, pizza pans, and pizza cutters. He's a man living alone. We have to keep it simple."

"Maybe we should pick up some paper plates." I laugh. "I don't know this side of him," I confess.

"That's why you're dating. You're going to get to know all sides of him."

"Yeah, but shouldn't we have done that before we added an actual title to this?"

"No. You do you, Parker. Who cares if you don't know if he likes to use paper plates? He's used them at our place without a problem."

"This is weird, right? Me buying stuff for his home?"

"Sounds like he let you do the same thing last night."

"He did, but he was with me."

"Maybe he saw that you have good taste, and he knows you're not going to do him wrong. I mean, unless we go back and get the dishes with the sunflowers. That's very manly." She laughs.

"No. I can't do that to him." I shake my head, fighting my own laughter.

"Okay, let's go to Walmart and get the groceries. My poor car is packed as it is. We don't have much room for more anyway."

"Let's do it." We climb in my car and drive the short distance to Walmart. "One cart should be enough, right?" I ask Autumn.

"I say we get two. One for food and one for everything else."

"Probably a good idea. It's hard to tell what you'll talk me into getting."

"I've got your back." She smiles and winks dramatically.

"Come on, goofball."

Once inside, we both grab a cart and head to the home goods side of the store to start. I keep running through my head of things he's going to need to be comfortable until all his belongings are delivered. I'm not going to go crazy. I just want to get what he needs to get him by.

"What about a rug for the shower?" Autumn asks.

"Yes. He's going to need that. Let's see if we can find a dark gray one." She holds one up, and I nod. "Toss it in the cart."

"He's a man. He's going to need one of these," she says, holding up a plunger.

I toss my head back in laughter. "Every house needs a plunger. Add it to the cart," I tell her.

"Oh, what about rugs for the front door?"

"Yeah, he's going to need those too." We turn back two aisles over and grab a couple of doormats. One for the mudroom, the front door, and the sliding door in the kitchen. That's enough for now. He can get more as he needs them.

"What else are we forgetting?" she asks.

"Silverware."

"He can eat with his fingers," she teases.

"Which of these looks like Holden to you?" I ask her, stopping in front of the shelf that holds silverware.

"These." She points at the same set I was thinking of.

"Agreed." I toss in two packs and move on down the aisle. "Grab some mixing bowls, and I'll get a cookie sheet and pizza pan."

"If you plan on doing any cooking, you might want to grab a casserole dish too."

"He probably has them at his old place."

"He was a bachelor who was never home."

"But he knows how to cook. He made us breakfast, remember?"

"Just because he knows how doesn't mean he did it. Besides, from what you tell me, it's a big-ass kitchen. He has the storage space."

She's right. After I add the pans, I grab a glass casserole dish as well. I toss in some kitchen towels, a couple of serving utensils and decide that's enough. "I think we're ready for food," I tell her. "I still feel like he's going to have double of all of this stuff. It's a waste of money."

"This is what he asked you to do. He said it was all hand-me-downs, so maybe he wants all new for his new house, new start, new girlfriend." She shrugs. "He's on a new kick right now."

"Stop." I laugh. "Come on. Groceries, and let's get out of here," I say as my phone rings. Fishing it out of my purse, I see Holden's calling.

"Hey," I greet.

"Hi. How's it going?"

"Well, I have a trunk full of stuff for your house, and we're at Walmart now getting some groceries and a few other small things."

"I need it all, so I'm sure whatever you have will be great."

"You might end up with a lot of duplicates when you move your stuff here."

"It was mostly all secondhand anyway. I've been thinking about just donating it."

"Okay. Well, is there anything specific you need or want to eat?" The question sounds very domestic, and it's something I've heard my mom ask my dad and vice versa many times in my life.

"Yeah, can you grab some towels and body wash? Whatever you think smells good is fine with me, and some shampoo?"

"I already bought towels, but I'll grab the other stuff. Food?"

"Water, milk, eggs, wheat bread, some fruit, really. Just grab what we'll need for tonight and the next few days. We can go out and fill up the fridge and pantry after that."

"Okay, well, I'll figure out a couple of quick meals and some snacks."

"Perfect. What time will you be here?" he asks.

"Well, we just started on the food, so probably an hour and a half to two hours. I still have to drop off at our place too."

"That's perfect. Thanks for helping me, Parker."

"Anytime. I'll see you soon."

"Drive safe, babe," he says before hanging up.

"What did he add?"

"Just some body wash and towels, but we're already all over that. He said just to grab for the next few days, and he can worry about getting stocked up later."

"What are you thinking?"

"I'm not sure. He said to grab whatever he thinks we might need."

"We, huh?"

"That's what he said."

"All right then, let's get to shopping."

It takes us another hour and fifteen minutes to grab food, spices, a case of water, and the things that Holden added to the list. This close to the holidays, this place is a madhouse. I did grab more than a few days' worth of food. I figured it was better to err on the side of caution.

Autumn and I had to do some shifting around, but we managed to get everything in the back seat without crushing the bread, bagels, and chips. I call that a success.

Now, to take Autumn home and drive to Holden's and unload. I'm exhausted after a full day of shopping. I hope he doesn't have any plans for us to go out tonight. I just want to stay in and relax. My place or his, I don't care either way. As long as we're together.

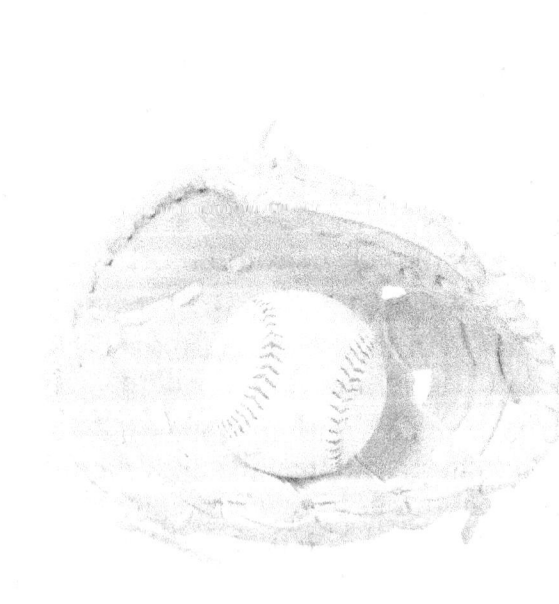

CHAPTER 20
Holden

I'M NOT USUALLY SOMEONE WHO likes to throw his weight around where money is concerned. I get paid a fuckton to play the sport I love, and if living expenses were not an issue, I'd play for free. With that being said, today I used my name, my position on the team, and the balance in my bank account to get shit done. No way would I have been able to accomplish everything I have without it.

First, I called a cleaning company. The house was spotless other than our mess last night, but I'd feel better about the fridge and the bathrooms being cleaned before we use them, and if all goes well, we'll be staying here.

Together.

Soon.

Second, I ordered some pictures to be developed online, so all I had to do was run in and pick them up. I grabbed a couple of frames while I was in there. Thankfully, the pharmacy is a one-stop shop.

Next, the furniture store. I picked out a new bedroom suite, and today must have been my lucky day because it was in stock in the warehouse and available for delivery next week. This is where my name, my career, and my bank account all helped me out. The manager is a fan of the Blaze, and after signing a million autographs for everyone in his family, and a hefty fee, he agreed to have the furniture delivered this afternoon instead of next week.

As I was leaving the store, a display caught my eyes, which led me to go back to the manager and make another purchase. The idea hit me out of nowhere, and I just went with it. That led me to the mall to finish up my shopping. Running into Parker and Autumn was a bonus. I almost convinced her to come with me, and she could pick out her gifts, but I wanted them to be a surprise, so I forced myself to walk away.

I'm glad I did. I ended up with something else that wasn't on my list, but I think it brings the earlier surprise full circle. I also grabbed her a coat. Funny story, I had no idea which coat she was looking at, but I looked at every store I went into. At the third clothing store, the saleslady who looked to be my grandma's age was very helpful. She even told me that the particular coat I was looking at was very popular, that a young lady spent a lot of time mulling over the possibility of purchase, but in the end decided not to. I showed her a picture of Parker, and she smiled and nodded.

Luck is definitely on my side today.

I bought the coat, and she graciously helped me pick out a hat, scarf, and gloves to match. I don't know if Parker wears that stuff, but the lady did me a solid, and she works on commission. It's the least I could do, and again, my bank account can take it.

After buying a few more things for Parker, I stopped at the gift wrap station. I gave them a generous tip when they got me sorted quickly and hightailed it home. I made it with barely fifteen minutes to spare before the furniture delivery truck was buzzing the gate.

It's been a flurry of activity all day, but no snafus have kept me from executing my plan. Everything is in place and where it should be. I'm excited for Parker to get here. I think I went a little overboard, but she's my first girlfriend in my adult life, and I know she has reservations about my past and my intentions. At least she did. I'm hoping that some of what I've accomplished today helps alleviate those fears.

My phone rings, and I rush to the kitchen, where I left it sitting on the island. "Hello?"

"Hey, I'm here. Can you buzz me in?" Parker asks.

"Sure. I'm sorry, I meant to give you the code. I'm going to open the garage door. You can pull in, and we can unload."

"Perfect. I feel like I should warn you. There's a lot of stuff in my car."

"Good. I need a lot of stuff."

"I hope you still feel that way when I get there. I kept all of the receipts so I can return any of them."

"I'm sure it's all perfect. Thank you for doing that. I want to be able to stay here, and with Christmas two days away, I know I couldn't have made this happen without you."

"You're welcome. I'm pulling into the garage now."

"I see you." I laugh and end the call, sliding my phone into my back pocket. She parks, and I rush to her door to help her out. My arms slide around her waist, and my lips settle on hers. "I missed you."

"I missed you too. Come on. We have work to do." She pulls open the back door and starts handing me bags. It takes us both several trips to get everything carried into the house.

"Wow, you did work today." I look at everything she bought as we unbag it.

"I tried not to go overboard, but if you want to stay here before all of your things are moved from your old place, there are things you're going to need."

"You did great, sweet pea. This is exactly what I needed." We work together to put away the groceries.

"I thought I could bring my Crock-Pot over tomorrow and maybe make some chili. There will be leftovers so you can eat it for a couple of days."

"That sounds perfect, but why didn't you just buy a Crock-Pot?"

"I wasn't sure if you already had one."

"That's one thing I do have, but I think I've heard my mom say you can never have too many." I smile at her.

"They are convenient," she agrees.

"I see you picked up our mess from last night," she says as she stands at the island and tears off the tags from the new towels she bought. "And I'm going to take these home with me tonight and wash them."

"Damn," I mutter. "I should have bought a washer and dryer today. I didn't even think about it."

"Well, we should probably run to my place and wash your bedding before you sleep on it tonight too."

Glancing at my watch, it's just after seven. I don't want to run out again. I want to give my girl her presents. "How about we deal with the sheets not being washed for one night, and tomorrow we can go out and buy a new washer and dryer."

"Are you sure you want to sleep on itchy sheets?"

"Trust me. If you're lying next to me, I'm not going to give a fuck about the sheets."

"Oh, I'm sleeping here tonight?" she asks, surprised.

"I was hoping you would."

"I have no clothes, and we don't have towels."

"We'll get up early and go to your place to shower, and then we'll go shopping."

"You realize tomorrow is Christmas Eve, and the crowds are going to be insane."

Shit. She's right. Pulling my hat from my head, I toss it on the counter. I have to think of something. Pulling my phone out of my pocket and the card from the furniture store earlier, I dial the manager I was working with. "Kyle, hi, this is Holden Bailey. I was hoping for a favor."

"What can I do for you, Mr. Bailey?" he asks. I can hear the eagerness in his voice.

"I need a washer and dryer. Is it possible to get that delivered tonight? It slipped my mind earlier today when I was there." Before he can refuse, I toss in what I know will get this done. "I'll add two tickets for you to opening day."

"Let me see what we have in stock. Front load or top load?"

"Parker, front load or top load?" I ask.

She shrugs. "We have top. The front seem to make clothes smell moldy."

"Top load, and all the bells and whistles," I relay to Kyle.

"Be right back." He places me on hold.

"Come here." I hold my hand out for Parker, and she steps toward me. I wrap my arms around her, and she rests her head against my chest. I don't know why it feels so good to have this woman in my arms, but fuck, she relaxes me, and dare I say, she feels like my missing piece.

"Right, we have a dark gray set of top loaders, all the bells and whistles. We can be there within the hour."

"Perfect. And Kyle, I'm going to need another favor."

"What's that?"

"I need everything it's going to take to hook it up. I need it installed, as well as some laundry detergent and fabric softener."

"Sure, we have all of that here. My wife says it's too expensive—" he starts to ramble.

"That's fine. I just need it all tonight."

"Done. How would you like to pay for this?"

I shuffle to grab my wallet out of my pocket and give him my credit card number. "I'll see you soon," I say, ending the call and sliding my phone and my wallet back into my pocket. "Done. We can do laundry here tonight."

"I still don't have any clothes," she reminds me.

"You can borrow some of mine to go home in tomorrow. I brought some over with me today. I have sweats that will be way too big, but we can figure it out."

"We'll see," she says, not committing.

"That's not a no, sweet pea."

She tosses her head back in laughter. "That's not a no."

"Come on. I have something I want to show you." Holding my hand out for her, I wait until she links her fingers with mine, then lead her upstairs to the master bedroom.

"Is this where you tell me all the magic happens?" she teases.

"Well, there has been no magic-making as of yet, but I'm sure we'll get there." I wink, and her cheeks flush. Pushing open the door, I step back, allowing her to enter.

"Wow. Holden, this is beautiful." She runs her hands over the wood of the four-poster bed.

"I was hoping you'd like it." She moves around the bed to the nightstand and stops. I know she's spotted her first gift, and I wait patiently for her to acknowledge it.

"When did you take this?" she asks, her voice laced with emotion. She reaches for the framed photo of her and inspects it.

"You were studying at Cup of Joe, and I remember thinking how beautiful you looked that day."

"Holden, my hair was tied up with a pencil, I had no makeup on, and I'm wearing a ratty Blaze sweatshirt."

"Exactly. No filter needed. Just you, Parker Monroe. I wanted to capture the moment."

She places the frame back on the nightstand and turns to look at me. Tears shimmer in her eyes. She blinks them away, and although I hate to see her tears, even happy tears, I want to smile because my plan is working. I'm making her see that this, that *she* is more to me.

"There's more. Take a look in here." I point at the door of one of the matching his and her closets.

Cautiously, she steps toward the door and turns the knob, stepping inside. "A housecoat and hangers?" She turns to look at me over her shoulder.

"Your housecoat and those hangers are for you too. You can leave as little or as much stuff here as you want. This closet is yours as far as I'm concerned. You have a dresser out here as well."

"Holden—" Her voice cracks.

I step up behind her, wrapping my arms around her waist. "This is my home, and I want you here. I know that if I were to ask you to move in with me, you'd tell me I'm crazy and that we're moving too fast. So this is my compromise. This is me telling you that you are welcome here. I want you in my space, in my home, and in my arms as much as possible." I place a tender kiss on her neck, and she shivers at the contact.

"I don't know what to say."

"You don't have to say anything. Besides, I'm not finished. I have something else to show you." With her hand in mine, I lead her back downstairs into the home office. "This is for you," I tell her as I move back, letting her step into the room.

She gasps. "What?" She turns to look at me, and the tears are back.

"I want you here, and I know once the season starts, life is going to get crazy. I know you have one more semester of school,

194 | KAYLEE RYAN

and I thought you'd like a nice quiet place to study. I already want to spend all my time with you, and I can only imagine that's going to intensify the more that I do. So I thought you could study here."

"Holden, I don't know what to say." Her eyes scan the room as she looks at the new office furniture.

"The computer is new," I say, pointing at the new iMac that's still sitting in the box. "That way, if you forget your laptop, you have options, or you can do research or shop online. Hell, I don't care what you do with it. I just want you here. Close to me."

A sob wracks her small body, and my feet are moving. When I reach her, I pull her into my arms. I don't say anything because I don't know what to say. This is not the reaction I was expecting. Instead, I move us to the small loveseat. I thought I could sit in here with her sometimes. My need to be close to her is over the top, but I'm embracing it.

I pull her onto my lap and hold her close. "I'm sorry," I say, running my hands up and down her back. I don't really know what for, but something I've said or maybe this room altogether has upset her in some way.

She lifts her head, giving me a watery smile. "You have nothing to apologize for. This just kind of hit me in the feels. When my parents were dating, Paisley was four, if I remember correctly. My mom was a single mom working and going to school. Dad took Paisley shopping and came back with shoes for her because she needed them and apparently told Dad she had to wait a few more weeks. To hear Dad tell it, he spoiled his girls that day. Paisley got what she needed and then some, and so did my mom. But one of the things he bought her was a laptop. Hers was apparently a piece of junk and took her a ton of extra time to finish her assignments because it was so slow. This"—she motions around the room—"reminds me of that. Of the love they have for one another."

"Your dad is a good man."

"He's the best. My sisters and I have always said we want a man like our father in our lives. That we want to be loved like

OUT OF REACH BOOK THREE

that, and then you do this, and it's so much like something my dad would do." She looks back at me, her blue eyes full of emotion. "I know we're not there yet. Love is a huge declaration, but this gesture... you're not the man I once thought you were Holden, and I'm sorry for judging you."

"You know better now," I say, poking her in the side to lighten the mood. "A lot of that was on me. I knew what the media would say, but I listened to my agent, who claimed any press was good press and rolled with it. I never imagined I'd find a woman who would capture my attention, and I'd end up regretting letting it happen. That's not who I am. Not anymore. You've changed me."

"It's so fast. All of this is happening so fast."

"Is it? I know you felt it that night all those weeks ago, and I know I did as well. We've been dancing around it."

"I feel like I just got you."

"Technically, yes, but you've had me. There's been no one else for me since the moment I laid eyes on you that first night at the club."

"I should care about the media stories and your reputation, but I kinda don't," she says, smiling up at me. "I'm happy."

My forehead presses against hers. "That's all that matters, baby."

"I can't believe you did all of this for me."

"This doesn't even touch the surface of what I would do to spend time with you."

"Creeper," she teases.

"Only for you," I say, kissing the corner of her mouth. The buzzer for the gate sounds. "That's the delivery guys. I need to handle this. Check it all out. I'll be back." She stands from my lap, and I head to let the delivery guys in through the gate.

"Holden?"

I stop and turn to face her. "Yeah?"

"Thank you for this. For being the amazing man you are."

It's as if her words are a vise around my heart. I don't say the words out loud, but dammit. I'm falling hard for her. "Right back at ya, baby," I say, then turn and walk away.

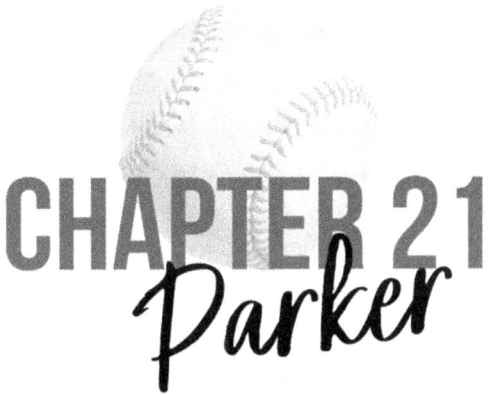

CHAPTER 21
Parker

I'M NERVOUS AND CAN'T STOP twisting my hands together. Holden insisted on driving since the weather report claims we could get some snow flurries today. He claims his truck will do better in the snow.

"Hey." He reaches over and places his hand over mine, and I stop fidgeting. "Are you sure you want to do this? I can drop you off and come back and pick you up."

He says the words, but I know he doesn't mean them. He's told me multiple times how excited he is for me to meet his family later today. I'm just nervous because I know my dad. I know how he treated Cameron the first time he met him, and I don't want his overprotectiveness to ruin Christmas.

"No. I want you to come with me. My dad, he's just really overprotective of us."

"I can handle it, Parker. I promise."

"I know you can. I just don't want him being an ass to you. Turn left here, the second house on the right." He does as I say and pulls into the driveway.

"Babe, I understand it. He's your dad, and my reputation, well, it's not exactly stellar. I can take whatever he gives me. I promise."

"Okay. Well, please don't hold it against me."

"The only thing I'm holding against you is me," he says with a wag of his brows.

"Come on, player," I tease. Just like that, he's eased my fears.

Climbing out of his truck, I grab the bag of gifts for my family, and Holden grabs his. He brought wine for my parents and a bottle for Paisley and Cameron as well. He got Peyton a gift card to the mall, and Jett got some kind of remote-controlled car. He picked everything out on his own.

"You didn't have to do that, you know." I point at the bag in his hands.

"Oh, so you're telling me that the bag in the back seat isn't for my parents?" I can't say that, so I just shrug. We step up to the porch, and he presses his lips to my temple. "It's all going to work out. They might not like me at first, but I'll win them over. It worked with you."

Instead of a reply, I push open the door just like ripping off a Band-Aid. We might as well get this over with. The house is bursting with activity. Taking off our coats and kicking off our shoes, we leave the presents in the foyer and go in search of my family. It's not much of a search. I know that they're going to be in the kitchen and that Mom will be serving her french toast casserole, bacon, biscuits and gravy, and hash brown casserole.

Dad thinks bacon should be its own food group. I love french toast casserole, Peyton loves biscuits and gravy, and Paisley loves hash brown casserole. Jett takes after his aunt Parker and prefers the french toast casserole, and Cameron, much like Dad, loves the bacon and all of the others. They always sample a little of each.

"Merry Christmas," I say, keeping my death grip on Holden's hand. My family stops talking and returns the sentiment. Mom comes around the counter and pulls me into a hug, and then to my surprise, she does the same to Holden.

"It's so nice to finally meet you," she tells Holden. Not that I'm surprised. I called her on my way to Holden's after shopping all day, and just as I suspected, Mom invited Holden and said she would take care of my dad. I make a mental note to remind Peyton that Mom is her ally when she finally decides to bring a guy home.

"It's nice to meet you as well, Mrs. Monroe," Holden replies politely.

"I'm Peyton." My younger sister waves at him.

"Nice to meet you." He nods, then turns to face my father. "Mr. Monroe," he says, offering my dad his hand.

Dad takes it, and with an elbow nudge from Mom, speaks. "Nice to meet you."

"Where's Paisley?" I ask, taking a seat at the island. Holden stands next to me and settles his hand on the small of my back. His silent support for me makes me smile. I should be supporting him after the cool greeting he received from my father.

"They're on their way," Mom answers. "Jett was having fun playing with all his new toys. It took them a little longer to get him out the door." No sooner than the words are out of her mouth, the front door opens, and Jett's laughter greets our ears.

"Grandpa!" Jett yells as the pitter-patter of little feet comes roaring down the hallway. "Look!" He runs to my dad, who is bent down to catch him in his arms. He stands, and his smile is as wide as Jett's. "I gots a dinosaur. Rawr!" Jett pretends like the animal is going to eat my dad's ear.

"Wow!" Dad exclaims with all the excitement that my nephew is expecting. "Santa was good to you."

"Hims was. I got lots and lots of toys." He nods.

"Hey, everyone," Paisley says, her hands resting on her tiny baby bump. "Hi, Holden. Glad you could join us."

"Wait. You two know each other?" Dad asks.

"He's my teammate," Cameron says, coming to his wife's rescue.

"Merry Christmas," Holden tells them.

"Time to eat. Everyone, grab a plate," Mom says.

I remain seated and let Paisley and her family grab their food, with Peyton following them. "You ready for this?" I turn to ask Holden. "I'm telling you my mom's Christmas morning breakfast spread is somewhat of a religious experience," I boast.

"After you, sweet pea." He smiles at me as he offers me a hand to help me down from the barstool I've been perched on. Together we fill our plates, and I notice that Holden samples a little bit of everything, just like Cameron and my dad. It makes me smile. He fits in with them so well. I just hope they're both willing to give him a chance.

"So, Holden, what does your family do for the holiday?" Mom asks once we're all seated.

"We do dinner and gifts at my aunt Lottie's every year."

"You're from around here, right?" Mom asks.

"Yes, ma'am. I moved away for college and then was drafted to the Tomahawks."

"Well, we're glad you're here."

"Thank you for having me."

"I can't believe you're leaving early," my dad grumbles from his place at the head of the table."

"Easton," Mom warns.

"What, queen?" he asks her. "It's not going to be the same without all three girls being here."

"Dad, we're staying for dinner and leaving after. That's us spending all day here," I defend.

Holden turns to look at me. "Babe, we can reschedule with my family. If you want to stay, we stay." He doesn't bother to lower his voice.

"No. We told your parents we would be there, and we will be."

"I think it's a great idea," Dad chimes in.

"Dad?" Paisley says.

"What's up, princess?" he asks.

"Do you not remember what happened with Cameron and me? Back off a little."

"I don't know what you mean. I just think having my duchess here with her family is a good idea. Cameron is here."

"And so is Holden. And last year, when Cam and I had to leave early to have Christmas with his mom, you didn't act like a child."

"I'm just saying—" Dad starts, but Mom speaks up.

"Easton, a word." Her voice is tight as she pushes back from the table and stands, stalking off toward the kitchen.

"Don't let him get to you," Paisley tells Holden.

"He did the same thing to me," Cameron tells him. "You want one of the Monroe sisters, you have to stand up to him."

I turn to look at him. "I'm sorry."

His hand rests against my cheek. "You have nothing to be sorry for. I'm sure when I have a little girl, no matter how old she is, I'll act the same way."

"He's out of control," Peyton tells us. "I'm the baby. He's going to flip out when I'm in this position."

"I guess you haven't asked him about spring break yet?" I ask my little sister.

"No, and I'm sure as hell not asking him today."

"We'll be there when you do," Paisley tells her. "Three strong and he won't be able to turn you down."

"I'm eighteen," Peyton defends. "I'll be nineteen in six weeks."

"Yeah, but as you said, you're the baby. You're his last hope at holding on and keeping us young."

My parents come back to the table, and all talks of spring break are dropped. Mom and Dad take their seats. Everyone is quiet until I hear Holden clear his throat.

"Sir." Dad stops eating and looks up at him. "I know the media portrays me as having somewhat of a wild lifestyle, but I promise you, as I'm sure you're aware, that you can't believe everything you read. I care about your daughter, Mr. Monroe. I would never do anything to hurt her." He turns his head to look at me. "All I want is for you to be happy. If you want to stay, we'll stay."

"Why can't you go without her?" Dad asks.

"Easton!" Mom scolds, and I swear I see flames coming out of her ears.

"It was an honest question," Dad defends.

"I could, sir, but it's Christmas, and I want to spend my day with Parker. So if she decides we stay, we'll stay and meet up with my parents later tonight or tomorrow."

"We're not staying," I say firmly. "Dad, do you even hear yourself right now? You're acting like a toddler. Holden is willing to not see his family to keep you happy."

"No, sweet pea, it's not for him. It's for you. This decision isn't for him. I'll do whatever you want. Your opinion is the only one that matters to me." He turns his eyes back to my dad. "It's not that I don't want your approval, Mr. Monroe, but I don't need it to care about her."

"You're welcome here anytime, Holden, and Parker, you told us you were splitting your time, and we understand that's how this works. At least I do. Your father needs a little refresher of how it works to juggle family commitments."

"You've been retired too long," Peyton teases our dad.

"Lady"—he shakes his head—"I'm not that old."

"You sure about that, *old* man?" she asks.

"I think Peyton might be onto something," Mom chimes in.

"Jett, what else did Santa bring you?" Dad asks, ignoring everyone but his grandson.

Jett rattles on about all the cool things Santa brought him, and that's pretty much the only conversation for the rest of breakfast. Jett steals the show, and I'm grateful for the reprieve.

"Present time?" Jett asks when Mom stands.

"Almost, sweetie. Let Grandma get everything cleared away."

Holden and I stand and begin to help her. He takes a load of dishes into the kitchen, and I stay behind to talk to my dad.

"I'm disappointed in you. I'm an adult, Dad. I can vote, I can buy beer, and I can choose the company that I keep. Holden is a nice guy, and he's good to me. Holden is a part of my life, Dad. You need to accept that or plan on seeing a lot less of me." With that, I take the dishes in my trembling hands and move to the kitchen. I stop as soon as I enter. Holden has his sleeves rolled up and is rinsing off dishes, then handing them to my mom as she loads the dishwasher.

"Your mother likes him," Dad whispers from behind me.

"I like him too."

"All right, duchess," he concedes. "I'll do better."

"See that you do," I say, stepping into the kitchen.

"I'll take those." Holden grins, and I hand them to him.

"Parker, this one's a keeper." Mom laughs.

"He cooks too," I tell her.

"Even better."

"And he spoils me." I'm aware Dad is still standing in the doorway, listening to this all go down. "He set up an office for me at his place so I could get peace and quiet to study next semester." I don't tell her about the housecoat. Not that I wouldn't, but I don't need to send Dad into orbit. I'll hold that off until it's just Mom and me.

Once the kitchen is cleaned, we head to the living room for gifts. Dad sits on the couch with Mom curled up next to him. Cameron and Paisley are on the loveseat, and Peyton is on the floor with Jett. Holden is sitting in the chair, and I'm on the floor resting between his legs. He's playing with my hair, and I see Dad's eyes scanning more than they should be. I don't care, though. Holden and I are together. Dad just needs to learn to deal.

CHAPTER 22
Holden

PARKER KEEPS CHECKING HER WATCH. I've told her a few times we could cancel. I don't want to, but I will. We can have Christmas with my parents tomorrow. I hate that this is stressing her out.

"It's about that time. We should head out."

"Are you sure?" I ask her.

"Yes."

"I'll go start the truck." With a gentle squeeze of her shoulders, I stand from the chair I'm sitting in and move to the foyer to start the truck. We finished dinner about an hour ago, and it was delicious. I've had a good day today getting to know her family, even when her father glares at me.

At the front door, I dig my keys out of my pocket and hit the remote start. The lights on my truck turn on and illuminate the driveway. Satisfied that it's started, I turn to go say goodbye but freeze when Easton steps into the foyer.

"You're not good enough for my duchess," he says bluntly.

I nod. "I happen to agree with you. However, I know with 100 percent certainty that no one will care for her like I do."

"You can't know that."

"You see, that's where you're wrong. I'm not going to stand here and tell you that I'm in love with her. She deserves that declaration before you or anyone else."

"She's my little girl."

I nod again. "I understand that. I know that she's your duchess, but sir, what you fail to realize is that she's my queen." I hear a gasp come from the hallway, and I know that Parker and potentially the rest of her family are listening in on this conversation.

Easton looks like I slapped him across the face. "Your queen?"

"Yes, sir. We can agree that I'm not good enough for her, but I'll make sure every damn day that I'm making choices that might get me there."

"You barely know her."

"I know enough. I know that she was scared as hell to come here today, to spend Christmas with her family for fear of your reaction to us dating. I know that she has to be able to zone out when she studies and block out the world. I know that she loves pumpkin spice lattes and that she gets so lost when she studies that she forgets to eat. I know that she's loyal to those she cares about and that she knows how to be silly and have fun. I know that she loves you very much." He closes his eyes and nods, but I'm not done. "And I know that she might be your little girl, but she's the woman who wormed her way inside my chest and wrapped herself around my soul."

"H-Holden?"

I turn to see Parker standing in the doorway. Her mom and sisters are surrounding her. There are tears in her eyes, but the smile that tilts her lips tells me they're happy tears. I'm caught off guard when she rushes toward me. I barely have time to brace myself when she launches herself at me, wrapping her legs around my waist and her arms around my neck. The next thing I know, her lips are on mine.

It takes control that I didn't know that I possessed to kiss her slowly, aware her family is watching us. When she pulls back, her watery smile hits me deep in my feels. "I'm ready to go."

"Okay, baby," I reply softly. Setting her on her feet, I make sure she has her balance before I move my attention to her mom and sisters. "Thank you for having me. Brunch and dinner were delicious. And thank you for the cologne, the sweatshirt, and the lounge pants," I tell them. "Merry Christmas. Mr. Monroe, thank you for having me."

Easton nods. "Drive safe."

I help Parker into her coat and take the bags of gifts her mother hands me. "Merry Christmas to you too." She smiles and links her arm through her husband's.

Hand in hand, Parker and I make our way to my truck. I open the door for her and wait for her to get buckled in before closing the door. After loading the bags into the back seat, I hustle around to my side.

Once I'm behind the wheel, I turn to look at her. It's dark outside, but I can still make out her features from the lights in the dash. "You ready?"

"Holden." She reaches over and places her hand on my arm. "Thank you for what you said in there."

"I meant it. Every word." She swallows hard. "I understand that he has a hard time letting go, but that's just it. I'm not going to let go, so he's going to have to get used to me being around."

"You have a way with words, Holden Bailey."

"Only with you." I give her a smile and put the truck in

reverse. We have one more family Christmas to get through, and then I get her all to myself. After the shit show of me squaring off with her father, I just need to hold her.

"Okay, so it's your parents and your aunt Lottie and uncle Lee. Who else am I meeting?"

"That's it for tonight. We always just do something small. Aunt Lottie and Uncle Lee never had kids, and this just turned into a tradition for us."

"Okay. So four, that's not too bad."

"Hey." I wait for her to look at me. "They're going to love you. I promise." I slide my hand around her waist and knock on the door.

My aunt Lottie opens the door, and her smile is bright. "Holden!" She steps back and motions for us to come in. "Let me take your coats. You must be Parker. It's so nice to meet you. Merry Christmas," Aunt Lottie rambles on.

My mom appears in the doorway and wraps her arms around me in a hug while Aunt Lottie takes our coats.

"Mom, this is Parker, my girlfriend. Parker, this is my mom, Ashley."

"It's nice to meet you," Parker says and chuckles when my mom pulls her into a hug as well.

"We've heard so much about you. I'm so glad that you could join us. Merry Christmas," Mom tells her.

"Aunt Lottie, this is Parker," I introduce properly when she comes back into the room.

"So nice to meet you, sweetheart." She, too, gives my girl a hug. "Come on in. Are you hungry?"

"No, ma'am. But thank you," Parker declines politely.

"Depends. Did you make your peanut butter cookies with the peanut butter cups in the center?" I ask.

"You know I did."

"Then, yes, I'm starving," I say, and all three of the women laugh.

"You go introduce your girlfriend, and I'll grab you a few from the kitchen." Aunt Lottie motions for us to head into the living room, where I know I'll find my dad and my uncle Lee kicked back on opposite ends of the reclining couch with full bellies, shooting the shit, just like every year.

My arm slides around her waist again, and I press my lips to her temple. Together, we make our way into the living room, and just as I suspected, Dad and Uncle Lee are sitting on the couch, feet propped up, and I wouldn't put it past them to have their pants unbuckled under their shirts.

"Tighten up, fellas. There's a lady in your presence," I call out, making them laugh. My dad is the first to stand and greet us.

"Merry Christmas, son," he says, hugging me before moving to Parker. "You must be Parker. It's so nice to finally meet you," he says, pulling her into a hug just as tight as the one he gave me.

"Step back from the lady, Stephen." Uncle Lee pushes on his arm and pulls Parker into a hug. "Heard a lot about you. Merry Christmas and welcome," he says, pulling away and hugging me tightly. "Been too long, Holden," he says before letting me go.

I lead Parker to the loveseat and nod for her to sit before taking the bag of gifts and placing them underneath the tree.

"Here you go," Aunt Lottie says, handing me a plate full of peanut butter cookies.

"You trying to put me in a sugar coma, woman?" I ask. "Coach would have my ass if he saw me eating all of these."

"They're not all for you. Share them with Parker."

"Oh no, you handed these to me," I tell her.

"Don't mind if I do." Parker grabs one of the bite-size cookies, well bite-size for me, and shoves the entire thing into her mouth. Her hand covers her face as she chews, and the moan that she releases as she swallows has my dick jumping behind my zipper. Now is not the time to go there.

"Cookie thief," I tease.

"They're so good." She smiles up at me as she reaches for another. This time, all I can do is shake my head at her.

"You ready for the season?" Uncle Lee asks.

"I'm ready. The new team and teammates thing is a little nerve-wracking, but I'm always ready to play the game I love."

"You're going to do great. We should hang out with Cam and Paisley before spring training starts so you two can get to know one another better."

"Cam?" Uncle Lee asks.

"My brother-in-law is Cameron Taylor."

"Well, I'll be. That must mean—" He stops as if mentioning her dad is rude.

"Easton Monroe is my dad." She smiles at him.

"You finally found one worth keeping." Uncle Lee chuckles.

"Hey!" I pretend to be offended, but he's not wrong. I wasn't looking before Parker, but now that I've found her, I'm definitely going to do everything I can to keep her.

"He's not wrong," Parker says, joining in on the banter.

"Do you play?" Mom asks.

"I do, actually. Softball. This is my last year of college."

"What's your major?" Aunt Lottie asks.

"Public relations. My uncle Drew, he's the GM for the Blaze, has offered me a position with the team when I graduate."

"That's wonderful," Mom comments.

"Yes and no. I'm grateful for the opportunity, but I don't want people to think the position was handed to me. It's entry-level, and I have to prove myself to work my way up," Parker explains.

"Well, I say take every advantage you can get. As long as you're not hurting anyone else, life is full of events that lead you to your next chapter. There's nothing wrong with taking the help he's offering," Dad tells her.

Parker nods. "That's a good point."

"Well, now that we're all here, who's ready to open some presents?" Uncle Lee asks. He stands and begins to pass out presents from under the tree.

"Will you grab ours?" Parker asks.

I can see she's uncertain about her gifts, but we both decided on the same things for our families. Grabbing the bag we set under the tree, I pull out the two bottles of wine and hand them to Mom and Aunt Lottie. "These are from Parker," I tell them. They gush over the wine and thank her.

We take turns opening gifts, and to Parker's surprise, my parents got her a sweater, and my aunt and uncle gave her a gift card for a massage. We laugh and cut up, and once all the wrapping paper is cleared, we settle in to watch *A Christmas Story*. It's a tradition, and the five of us can recite it word for word, but we still watch it every year.

"Parker, have you ever seen this movie?" Dad asks.

"Yes. My sisters and I watched it every year growing up. It's been a few years, though."

I make a mental note that she and I need to start our own holiday tradition, starting this year. My mind is racing with the possibilities when Aunt Lottie's voice breaks into my thoughts.

"Here we go." Aunt Lottie turns down the lights, and she and my mom squeeze onto the big couch and snuggle up to my dad and uncle. Not together, but you know what I mean. This year is the first year that I have my own snuggle partner, and I happen to like it a hell of a lot. More than I ever thought I would.

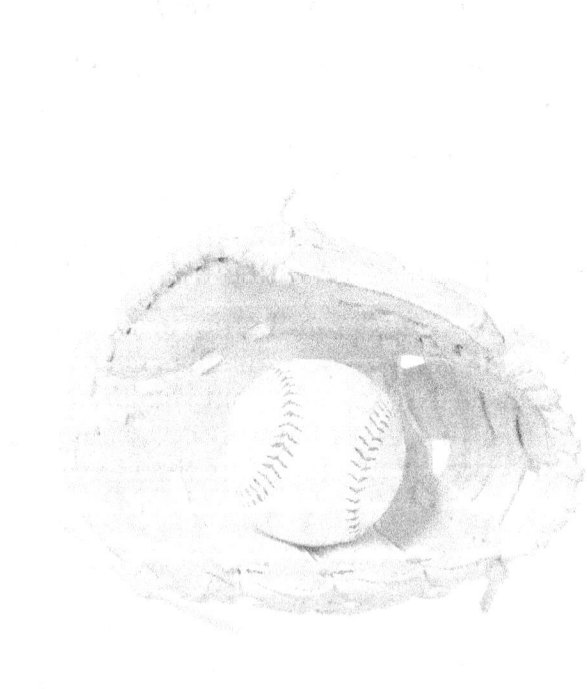

CHAPTER 23
Holden

"I LOVE YOUR FAMILY," PARKER says from the passenger seat of my truck. We're headed back to my place. At least that's my plan. I haven't asked her yet if she wants to stay with me, and I don't think I'm going to. I think I'll just drive us to my place and see what she says.

"Today was a good day." Even though her dad did a little flexing, it was still good to get to see her with her family and get to know them. What was even better was seeing her get to know my family. She fits in with us, and snuggling with her while watching my family's favorite Christmas movie? Well, that turns me into a sap I never thought I'd be. I can recall countless times I've ridden my friend's and teammate's asses for going all soft over the women in their lives. Now I get it. I mean, I grew up watching it with my dad, but he was Dad, and it was for my mom, so that made it okay.

"It was. I just wish my dad wasn't such an ass to you."

"He'll come around." And if he doesn't, that's his problem, not mine. If he can't see how much I care about her, then that's on him.

"You don't know that."

"I do know that. He's going to see what you mean to me." At least, I hope he does. Either way, I'm going to continue to be respectful to him. No way would I ever want to put her in the position where she might have to choose. Part of it is the fear of losing her, and the other part can't stand the thought of her having to make that decision. However, I'm hopeful that he'll come around. He seems to have finally accepted Cameron. Maybe one day, that will be me.

"You're not sick of me yet?" she asks when I pull up to the gate of my house.

"Never. Besides, I have your gifts to give you."

"Oh!" Her eyes light up. "With everything going on, I forgot about you and I exchanging gifts."

"Exactly." Pulling my truck into the garage, I shut off the engine and hit the button on the ceiling to close the garage door. "Come on. You've got presents to open." Not having to be told twice, she reaches for her handle and carefully climbs out of the truck.

Inside, we tear off our shoes and coats and make our way to the living room. I hit the switch that turns on the lights for the Christmas tree, and the room is lit with an intimate glow.

"Come sit." Parker is already sitting on the floor in front of the tree, with the remaining presents in two piles. "These are yours," she says, pointing at the pile in front of her. "And these have my name on them. And I'd just like to add that you've already done so much for me these aren't necessary. You built me an office and bought me a computer."

My girl is a breath of fresh air.

"I like spoiling you. And those things are selfishly for me too. I'm hoping that means I get to see you more."

"That's not why I'm with you, Holden."

"All the more reason to do so." I lean over the small stack of presents and press my lips to hers. "Now, how are we going to do this? One at a time or all at once?"

"I say we go one at a time. You first." She points at the pile of gifts with my name on them.

Grabbing the first gift, I slowly pull off the ribbon and begin to tear at the paper. When I lift the lid from the box, I sift through the tissue paper and pull out a jersey. A Blaze jersey. I hold it up, take in the front before turning to look at the back, and my name, Bailey, is embordered on the back. "How did you get this?"

"So, I might have called in a favor to my uncle Drew."

"When did you have time to do that?"

"I might have shot him a text a couple of days ago and asked if the orders for your replicas had come in yet. I know they ordered during the off-season, and I was hopeful yours was included in that order since he knew of the trade."

I stare at the jersey and try to remember the anger I had when I found out I was traded. I haven't even stepped foot onto the field with my new team, but already the Blaze feels like home. Maybe it's my hometown, and maybe it's the girl sitting across from me. Either way, the anger is gone, and dare I say, it's replaced with happiness. I'm more content at this moment, in this time in my life, than I can ever remember being in the past.

"Thank you, Parker," I say, my voice a little higher than normal.

"There's something else in there." She smiles.

I reach into the box and pull out another jersey. This one is much smaller than the one before it. "That one's mine," she says, leaning over to grab it from me. She holds it to her chest. "I have to represent, right?"

"You're damn right you do." I lean forward, and she meets me halfway for a kiss that has my cock twitching in my jeans.

"Your turn." I pull away from her lips before I toss her over my shoulder and carry her to my room.

She smiles and reaches for the smallest box. I watch her as she opens the scarf and gloves. "I love them. Thank you so much. You know they actually match that coat I was looking at the other day. Maybe I'll go back and see if it's still there."

Her comment has me biting down on my cheek. I can't wait until she opens the coat. "Open another one," I tell her, anxious for her to choose the largest of the packages.

"Nope. It's your turn."

Reaching for another box, I tear at the paper much faster this time and inside is a Blaze ball cap. "You heard Uncle Lee razzing me about not supporting my team tonight. I love it. Thank you."

"I did hear him. I almost cornered him and told him that I had you covered but decided not to."

"It's perfect. Thank you."

She reaches for another box, and this time, it's the perfume I bought her. She sprays a little on the inside of her wrist and offers it to me to smell. We go back and forth like this a few more times. I open a set of pajamas with baseballs all over them and a sweater. Parker opens the pair of small gold hoop earrings and the Blaze sweatshirt that I had my name and number added in a heat press to the back at the mall.

"Last one," I say, pushing the large box toward her.

"You've already gotten me too much," she protests.

"Just open it, sweet pea." Doing as I say, she reaches for the box and rips it into the paper. When she pulls off the lid and reaches in to pull out the coat, she gasps.

"H-How? How did you know?" she asks, hugging the coat to her chest and staring at me.

"I didn't. I was looking at coats, and the saleslady said it was popular and that a young lady was eyeing for a long time just before me. I showed her your picture, and she confirmed it was you. So I bought it."

"You're something else, Holden. I can't believe you were able to track down the exact coat I was looking at. I don't even need it. I have so many, but I really love it. Thank you."

"You're welcome."

She climbs over the boxes, and I open my arms for her as she settles on my lap. She links her hands behind my neck and pulls me into a kiss. I want to get lost in it, in her, but we're not done yet.

"I have one more gift. This one is for both of us as well."

Her blue eyes light up. I reach behind me, where I shoved the small box, and hand it to her. "What is it?"

"Open it." She pulls the lid from the small box and lifts the ornament. I watch as she traces over our names and the year, and the words, *our first Christmas*. "I thought maybe we could start our own tradition."

"Ornaments?"

"Yeah, one for every year."

"You know you're talking about the future, right?"

"That's the plan."

"You're making it impossible for both my head and my heart not to get attached to you."

"Perfect. Once your soul is on board, you'll be caught up to where I am."

"And where's that?"

"You're not ready to hear it. Not yet," I say before softly pressing my lips to hers.

"We should put this on the tree." She stands and offers me her hand, pulling me from the floor. "It's going to stick out like a sore thumb on this matching tree." She laughs as she chooses a branch in the middle to hang the ornament. They're all matching, just like you would see at a department store, but I'm hoping that's going to change. We have years to add our own personal ornaments. Maybe we'll get a special tree just for sentimental decorations.

"Well, we're just going to have to buy another tree just for our ornaments."

"That's silly."

"Is it? There are all kinds of life-changing events that we can purchase ornaments for."

"Oh, Holden." She wraps her arms around my waist and buries her face in my chest. I return her embrace and savor the moment. I never want to forget what this feels like. It's not the house, or the tree, or the new furniture, but the woman in my arms who makes this place feel like home.

"Will you stay?" I ask.

With her head tilted back, she smiles up at me. "I'd love to."

That smile of hers has my heart constricting in my chest. "Let me lock up and turn off the tree."

"We should clean up first."

"Nah, leave it. It will be here tomorrow. Right now, all I want to do is hold you." That's not entirely true. I want to do more than hold her, but no way am I going to make her feel pressured. "Go on up and get ready. I'll be right there."

She nods and stands on her tiptoes, her lips meeting with mine. "Thank you for an amazing day, Holden."

I swallow hard. "We have many more ahead of us." After another quick kiss, I pull away from her. She heads upstairs, and I make sure the house is locked up and turn off the tree. The past three days have been crazy getting everything set up to be here, but this moment was worth it all. I wouldn't change a single second of any of it.

CHAPTER 24
Parker

I HAVE TO FORCE MYSELF to walk slowly up the stairs. Once I reach the landing, I sprint into his room and rush to the bathroom. I quickly brush my teeth and strip out of my clothes to freshen up. Swiftly, I turn off the bathroom light and rush to the bed, diving under the covers. My heart is racing, and my palms are sweating. I've never been this bold with a man, and it's fitting that it's Holden, the one person I was fearful of shattering my heart. He's not the man I assumed him to be. He's so much more. He's good to me, and I can see it in his eyes when he looks at me. This isn't a game to him. This player is hanging up his hat for me.

I want to show him that I'm in this. He says I'm not ready to hear how he feels about me, and maybe he's right. Because I know I'm falling in love with him, but I'm too damn scared to say the words. Instead, I'll show him what he means to me with our bodies, and hopefully, one day soon, I'll get the courage to come out and tell him that my heart, my body, and my soul are all his.

I hear him enter the room and close the door behind him. The sound of his belt unbuckling has me clenching my thighs together. I'm debating on letting him change into pajamas or just tell him now what I have planned.

"Hey, Holden?"

"Yeah?"

"Can we maybe not do the pajamas thing?" I ask quietly.

I can hear him moving, and then the bed dips next to me. "What's going on in that pretty head of yours?"

"I just—" I start but then stop. What do I tell him? That I can't think about anything other than being pressed skin to skin. That I think about his lips tracing every inch of me? That I've fantasized about his making love to me?

He leans in close and rests his palm against my cheek. "Don't ever hide from me, Parker. My career is going to make this difficult enough as it is. I want you to always be open and honest with me. Tell me what you want, baby."

"You," I blurt. "I want you."

"You have me. All of me."

He's not getting it. With a deep breath, I slide my hand out from under the blanket and reach for his hand that's resting on my cheek. Moving his hand under the covers, I place it on my chest.

He sucks in a breath. "Jesus," he whispers. He runs the pad of his thumb over my hardened nipple.

"I want you," I repeat.

"You sure about this? Parker, I don't know—" He swallows hard. "I know I don't have the willpower to sleep naked next to you. I just... I don't have it in me. I want you with a ferocity I've never known before."

"I'm not asking you to sleep next to me. Well, I am—but I want something from you first."

"Tell me." His words are breathless as his thumb continues to stroke my nipple, stoking the flames of desire inside me.

"I want you to make love to me." I'm aware that I used the word love. His eyes widen, and that tells me he is as well. We might not have said the words yet, but it feels like we're heading in the same direction. I can feel it like a balm to my soul that we're both falling into this with our eyes wide open.

"You sure about this? We can wait."

"I don't want to wait."

He nods once, pulls his hand from beneath the covers, and stands. My eyes trail his every move as I watch him remove his jeans and sweater. He's standing before me in socks and underwear. My eyes are eager as I follow his motions, watching him slowly remove one sock and then the other. Next, his fingers slide into the waistband of his boxer briefs, and I lick my lips, more than ready to unwrap this final gift, but he halts his movements.

"What's wrong?" My voice sounds a little panicked, worried he's going to back out. I'm already dripping wet for him, and he's barely touched me. If he backs out now, he'll give me the woman's equivalent to blue balls.

Please don't let him back out.

"Condom," he croaks. "I don't have a fucking condom."

It's on the tip of my tongue to tell him that we don't need them. I've been on the pill for years, but as much as I want this to work between us, it's still new, and well, I think we need them for now. "My purse."

"What?" he asks.

"I have a new box. Autumn insisted I buy them when we were out yesterday. I told her I wouldn't need them, but I bought them anyway. They're in my purse."

"Where's your purse?"

"Kitchen."

He bends over and kisses me hard. "Don't move." With that, he's gone.

I hear his feet pound down the stairs, and the noise matches that of the rhythm of my heart thumping in my chest. Sliding my arms back under the covers, I focus on my breathing, willing myself to calm down. I've barely started the process when I hear Holden's footfalls on the steps once again. The click of the bedroom door closing sounds throughout the quiet of the room. Holden makes his way to his side of the bed, and I hear him tearing open the box, and I watch from the moonlight spilling into the room as he pulls a foil packet from the strip and tosses it on the bed before placing the box on the nightstand.

His fingers once again slip under the waistband of his boxer briefs, and he pulls them to his ankles, kicking them across the room. The cover is lifted, and he slides in beside me. I don't wait for him to reach for me. Instead, I move and meet him in the middle. I'm lying on my back, and Holden is hovering over me.

"You sure?" he asks again.

"Are you going to make me beg, Bailey?" I tease, trying to lighten the mood a little.

"As enticing as that sounds, it's not necessary. I'll forever give you everything you want." He leans down and captures a nipple into his mouth. "Everything you need." His hot breath brushes over my breasts, making me shiver.

Burying my hands in his hair, I close my eyes and just feel. I savor every swipe of his tongue and every press of his lips. His hands are everywhere, and the actions combined have my body burning with desire for him.

He kisses his way down my belly, his head now fully under the covers. My hands are still buried in his hair, and I arch off the bed with the first swipe of his tongue against my clit. He moves my legs over his shoulders and begins to torture me with his tongue. It's exquisite and, dare I say, life-changing the talent the man has with his tongue.

I try not to think about the practice he's had or my lack of experience where this particular act is concerned. There have only been two other guys to go down on me, and from what I'm experiencing right this moment, they didn't know what the hell they were doing.

Pulling back the covers, I lift my head to watch.

"You good, sweet pea?" he asks.

"So good," I say, burying my hands back into his locks. He winks and gets back to work. I watch him, and the sound he's making—as if this is the best thing to ever happen to him—only heightens my desire. When he slides one long thick digit inside me, a moan unlike anything I've ever heard before tumbles from my lips.

He adds yet another finger, his mouth never stopping the delicious rhythm against my clit. All that I can do is hold on. My head drops back to the pillow, and my legs hug him tighter as I feel the fire of my pending orgasm race through my veins. With each stroke of his tongue and with each thrust of his fingers, I grow closer and closer to the edge. Heat from my core spreads throughout my body.

"H-Holden," I pant.

"Let me have it, Parker. Give me your pleasure," he commands.

As if my body was waiting for his permission, I cry out as ecstasy like I've never felt washes over me. My body arches off the bed, and a low moan rips from my throat as everything tingles and crashes like waves against the shoreline.

Spent, my body sags against the mattress, and I can't help but laugh when I realize we're going to have to change the sheets, and we just washed them.

"Not the reaction I was hoping for," Holden says as he kisses his way back to my lips. He kisses me softly, and I can taste myself. It's not something I'd ever done before him, but with Holden, it seems my guard is nowhere in this room. He's getting all of me unfiltered and unashamed. He makes me feel sexy and wanted, and tasting myself on his lips is more erotic than I ever thought possible.

I reach for his cock, and he moves just out of reach. I make a grunt of protest, and he chuckles. "As much as I want to feel the softness of your hands wrapped around my cock, I can't. Not right now."

"Why?"

"Because when I come, I want to do it inside your sweet pussy. I've been jacking off for weeks thinking about you, and I need the real thing. If you're sure that's what you want?"

"I'm sure." I pat around the mattress until my hands land on the condom and hand it to him.

His blue eyes smolder in the moonlight as he sits back on his legs and tears open the wrapper, sliding the condom over his length. He moves with the grace of the professional athlete he is, and his arms are now resting on either side of my head while he hovers over me.

My hands rest on his cheeks, and with the light of the midnight sky shining through the window, I know he can see me when I look into his eyes and say the words for the second time tonight. "Make love to me."

He nods once before reaching between us and aligning himself at my entrance. Carefully, he lowers his weight against me, and I savor the feeling. "Merry Christmas, baby," he whispers as he pushes inside me.

One slow stroke in, one identical slow stroke out. Over and over again, he sets the pace. Not once does his gaze leave mine, and I can't seem to find it in me to look away. It's almost as if this is an out-of-body experience.

The moment is intimate.

It's ours.

"Kiss me," I breathe. I need a break from the intensity of his stare and the way it makes me feel. I'm on the brink of shouting that I love him, and although to some, it may be too soon, the rapid beat of my heart and the way he's making my body sing with pleasure for his tells a completely different story. He's mine, and I'm his, and we feel what we feel.

His lips press against mine, and his tongue prods past my lips, and I'm grateful. Not only for the taste of him on my tongue, the taste of us, but for the moment, giving me time to gather my senses before I confess my undying love and he runs far, far away. I'm not ready to lose him, so I'll keep my confession to myself. It's better this way. I can let the love we share simmer and grow, and when I'm ready to tell him, and when he's ready to tell me, that will make that moment even better.

I've never had multiple orgasms, but it looks like Holden is the exception to my every rule. The fire begins to ignite, only this time the flames grow taller and faster. I'm racing toward the edge and hope that he's with me.

"I'm so close," I pant.

"Thank fuck. Baby, I'm barely hanging on here," he confesses.

"More," I say, wrapping my legs tighter around his waist. "Faster."

"You wanted me to make love to you," he says, ignoring my request to move faster.

"You are."

"Slow," he says, smiling down at me.

"We've already broken all our rules, Holden. Why stop now?"

"Because this moment, it's changing my life. *You're* changing my life, and I need you to know that. I need you to see that this is more, Parker. So much fucking more," he says, his brows furrowed as he continues his slow, torturous pace.

"We're more," I agree with him. "And we have many more days like this ahead of us."

"Years," he corrects.

"Then move, Bailey. Show me what you can do."

"Fuck," he groans. "Are you sure? This won't last much longer."

"I'm sure. Give me all of you."

My words, or maybe my acceptance of his, are all he needs to unleash everything he has. My arms and legs are wrapped around him tightly as he thrusts hard and fast. There's no more talking as he takes what he needs and, in the process, gives me what I need as well.

The fire inside me now burns at an accelerated pace, and before I know it, I'm calling out his name, digging my nails into his back. He rocks into me one last time and stills. I open my eyes in time to see his head thrown back and his jaw clenched tightly as he releases inside me.

His arms quiver as he tries to hold his weight off me. "You okay?" This time I'm the one concerned.

He lifts his head, and a slow smile pulls at his lips. "I've never been more okay in my entire life. You've ruined me, Parker. Ruined. Me." He drops a kiss to my lips and slowly pulls out of my body. Immediately, I miss the connection. "Let me clean up. I'll be right back."

I know I should do the same, but my legs are jelly, and from the way he's wobbling his way to the bathroom, I'd say he's feeling the same way. A few minutes later, he's sitting next to me on the bed, tapping my thighs for me to open as he helps clean me with a warm washcloth. Once he's satisfied, he tosses the rag through the bathroom door—not a single care where it lands—and crawls over top of me, pulling the covers over us.

I'm back in his arms where we both want me to be. "In case we weren't clear in all our previous conversations, you're mine, Parker. It's going to take the world ending for that to change."

I don't know what to say to that other than "I'm falling in love with you," so instead, I say nothing at all. I snuggle into him and let the rhythm of his heartbeat lull me to sleep.

CHAPTER 25
Holden

THE PAST FOUR MONTHS HAVE been nothing short of incredible. If you'd have asked me that first night four months ago where I'd be today, I never would have said, "madly in love with Parker Monroe," but here I am.

Parker and I have settled into a routine of sorts, but that's all about to change. I have to report to spring training in just a few days, which means I'm leaving for Florida, and my girl and my heart will still be here in Tennessee.

This weekend is Valentine's Day, and although I know it's cliché, I plan to tell her that I'm in love with her. So many times over the past couple of months, I've almost said the words. In fact, there are times when we're in bed at night—and I know from her even breaths she's sound asleep—that I've whispered them to her. That changes this weekend. I'm having a hard time with leaving her, and no way am I going to just jet off to spring training without her knowing that she is the absolute love of my life.

Hands down.

No question.

She's my game changer.

I knew that October night all those months ago when I saw her for the first time that she was different. I just didn't know that she was not only going to change my life but alter who I am as a person. Hell, even the media portray us as a baseball royalty couple, second place of course to Cameron and Paisley. And to hear Easton tell it, we are in third place. He is the king of the family, after all. His words, not mine. Not to mention I now have a new agent, who is not of the frame of mind that all press is good press.

I want to be better for her. I want to show her every single day that nothing is more important to me than her.

Not even baseball.

If it were not for the fact that it's only been four months since I've known her and that I know she wants to graduate from college first, I'd be asking her to marry me tonight—confessions of love and promises of happily ever after. I've considered it, and hell, I even bought a ring. I was out shopping last week for today, and I saw it. I just knew it was meant for Parker. I bought it with the intention of proposing tonight, but I talked myself out of it. There's no rush. I'll let her focus on her last semester of college, and then all bets are off.

My phone rings, and I smile when I see it's Cameron. He's not only just my teammate but someone I consider a close friend and my girl's brother-in-law. One day soon, he'll hold all of those titles for me as well.

"What's up, man?" I ask.

"Paisley's not feeling well. She thinks it might be the Mexican that we had last night that's not agreeing with her."

"Shit. Okay, well, we need to change it up then."

"Nah, man, you and Parker go on without us."

"No. Parker is excited for all of us to get together. She doesn't buy into Valentine's Day." Which is why today is perfect for telling her that I'm head over ass in love with her. She knows that I know how she feels about the holiday, and she won't be expecting it, especially since we had plans with Cam and Paisley.

"No. We can figure this out."

"Paisley wants to stay close to the house, just in case."

"I can work with that."

"Jett's still here."

"Okay. Here's the deal. You need to get on the phone and use your Cameron Taylor charm to organize dinner. I can pick it up if I need to. I'm going to swing by your place and pick up Jett to drop him off at his grandparents. While I'm gone, I'll pick up what we need. We're going to transform your basement."

"Without my wife knowing?" he asks.

"We're sure as hell going to try to do this without either of them knowing."

"We're going to need help."

"I know."

There's a beat of silence on the phone before we both say, "Easton," and laugh.

"He's coming around with me, and since you and Paisley are involved, I think he'll help us. I'll get Larissa to have Peyton help too when she gets home. I can't call her right now. She's with Parker getting their nails done."

"Got it. Yeah, Paisley was supposed to go as well but decided not to. Larissa stayed home in case Paisley needed her."

"All of that could work in our favor. I'm on my way to your place now. You start thinking about food."

230 | KAYLEE RYAN

"Sounds good. See you soon. I'll get Jett ready. Paisley is resting, and she'll never know. I hope." He laughs softly.

"We've got this, Taylor," I pep talk him before ending the call. Grabbing my keys, I lock up the house and head to pick up Jett.

"Grandpa!" Jett launches out of my arms and into Easton's. "Uncle Holden bringed me."

Not gonna lie. When the kid refers to me as Uncle Holden, something softens in my chest. He was confused as to what boyfriend meant, and since I was Aunt Parker's boyfriend, I should be an uncle. I was fine with it, and so were his parents, so we just rolled with it.

"I see that," Easton says, bouncing him on his hip. "Is everything okay?" he asks me. "My princess said she was fine when we talked to her earlier."

"Everything is good. We just decided to bring dinner to their place and surprise the girls."

He nods, and dare I say, a small smile plays at his lips.

"Parker was looking forward to tonight, so Cam and I are changing things up a bit. Are you still good to keep Jett?" I ask.

"Always." Easton hugs his grandson to his chest. "Go see Grandma. She made cookies last night."

"Cookies!" Jett races off in search of Larissa.

"So, change of plans, huh?" Easton asks.

"Yeah, we're going to bring dinner to them. I need to grab a few things, a tablecloth, fresh flowers, candles, but we're going to make it happen. We're setting it up in Paisley and Cam's basement."

"Need any help?" he offers.

I don't, but this is an olive branch from her father, and I'll be damned if I pass it up. "Sure, I was thinking about getting one of those outdoor gazebos, the one with a cloth top, and keep the top off, and hanging lights around it to help set the mood."

He nods. "I like that. What else you got?"

"Well, Cam is taking care of dinner, and I just need to grab it on the way over.'"

"No. That won't do. I'll call Cam and let him know that I'll be picking up dinner. That will spoil the surprise for my duchess. Just tell me what time to have it there, and I'll do a drop-off."

"That would be great. Thank you."

"Sure, anything for my girls. How about I run out and pick up some lights and flowers while you grab the gazebo?"

"Sounds like a plan. Oh, can you get Larissa and Peyton in on this as well? Maybe have Peyton stall Parker as long as she can. Or maybe not tell Jett and have him call and say he misses them? You know they can't refuse him."

"Great idea. Go on, get moving. I'll be in touch." He holds his hand out for me to shake, and I take it.

That's not at all how I expected this drop-off to go, but I'm thrilled that it happened. I never blamed Easton for his coldness toward me. I knew deep down it was more about no longer being the only man in his daughter's life than it was the man I am. He knows I love her. Hell, she knows I love her, and I won't stop until the entire world knows it too.

I might not have said the words, but I've always believed that actions speak louder, and I try to show her every day that I love the hell out of her. No matter who's around or who's watching. Parker comes first, always.

"I can't believe you two actually pulled this off without either of us finding out," Parker says as she lays her napkin on the table.

"Oh, we had help," I assure her.

"Who schemed against us?" Paisley asks, humor in her voice as she rests her hands on her baby bump.

"Your dad, your mom, and your little sister." Cam lets the cat out of the bag.

"Our dad?" Parker asks, surprised.

I tell her about how I dropped Jett off, and he offered to help, and how everyone just rallied after that to help us pull this off.

"I knew he'd come around." Paisley smiles at her sister.

"Well, ladies, the night's not over. We promised you dinner and dancing," Cameron reminds them.

The lights in the basement are already dim. The glow from the candles placed around the room and the table, along with the string of lights that Easton helped install, give us plenty of romantic lighting.

Cameron stands and pulls Paisley's chair out for her. "May I have this dance, Momma?" Paisley smiles up at him like he hung the moon, and for the first time in my life, when I see a couple who shares that look, I know how it feels to be on the receiving end, because when I turn to look at Parker, she has the same look on her face and it's directed right at me.

The look, that same smile she's always held just for me, reaches into my chest and squeezes my heart. Every. Damn. Time.

"Sweet pea?" I stand and offer her my hand. Pulling her to her feet, I'm quick to wrap her in my arms and begin a slow sway side to side. The music turns up a little louder, and I glance over to see Cameron sliding his phone back into his pocket.

Song after song, the four of us are lost in our own little worlds. Nothing matters but being in each other's arms and cherishing the moment.

"You know, I'm kinda glad our plans changed for tonight," Parker says.

"Yeah?"

"This is so much better. Being here with you. Just you. No fear of cameras or fans asking for autographs."

"But I like when they take pictures of us."

She playfully rolls her eyes. "I'm convinced now, Holden. You've hung up your playboy hat."

"Yeah, but I need to keep reminding the world that I'm happily taken."

"What am I going to do with you?" she asks.

Love me. "Kiss me," I say instead, as the lyrics to "I Cross My Heart" by George Straight fill my ears.

Pulling out of the kiss, I bend so my lips are next to her ear and sing every word to her. Her hands grip the back of my shirt, and I know that this is it. This is my moment. Our moment. As the last verse plays, I stop moving and cradle her face in my hands.

"I love you, Parker."

Tears shimmer in her eyes, but her smile is as bright as the sun. Her lips tremble as she replies, "Oh, Holden, I love you too."

I kiss her with all the love I have, and it's not until I see the flash of the camera from the corner of my eye that I remember that Cameron and Paisley are here, and Cameron knew to snap a photo of us once I told her. It was his idea, and when I asked him how he would know the right moment, he replied, "Don't worry, I'm madly in love with a Monroe sister. I'll know."

"What are you doing?" Parker laughs.

"Documenting the moment." Cameron grins at her.

"Just because your relationship was caught on camera doesn't mean mine needs to be," she teases.

"Best fucking day of my life," he says, leaning down and kissing Paisley's swollen belly. A jolt of envy washes over me. One day soon, that will be us, and it will be our baby on the way. I can't fucking wait to see what the future holds for us.

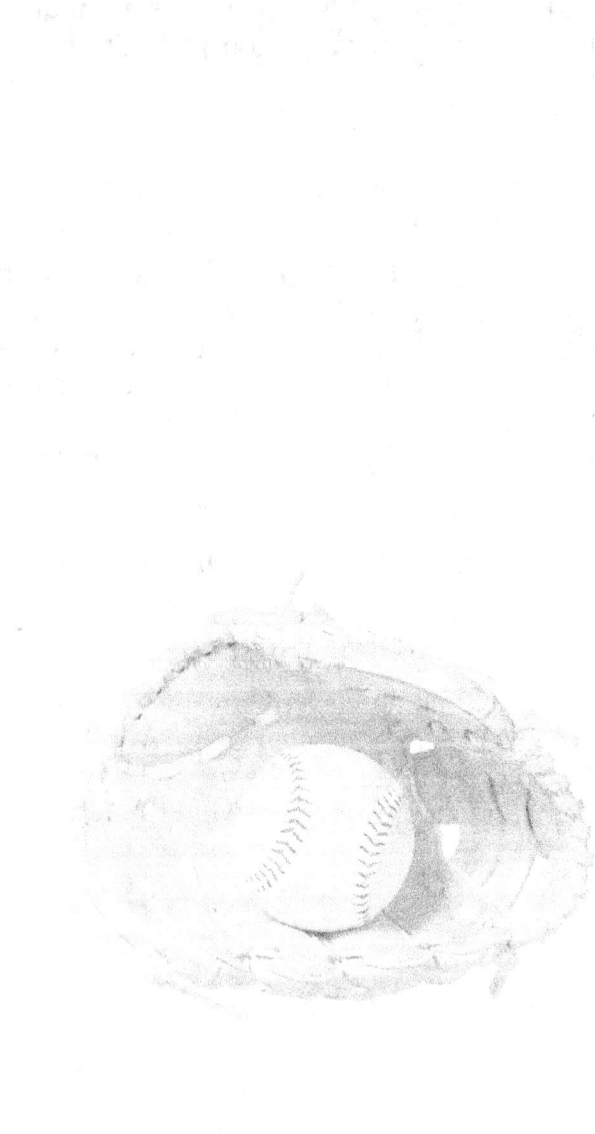

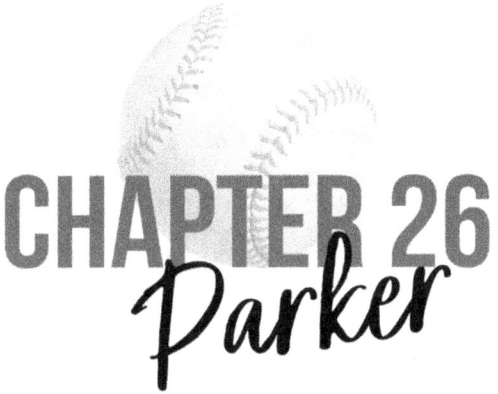

CHAPTER 26
Parker

"I CAN'T BELIEVE WE'RE HERE," Peyton says from her seat next to me on the plane. Our flight just landed at the Ft. Myers airport. We're both on spring break from college, and I'm flying down to see Holden.

He left a month ago this week, and it's been hard not being able to see him. This is the last week of spring training before he's back, but waiting another week to see him didn't work for Holden or for me. He bought me a plane ticket to come and see him since there are no classes.

When Peyton found out I was coming, she begged my parents to let her go. She and her friends had been planning a trip to the beach for spring break, and my parents were hesitant to let her go. All it took was me promising to keep an eye on her, and Dad loosened up the reins a little and agreed. We both had to promise to call him every day. I'm turning twenty-two soon, and Peyton is nineteen. Dad doesn't care, though. He's a papa bear, no matter how old we are.

"Don't forget to call Dad. I wouldn't put it past him to send a search party," I say, only half joking.

"Don't even joke about that," Peyton grumbles. "What time is Autumn meeting you?"

"She flew down with Kate last night. I waited for you to be out of your last midterm so we could fly together."

"Best big sister ever," she says dramatically.

"I'll be sure to tell Paisley you said so," I taunt.

"I love you both equally." Peyton grins.

"So, are your friends here yet?" I ask her.

"Karina is here. She flew down with her parents. Their flight was this morning at six or something like that. They're staying in the same hotel as us, so I told her I'd call when we were checked in."

"Do you have your pepper spray?" I ask her.

"Yes, Mom."

"Peyton, you're beautiful, and so is Karina. I don't want the two of you getting abducted or worse. This world has some crazy-ass people in it."

"I know. I promise we'll be careful, and I'll check in with you often. We're really just planning to hang by the pool and on the beach. No crazy partying or drinking. Besides, Karina's parents are here."

"Yeah, Dad was excited to hear that."

"It wouldn't surprise me if he's already called and talked to them." She snorts out a laugh.

"*That* is a bet I'm not taking." I join in her laughter. Our father is just over the top most of the time.

"When do you get to see Holden?"

"I want to get checked in and make sure you've met up with Karina, and then I'm going to go to where they're practicing. I bought a ticket for today, but he doesn't know. He thinks he doesn't get to see me until later tonight."

"Look at you going all out to surprise your man."

"It's just as much for me as it is for him. I miss him."

"There isn't a single doubt in my mind that the man isn't going out of his mind with missing you. He's crazy about you. You and Paisley managed to actually find men who love just like Dad loves Mom."

"Yours is out there too. He'll come into your life when you least expect him to. Trust me. I wasn't expecting Holden, and we know Paisley wasn't expecting Cameron either. Life just tosses him into your path."

"Well, I know one thing. I'm holding out. I want that kind of love. I want a man who looks at me the way Holden looks at you. I won't settle for less."

"That's my girl," I say, giving her a hug. The flight attendant tells us we can exit the plane, so we reach overhead to grab our bags. Nervous energy courses through me. I miss Holden more than I ever thought I would or even could. I can't wait to feel his strong arms wrap around me.

"So he has no idea you're coming today?" Autumn asks.

"No. I wanted to surprise him by coming to watch practice. He's not expecting me until tonight."

"How did you manage to actually pull that off?" she asks. "That man is all up in your business." She wags her eyebrows as we make our way into the stadium.

"Well, it helps that it's been a month since we've seen each other in person. Otherwise, you're right. I doubt I could have pulled it off." I smile because Holden and I have become so close that I'm not sure where he begins and I end. We just fit together.

We make our way to the field to find our seats, only to find it mostly empty. "Excuse me, sir," I say to a man and his two young sons. "Is training over for the day?"

"It is. They were only scheduled until two today."

"Thank you."

With a heavy sigh, I turn around and head back up the steps with Autumn hot on my heels. "It's what, twenty minutes after two? He still has to be here. They have to shower and get speeches and shit, right?" she asks.

"Possibly, but I don't think I can get to where he is. I have a general admission ticket."

"Yes, but didn't you tell me that your boyfriend insisted that he put you on the approved guest list for the entire duration of spring training just in case you were able to get down here to see him sooner?"

"He did, but I think that's just tickets at will call. My schedule with classes and softball just never seemed to match up. I hate that we're only here for four days, and I have to get back for a practice and a game."

"Then why did you buy the ticket today?"

"I don't know." I laugh. "I got caught up and forgot he had added me to the approved list."

"Well, let's go see if we can find him. The worse they can do is kick us out. Most of the fans are gone, so I think we can make it happen. Come on."

"Where are we going? The locker rooms are that way."

"I love that you know your way around most stadiums."

"I came here a lot to visit my dad during spring training," I remind her.

"Then this is going to be a piece of cake." She hits the button on the elevator, and the numbers change. Excitement stirs in my belly. I can't wait to see him. It's been too damn long.

As soon as we exit the elevator, I hear voices. Autumn stops so we can see if we need to hide from whoever it is, but when we hear my name, we glance at one another and then step a little farther down the hall to listen.

"Pussy whipped," a male voice says with a laugh.

"Never seen anything like it," another adds.

"Harp on me all you want. I'm the one who has a beautiful woman warming my bed at night."

Holden.

"Yeah, well, I do too. Only I get the variety," one of the voices comments.

"Been there done that, fellas. Not interested."

"Come on now, what we really need to be talking about is the bet," a new voice chimes in.

"Bet?" Autumn mouths, and I shrug. I move to step around the corner, but she grabs my arm to stop me and places her finger over her lips. With a roll of my eyes, I move to stand next to her again and indulge her in this little stakeout session she's got going on. I'm not sure what kind of juicy gossip she's looking for, but I'm giving her two minutes tops, and I'm going to my man. It's been too long, and I don't think I can wait a second longer than that. He's right there!

"What in the fuck are you talking about?" Holden asks.

"Come on, Bailey. Don't play dumb."

My stomach sinks. I don't think I'm going to like whatever is about to go down.

"We all heard you that day. Hold on. I even recorded it. Here, listen to this," the guy says as the recording begins to play.

"What do you think, Bailey? Think you can execute the play?" a male voice asks.

"I'm not only going to execute it, but I'm also going to fucking excel at it. Watch and learn, boys. Watch and learn," a voice I know without a doubt is Holden's replies.

My eyes instantly burn with tears. How could he do this to me? I thought it was real. I thought what we had was real. "Oh God," I cry out, slapping my hand over my mouth.

"Come on." Autumn slides her arm around my shoulders. "Let's get out of here." We turn to leave, and no matter how hard I try, I can't keep the tears at bay. The floodgates of my broken heart have opened, and I don't know that I'll ever be able to make it stop.

"What the fuck?" I hear shouted behind us, then heavy footfalls. "Parker!" Holden calls out, but I don't look back. Autumn and I keep facing forward as we wait for the elevator to open its doors.

"Parker, sweet pea, what's wrong? What are you doing here?"

"What's wrong? What's wrong?! It was a bet! A fucking bet, Holden! You win. You played me like I originally thought you would. I fell for it. Every whispered word, every touch, every promise of the future. Every. Fucking. Word. I fell for it, and look where that got me."

"Parker—" He reaches for me, but I move out of his reach.

"Don't fucking touch me. You don't get to touch me. Not anymore. I'm not yours, and you're not mine." My voice breaks as the elevator doors slide open, and Autumn leads me inside. He moves to step on with us, but I scream, "No!" at the top of my lungs. "Forget you know me," I say as the doors slide closed. I hear his screamed, "Fuck!" as the elevator carries us to our next destination. Anywhere but here.

When we step off the elevator, I'm thankful there isn't a crowd of people and, even worse, photographers to witness the hot mess that I am. My tears are falling hard and fast, and my breathing is so rapid, I fear I may pass out.

Autumn manages to get me into her rental and pulls a stack of napkins that have been there for who knows how long from the glove box and sets them in my lap. "I'm so sorry, Parker." Her voice is soft, and I know she's hurting. She encouraged me to let loose, and this is what happens when I do. But this isn't

Autumn's fault. No, this is Holden. He shattered my heart all on his own.

"I thought he loved me," I say through my tears. "He told me that he loved me."

"I know, sweetie," Autumn says, rubbing my back. "If it makes you feel any better, I truly believe that he does love you."

"I was a bet to him. A fucking game. Once a player, always a player," I sneer.

"Maybe," Autumn says. "But I see the way he looks at you. If it was about sleeping with you, he could have bailed months ago. Maybe it started that way, and you made him fall in love with you."

"It was always the chase. Everything is a game to him. Hell, I should have stuck around to see what he won."

"I don't know, Parker, did you see his face? He looked destroyed."

"Whose side are you on?" I ask her.

"Yours. Always yours, but you're upset, and so was he. He looked about like you do right now. I even think I saw a hint of tears in his eyes."

"Come on," I scoff. "Now you're just trying to be funny."

"Are you going to get that?" She nods toward where my phone has been going off like crazy in my purse.

Digging around until I find it, I look at the screen and see fifteen missed calls from Holden. I can't deal with him. I don't want to deal with him. He played me, made a fool of me. So, instead of talking to him like a mature, responsible adult, I do the only other thing I can think of at that moment and turn my phone off.

"Tell me what you need. What do you want to do?"

"Can you just take me back to the hotel?" I ask her.

"Sure thing." She puts the car in drive.

I cry silent tears all the way there, and thankfully, I'm able to sneak in the back entrance of the hotel. The last thing I need is my red blotchy tear-streaked face to be splashed all over social media. It's bad enough once the breakup is out. That's going to happen anyway.

I have no one to blame but myself. I knew better. I knew he was too good to be true. I opened my heart to him and gave him all of me. He was my everything, and to him, I was just a bet.

I was wrong. I'm not the one to blame. Holden is.

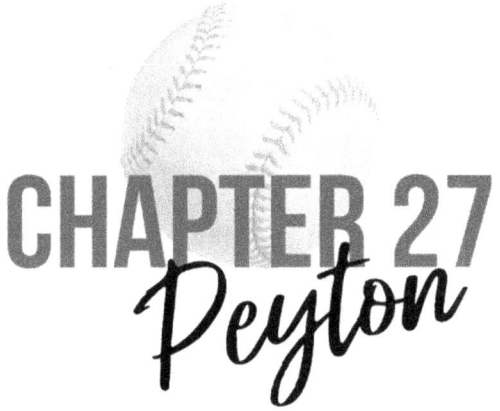

CHAPTER 27
Peyton

M Y BEST FRIEND KARINA AND I are sitting out by the pool, just soaking up the glorious Florida sunshine, when my cell phone rings. Assuming it's my dad, and knowing that if I don't answer, he'll send in the National Guard, I don't bother to look at the screen when I answer.

"Hello?"

"Peyton," a panicked voice asks.

I pull the phone away from my ear to make sure I'm not hearing things, and sure enough, it's Holden, and worry sets in. "What's wrong? Where's Parker?"

"Where are you staying?" he asks instead of answering me.

"Holden!" I shout. "What in the hell happened? Where is Parker?"

"I didn't do it, Peyton. I love her. Fuck me. I love that girl more than anything. I would never bet on her."

"What are you talking about?" I sit up straighter in my lounge chair. Karina does the same, sensing something is off. "Start at the beginning." He launches into the story and ends with a break in his voice.

"Peyton, I love her. Please, you have to help me."

"How do I know you're telling the truth?"

"My friends, they were there. The guy who recorded us was sitting behind us. He didn't hear the entire conversation. That clip he played, that was after I told them I wouldn't take that bet. I told them she deserved better than that. Fuck, Peyton, I didn't know it then, but I was already half in love with her. I would never do that to her. Please, you have to help me. I can't lose her."

I bite down on my bottom lip, and I consider my options. I know Parker was concerned about his reputation from the very beginning, and I know my sister. Hearing that clip crushed her. I also know that when she's not paying attention, he looks at her as if she's his entire world.

If I hadn't grown up watching my dad look at my mom that way, I might not have noticed. Nah, that's not true either. I recognized it when Cameron looked at Paisley, and I was just a kid then. I know he loves her.

"Don't make me regret this," I tell him.

"We'll name our firstborn after you," he offers.

I throw my head back in laughter. "Let's start with her forgiving you before you talk about knocking her up," I advise.

"I'll win her back, Peyton. There is no other option. She owns every piece of me."

"I'll text you the hotel and the room number."

"Thanks, little sister. I won't forget this," he says, ending the call.

"What's going on?" Karina asks.

"That was Holden. He was looking for Parker. I guess they had a spat." I love my best friend and roommate, but this is personal, and growing up, you never know who's listening or watching. Case in point is the mess Holden is currently in. "I'll tell you in the room." Better safe than sorry.

Grabbing our things, we head to the room so I can fill her in and I can check on my sister.

CHAPTER 28
Holden

I KNOCK SOFTLY ON THE door, which goes against my every instinct. I want to pound it off the fucking hinges. Whatever it takes to get to her. I have to talk to her, and if she thinks it's me at the door, I know I'll be standing out here in this hallway all night long. The fucked-up part is that I would do it.

For her.

The door opens, and there she stands. Her hair is piled in a knot on top of her head. Her face is red and blotchy, and there are fresh tears in her eyes. "Baby." My voice cracks. I reach for her, but she backs away. "P-Please, can I come in?"

Autumn appears next to her. "I'm going to go take a walk. You two should talk." Autumn gives me a warning glare, but something tells me that she might be on my side.

"Thank you," I tell her. She nods and pats my shoulder, and that gives me hope.

Parker steps back and allows me to walk into the room, closing the door behind me. "P-Parker." I swallow hard. "Please, can I explain?"

She gives me a small nod.

"Never. You were never a bet to me. The guys tried to make it a bet when they knew I wanted you. I told them that you deserved better than that, and you do."

"That's not what I heard."

"I know." I pace across her room, pulling my hat off my head and running my fingers through my hair. "The guy behind us, Rogers, he was eavesdropping, and he only recorded a part of the conversation. He wasn't even in on it. I had no idea he even recorded it until today."

"You played me, Holden. I gave you all of me, and in return, you played me." Her voice cracks, and so does my heart.

So many emotions are rolling through me. I'm frustrated because I want to just shake her to make her understand that she's the love of my life. I didn't bet on her, but I should have bet on us.

I'm pissed off at Rogers for recording our conversation, one that he wasn't a part of. If I lose her over this, teammate or not, I'm kicking his ass. Career be damned.

I'm so in love with her. She's all that I can see. Nothing matters to me but making her see what she means to me. I'd walk away from it all if it meant she would always be mine.

"You played me," she says again, dropping down to sit on the bed. Tears are still coating her cheeks, and it cracks my soul wide open. "I heard what you said."

"Dammit, Parker. Yes, that was me on that recording. I said those things, but you have to know that this is different. What we have is beyond the play. It might have started with the play and the thrill of the chase, but baby, I'm not playing. Not with you."

She closes her eyes as her tears continue to fall, and I feel her slipping away from me. Short of calling the guys, I don't know what I can do or say to make her understand, so that's what I do. Pulling my phone out of my pocket, I dial Wade.

"Hey, man, it's Holden. I'm going to text you a room number. I need you, Tucker, and Sonny to come here. And if you can track down the pencil dick Rogers, he needs to be here too."

"Done," he says, ending the call, and I shoot him off a quick text.

"What did you do?" she asks.

"The guys who I was talking to that day, they're going to come here and tell you what happened. They can tell you what I said."

"I heard what you said."

"No, sweet pea. You heard the tail end of a conversation. The one where I had already made up my mind that you were going to be mine. Hell, I was probably already half in love with you but too blind to see it."

Before she can reply, there's a knock on the door. I stand and go to answer it, but it's not who I was expecting. Instead, I find Cameron standing there with his hands shoved in his pockets.

"Hey," I greet and step back, letting him in.

"I ran into Peyton in the lobby. She told me what happened." He goes to sit on the bed next to Parker and pulls her into a hug. "You okay?" he asks her.

"No." Her voice cracks, and the fact he's comforting her and I'm not has me going crazy. I begin to pace the room. All I want to do is hold her and tell her what she means to me. I just want this all to go away.

"Do you want me to ask him to leave?" he asks, just as another knock sounds at the door.

I rush to open it, desperate for it to be the guys. I need this shit handled, and I need to hold her. Thankfully, when I pull open the door, all four of my teammates are standing there. "Get in here," I say, more forcefully than I probably should. When Rogers passes, I shoulder check him and glare, daring him with my eyes to fucking start something with me.

"Rogers, let's start with you," I seethe. "Can you please tell the love of my life what you heard that day?" I cross my arms over my chest.

"What I recorded is all that I heard. I got the tail end of the conversation, but it's obvious what was going on." He smirks.

I keep my arms crossed to prevent from knocking this fucker on his ass. I turn to Wade, and he nods.

"Parker?" he asks. She lifts her head, and he holds his hand out for her. "I'm Wade Hoffman. I was traded to the Blaze with Holden." He motions to Tucker and Sonny. "We all were."

She nods and shakes his hand, her manners winning out.

"I'm not here to sing his praises. I've played ball with him since he was drafted to the Tomahawks, and he's never been one to settle down, instead choosing, uh, variety," he says, and I glare at him.

How in the fuck is this helping me?

"Anyway," he says, ignoring my glare, "we were all giving him a hard time because the moment you walked into the room, he couldn't take his eyes off you. We were razzing him, which is what we do, and Sonny said he sensed a wager. We knew he was into you, and it was wrong of us to tease him with a bet. It's just what we do." He looks down at the floor.

"What did you say?" Cameron asks.

He and I might be friends, but she's his family. "Wade? Sonny? Tucker? I've already told her what I said. I want her to hear it from you."

"I can't really remember exactly," Tucker speaks up. "Something about you being better than a bet," he says directly to Parker. "He said no deal but then proceeded to tell us something about guaranteeing that you would be his."

"Thanks, guys," I say, my voice tight with fear that having them come here wasn't enough. One by one, they file out of the room, and even Rogers has the decency to look ashamed of what he did. Once the door closes behind them, I slouch against the wall. My heart is cracking wide open, bleeding on the carpet. Fear like I've never known grips at my chest as the thought of losing her becomes a real possibility.

"Parker?" Cameron says softly. "Tell me what you want me to do. Do you want me to kick him out? Kick his ass? You name it, and it's done."

I can't even be mad at him for it. I like knowing she has him in her corner. Cameron is a stand-up guy.

"No, I'm okay. We need to talk," she says. Her eyes stay trained on him, and I'm not going to lie, I'm scared as hell that she's going to tell me to go to hell.

"All right. Well, the team is staying here, which I'm sure you know, so if you need me, just call."

"Thanks, Cam."

"Anytime." He stands, kisses the top of her head, and walks away. He stops next to me and squeezes my shoulder. "Fight for her," he says, low enough for only me to hear.

"Always." I nod. I'll never stop fighting for her. For us.

The door closes with an audible click, and the sound echoes throughout the room. I can't take it any longer. I walk to where she sits on the bed and drop to my knees. I wrap my arms around her waist and bury my face in her lap. At first, she doesn't move a muscle, and I can feel the pain as my heart shatters in my chest. I swallow the lump forming in my throat. I don't know how I'm going to walk away from her.

When she runs her fingers through my hair, a sob breaks free from my chest. I battle against the tears that threaten to fall. Lifting my head, I look into her eyes, and I see it—the love we have for one another.

Fight for her.

"The moment I laid eyes on you, I knew you were special. Every moment from that night forward, you proved that theory to be correct. I love you so much, Parker. I swear to you, baby. I'm not the man I was the night we met. You changed me. You're the only woman I see. You're all I think about, and it's not just you, but our life together. Our future. I want all your moments, Parker. But it's more than that. I want them to be our moments. I want to give Jett cousins to play with, and I want to add ornaments to our tree every year for all our life's biggest accomplishments. I want to fill my house, the same house that only feels like home when you're there, with the pitter-patter of little feet. I want you to be my wife. I want to grow old with you." I pause to catch my breath, but when I go to speak again, she places her finger over my lips to silence me. My heart stalls as I wait for her next move.

"Holden." She pauses. "I believe you," she finally says. "I believe you, but the power I've given you scares me. The ownership of my heart. The thought of losing you, it cripples me."

"You won't," I say, standing. I pull her to her feet and move to sit on the bed, tugging her onto my lap. "I'm not me without you, Parker."

"I love you so much," she says, her voice cracking.

"Thank fuck," I mutter, before sealing my lips with hers. She kisses me back with an intensity we've never experienced. It's not until she pulls away and rips her tank top over her head that I know where this is going and why it feels so much more intense.

Makeup sex.

This is a first for us, and I'm here for it.

She scrambles to her feet, and I follow her as we frantically tear at our clothes. When we're both naked, we stand, staring at one another. All the fear and worry of the day fade away as I stare into her pretty blue eyes. The woman standing before me is my life, my future, and one day soon, my wife.

"On the bed, baby."

She grins and rushes to lie back on the bed. And that's when I remember I don't have a condom. "Fuck."

"What's wrong?"

"Condom," I mutter. Fuck me. I need her. The thought of getting dressed and leaving her here to run downstairs and buy some pisses me the fuck off.

"Holden?"

"Yeah?"

"We don't need them."

"What?" I smile. "Does that mean?" I climb on the bed and place my hand over her belly.

"No." She laughs. "I'm not pregnant, but I am on the pill."

"I know, but we always use them."

"Well, now we don't have to."

"I've never—" I shake my head. "Sweet pea, I'm not going to last," I tell her.

She shrugs. "Doesn't matter. We can just do it again."

"I love you, Parker Monroe."

"I love you too, Holden Bailey."

Climbing on the bed, I settle between her thighs. I bend my head to kiss her, and I sigh as her tongue tangles with mine. Her legs wrap around my waist, and her hands grip my back.

"Holden"—she smiles up at me—"it's called makeup sex," she teases.

"I want to savor you. And I know this is going to be a life-altering experience."

"One you can have every day of forever, but right now, I need you inside me. I need to feel you. To feel us."

I nod, and for the first time in my life, I slide inside a woman—not just any woman but the love of my life—completely bare. "I'm glad it was you," I say before pulling out and thrusting back in.

"Feels different. Better," she pants, as I unleash the worry and fear and stress of possibly losing her. I never want to go through that ever again. Never.

I grit my teeth to ward off my orgasm, but when her pussy grips my cock like a fucking vise, I know I don't have long. "Where?" I ask, and my girl knows what I'm asking.

"Inside me."

That's all it takes for me to come harder than I have in my entire life. I roll over to my back, not willing to pull out of her heat just yet, but needing to not crush her with my weight.

She props her chin on her hands that are resting on my chest. "When can we do that again?" she asks, smirking.

All I can do is smile up at her and thank my lucky stars for bringing her into my life.

EPILOGUE

Three months later

FUCKING RAIN DELAY. OF COURSE, the one day that I need to get my ass home after an away series and there's a fucking rain delay. That means I'm going to miss my flight, and if the information staring back at me on my cell phone is correct, there are no other flights out until the morning, which means I'm going to miss her graduation.

Fuck me.

I dread making this call. I hate disappointing her, but I don't see a way around it. Dialing her number, I walk to the showers in the locker room for some privacy while I wait for her to answer.

"Damn rain." She laughs. "How's it looking? I have the radar pulled up, and it doesn't look like it's done yet."

"It's not. Sweet pea—" I start, but she stops me.

"You're going to miss your flight."

"Yeah."

"I already looked. There are no other flights. That's the last one until eight o'clock tomorrow morning."

"I know." My gut twists, and I'm ready to say fuck the game and the fine and head to the airport.

"No." She laughs. "I can practically hear you thinking, Holden. This is your job. I know that. It's not a big deal. It's just a piece of paper. You'll see it when I hang it on the wall in the office."

Yeah, she agreed to move in with me after graduation. Little does she know she's playing right into my plans for us. "It's not fine, Parker. You worked your ass off for that degree, and I want to be there to watch you walk across the stage."

"Hey," she says soothingly. "This might be the first thing that you've had to miss, but it's not going to be the last. We know that this job takes you away, and that's okay. I know that you're here with me, even when you're not."

"That's not okay," I say, frustrated as hell.

"Holden? I'll be at your game tomorrow night. You know the one that Uncle Drew insisted I throw the first pitch as a celebration of my graduation from college and accepting the PR position with the Blaze. I'll bring my diploma, and you can see it then."

"That's not the same, and you know it."

"No," she agrees. "It's not the same, but do you know what is?"

"What?"

"The way you love me. It means the world to me that you want to be there, but I get it."

"I can't even FaceTime to watch it. I'll be on a fucking plane."

"That's fine. I'll have Dad record it so you and Cameron both can watch it. He knows what it's like. Trust me. This isn't new to me."

"I miss you."

"I miss you too. Now, when this rain clears up, I want you to go out there and kick some Badger ass, you hear me?" she says, trying to be stern and failing miserably. I can hear the humor in her voice.

"I'm sorry, Parker."

"It's fine. I promise."

"I don't know what I did in my past life for you to come into my life, but I'm so damn thankful for you. I know my career is hard."

"It's baseball," she says as if it's that simple.

"I love you."

"Love you too. I'll talk to you tomorrow, and hey, I'll be the one throwing the first pitch, you know, in case you weren't sure."

"You're going to do great," I tell her.

"Of course I am. I'm a Monroe. Dad even dug out one of his old jerseys for me to wear."

"Really? I was hoping you would wear mine."

"We'll see, player," she teases.

"Don't start," I warn her. "I need to get back. Good luck, babe. I'm with you in spirit."

"I know you are."

I end the call and stalk back to my team.

Parker

"PARKER ELIZABETH MONROE." MY NAME is called, and I walk across the stage to accept my degree with a smile on my face. When I turn for the camera, hoots and hollers ring out. My eyes scan the crowd for my family, and that's when I see him.

Holden.

He's standing on a chair, his hands cupped around his mouth as he screams for me. He's here. My legs can't carry me off the stage fast enough. Instead of going to my seat for the remainder of the ceremony, I run to him as fast as I can in these heels. I got my picture taken and walked across the stage. That was good enough for me.

He sees me coming for him and climbs down from the chair, opening his arms for me. I launch myself at him and bury my face in his neck. "How are you here right now?" I ask, pulling back.

"Cameron missed Paisley and the kids, so we chartered a plane. We landed about an hour ago."

"I can't believe you did that just to see me graduate." I kiss him softly. He's been gone for five days, and I've missed the hell out of him.

"Don't you know by now, sweet pea, I'd do anything for you?" he asks, sweeping my hair out of my eyes.

"What time do you have to be at the field?"

"Not for a few hours."

"Good," Dad says, placing his hand on his shoulder. "We're going out to eat to celebrate."

"Congratulations, baby."

Just when I thought this day couldn't be any better, he gives me the surprise of all surprises.

"Come on, you two," Dad says, leading our rowdy group out of the auditorium.

"And now for the opening pitch, please welcome Parker Monroe!" the announcer says over the PA.

I'm nervous as I walk out onto the field and wave at the crowd. It's one thing when it's your dad or brother-in-law on the team. It's a whole other ball game, no pun intended, when it's the team of the man you're madly in love with. As a last-minute decision, I switched to his jersey instead of one of Dad's. Holden earned it with the work he did to make it to my graduation.

To my surprise, it's Cameron who meets me on the mound and hands me the ball. "You ready for this?" he asks me.

"Pft, just like riding a bike," I say with confidence. If there is one thing I know my sisters and I can do, it's throw a baseball.

"Good luck." He taps my shoulder and jogs to the dugout.

My eyes scan the players, looking for Holden, but I don't see him. I don't want him to miss this, but I can't just stand here like an idiot delaying the game, so I wind up the pitch and let it sail. The crows grow wild, and I wave. A few of them start pointing behind me, and I worry that I ripped my pants or something. Turning, I look to see what they might be pointing at and gasp.

"Oh my God," I breathe when I see Holden kneeling behind me with a ring box in his hand.

"Hey, sweet pea," he says. His voice rings out over the entire stadium. "I love you," he says, his voice strong. "Will you spend all the days of your forever with me? Will you marry me?"

I nod because the tears are falling too fast, and the emotion in my throat is too thick to form words. He stands and slides a huge diamond on my finger. "Nice jersey," he says, his mic still on.

I shake my head and smile. He lifts me in the air and spins me around. "She said yes!" he shouts, and then his lips fall to mine. By the time we come up for air, there's a picture of us on every screen, and our families are on the field waiting to hug us and wish us congratulations.

When we finally walk off the field, Holden pulls me to the side and hugs me tight. "What do you think, babe? Did we take this beyond the play?" He winks, and all I can do is nod.

He might have been a player before he met me, but that's not who he is now, and I'm the lucky one who gets to spend the rest of my life loving him.

I cannot thank you enough for taking the time to read **Beyond the Play**. *Peyton's story is next.*
Be sure to sign up for my newsletter below to never miss a new release.

Other titles in the **Out of Reach Series:**

Beyond the Bases

Beyond the Game

Beyond the Play

Beyond the Team

Never miss a new release:
Newsletter Sign-up

Be the first to hear about free content, new releases, cover reveals, sales, and more. kayleeryan.com/subscribe/

Discover more about Kaylee's books
kayleeryan.com/all-books/

CONTACT
Kaylee Ryan

Facebook:

bit.ly/2C5DgdF

Reader Group:

bit.ly/2ooyWDx

Goodreads:

bit.ly/2HodJvx

BookBub:

bit.ly/2KulVvH

Website:

kayleeryan.com/

ALSO BY
Kaylee Ryan

With You Series:
Anywhere with You | More with You | Everything with You

Soul Serenade Series:
Emphatic | Assured | Definite | Insistent

Southern Heart Series:
Southern Pleasure | Southern Desire
Southern Attraction | Southern Devotion

Unexpected Arrivals Series
Unexpected Reality |Unexpected Fight | Unexpected Fall
Unexpected Bond | Unexpected Odds

Riggins Brothers Series:
Play by Play | Layer by Layer | Piece by Piece
Kiss by Kiss | Touch by Touch | Beat by Beat

Entangled Hearts Duet:
Agony | Bliss

Cocky Hero Club:
Lucky Bastard

ALSO BY
Kaylee Ryan

Mason Creek Series:
Perfect Embrace

Standalone Titles:
Tempting Tatum | Unwrapping Tatum | Levitate
Just Say When | I Just Want You | Reminding Avery

Hey, Whiskey | Pull You Through | Remedy
The Difference | Trust the Push | Forever After All
Misconception | Never with Me

Out of Reach Series:
Beyond the Bases | Beyond the Game
Beyond the Play | Beyond the Team

Co-written with Lacey Black:

Fair Lakes Series:
It's Not Over | Just Getting Started | Can't Fight It

Standalone Titles:
Boy Trouble | Home to You | Beneath the Fallen Stars

Co-writing as Rebel Shaw with Lacey Black:
Royal | Crying Shame

ACKNOWLEDGMENTS

To my family: It's been a tough year, but we made it through it. Thank you for being my rock. I love you.

Wander Aguiar: Thank you for another incredible image. It's always a pleasure working with you and Andrey.

Sommer Stein: Thank you for making each cover fit the Out of Reach branding. I love them all!

Lacey Black: My dear friend. Thank you for always being there with life, and work. I value our friendship, and our working relationship more than you will ever know. I can't wait to see what our co-writing journey takes us.

My beta team: Jamie, Stacy, Lauren, Erica, and Franci I would be lost without you. You read my words as much as I do, and I can't tell you what your input and all the time you give means to me. Countless messages and bouncing idea, you ladies keep me sane with the characters are being anything but. Thank you from the bottom of my heart for taking this wild ride with me.

Give Me Books: With every release, your team works diligently to get my book in the hands of bloggers. I cannot tell you how thankful I am for your services.

Tempting Illustrations: Thank you for everything. I would be lost without you.

Julie Deaton: Thank you for giving this book a set of fresh final eyes.

Jenny Sims: Thank you for helping polish this book to be the best than it can be.

Becky Johnson: I could not do this without you. Thank you for pushing me, and making me work for it.

Marisa Corvisiero: Thank you for all that you do. I know I'm not the easiest client. I'm blessed to have you on this journey with me.

Brittany Holland: Thank you for your assistance with the blurb. You saved me!

Chasidy Renee: Thank you for everything you do. How did I survive without you before now?

Erica Caudill & Kaitie Reister: Thank you both for your baseball expertise. You helped me so much with this series.

Bloggers: Thank you, doesn't seem like enough. You don't get paid to do what you do. It's from the kindness of your heart and your love of reading that fuels you. Without you, without your pages, your voice, your reviews, spreading the word it would be so much harder if not impossible to get my words in reader's hands. I can't tell you how much your never-ending support means to me. Thank you for being you, thank you for all that you do.

To my reader group, Kaylee's Crew: You are my people. I love all of the messages and emails you send me. I love the little book community we've created. You are my family. Thank you for all of your love and support not just with books, but with life. Thank you for being on this wild ride with me.

With Love,

Kaylee Ryan
AUTHOR